# "You're free to go, Ms. Diamond, but stay away from Lauren.

"My daughter is engaged to be married this summer. The last thing she needs or wants is a career in modeling."

Her composure slipped when he mentioned the engagement. He saw an instant of shock before she rallied, blanking her expression completely. The phone rang again as she came to her feet.

"Isn't that for her to decide, Sheriff?"

"You don't know when to quit, do you?" But she definitely had spunk, he'd give her that.

"This isn't the Middle Ages, you know. Women do have choices."

He grabbed his hat, answering his assistant's emergency call, and closed the distance between him and the woman. Flecks of blue and green shimmered in her eyes as excitement warred with apprehension. While she flinched slightly, she didn't back up or lower her gaze.

"Go back to New York, Ms. Diamond. You've overstayed your welcome in Darwin Crossing. If I find you around town again, I'll arrest you for loitering."

"And I thought New Yorkers were cold." She shot the words after him.

Noah sprinted for the gas station and his leaky truck. So she thought he was cold, did she? Well, cold was the one way Skylar Diamond definitely didn't leave him.

Dear Reader,

I was excited to be asked to participate in the TRUEBLOOD, TEXAS series with such a talented group of authors. Bigger than life, these bold men and women of the series are ready to tame and be tamed—by the right mates.

Noah and Sky's story presented a unique opportunity to delve into the complexities of more than simply a man and woman's relationship. How would it feel to discover the infant you had to give up at birth was about to marry? What would it be like to fall in love, only to learn the woman you love is the mother of your adoptive daughter? And what would happen if you discovered someone you liked and respected was actually your birth mother?

Writing this story was a challenging undertaking. But watching them struggle to become a family unit and overcome their problems was a voyage of discovery for all of us.

I hope you'll enjoy reading *The Sheriff Gets His Lady*. And be sure to watch for the next installment from TRUEBLOOD, TEXAS. I know I'm looking forward to it.

Happy reading!

*Dani Sinclair*

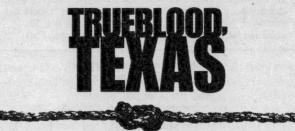

# TRUEBLOOD, TEXAS

## Dani Sinclair

### The Sheriff Gets His Lady

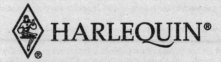

# HARLEQUIN®

TORONTO • NEW YORK • LONDON
AMSTERDAM • PARIS • SYDNEY • HAMBURG
STOCKHOLM • ATHENS • TOKYO • MILAN • MADRID
PRAGUE • WARSAW • BUDAPEST • AUCKLAND

Dani Sinclair is acknowledged
as the author of this work.

This one is for you, Roger—
my helpmate, lover and best friend.

Special thanks to Mary McGowan and Jacki Frank
for help beyond the call of friendship.
And for Chip, Dan and Barb as always

HARLEQUIN BOOKS
225 Duncan Mill Road, Don Mills,
Ontario, Canada M3B 3K9

ISBN 0-373-65085-X

THE SHERIFF GETS HIS LADY

# TRUEBLOOD, TEXAS

| | |
|---|---|
| The Cowboy Wants a Baby | Jo Leigh |
| His Brother's Fiancée | Jasmine Cresswell |
| A Father's Vow | Tina Leonard |
| Daddy Wanted | Kate Hoffmann |
| The Cowboy's Secret Son | Gayle Wilson |
| The Best Man in Texas | Kelsey Roberts |
| Hot on His Trail | Karen Hughes |
| The Sheriff Gets His Lady | Dani Sinclair |
| Surprise Package | Joanna Wayne |
| Rodeo Daddy | B.J. Daniels |
| The Rancher's Bride | Tara Taylor Quinn |
| Dylan's Destiny | Kimberly Raye |
| Hero for Hire | Jill Shalvis |
| Her Protector | Liz Ireland |
| Lover Under Cover | Charlotte Douglas |
| A Family at Last | Debbi Rawlins |

# THE TRUEBLOOD LEGACY

THE YEAR WAS 1918, and the Great War in Europe still raged, but Esau Porter was heading home to Texas.

The young sergeant arrived at his parents' ranch northwest of San Antonio on a Sunday night, only the celebration didn't go off as planned. Most of the townsfolk of Carmelita had come out to welcome Esau home, but when they saw the sorry condition of the boy, they gave their respects quickly and left.

The fever got so bad so fast that Mrs. Porter hardly knew what to do. By Monday night, before the doctor from San Antonio made it into town, Esau was dead.

The Porter family grieved. How could their son have survived the German peril, only to burn up and die in his own bed? It wasn't much of a surprise when Mrs. Porter took to her bed on Wednesday. But it was a hell of a shock when half the residents of Carmelita came down with the horrible illness. House after house was hit by death, and all the townspeople could do was pray for salvation.

None came. By the end of the year, over one hundred souls had perished. The influenza virus took those in the prime of life, leaving behind an unprecedented number of orphans. And the virus knew no boundaries. By the time the threat had passed, more than thirty-seven million people had succumbed worldwide.

But in one house, there was still hope.

Isabella Trueblood had come to Carmelita in the late 1800s with her father, blacksmith Saul Trueblood, and her mother, Teresa Collier Trueblood. The family had traveled from Indiana, leaving their Quaker roots behind.

Young Isabella grew up to be an intelligent woman who had a gift for healing and storytelling. Her dreams centered on the boy next door, Foster Carter, the son of Chester and Grace.

Just before the bad times came in 1918, Foster asked Isabella to be his wife, and the future of the Carter spread was secured. It was a happy union, and the future looked bright for the young couple.

Two years later, not one of their relatives was alive. How the young couple had survived was a miracle. And during the epidemic, Isabella and Foster had taken in more than twenty-two orphaned children from all over the county. They fed them, clothed them, taught them as if they were blood kin.

Then Isabella became pregnant, but there were complications. Love for her handsome son, Josiah, born in 1920, wasn't enough to stop her from growing weaker by the day. Knowing she couldn't leave her husband to tend to all the children if she died, she set out to find families for each one of her orphaned charges.

And so the Trueblood Foundation was born. Named in memory of Isabella's parents, it would become famous all over Texas. Some of the orphaned children went to strangers, but many were reunited with their families. After reading notices in newspapers and church bulletins, aunts, uncles, cousins and grandparents rushed to Carmelita to find the young ones they'd given up for dead.

Toward the end of Isabella's life, she'd brought together more than thirty families, and not just her orphans. Many others, old and young, made their way to her doorstep, and Isabella turned no one away.

At her death, the town's name was changed to Trueblood, in her honor. For years to come, her simple grave was adorned with flowers on the anniversary of her death, grateful tokens of appreciation from the families she had brought together.

Isabella's son, Josiah, grew into a fine rancher and married Rebecca Montgomery in 1938. They had a daughter, Elizabeth Trueblood Carter, in 1940. Elizabeth married her neighbor William Garrett in 1965, and gave birth to twins Lily and Dylan in 1971, and daughter Ashley a few years later. Home was the Double G ranch, about ten miles from Trueblood proper, and the Garrett children grew up listening to stories of their famous great-grandmother, Isabella. Because they were Truebloods, they knew that they, too, had a sacred duty to carry on the tradition passed down to them: finding lost souls and reuniting loved ones.

# *PROLOGUE*

NOAH BEAUFORT CLIMBED into his truck and started the engine while the warden's warning played in his head.

*Francis Hartman was released this morning, Noah. You need to be aware that the last thing he told his cellmate was how much he was looking forward to seeing you again.*

Francis Hartman had graduated from armed robbery to paid muscle for a drug distributor in Dallas. Noah's last undercover assignment with the Dallas P.D. had netted him, along with a number of other people. Unfortunately, Hartman had enough money for a good attorney. Noah wasn't surprised he was out already.

Threats were something every lawman faced. Noah wasn't overly concerned, but with his daughter living at home this semester, he couldn't dismiss the threat completely.

He was thinking about that when he started backing up—right into another car. Braking sharply, Noah cursed his inattention. Putting the truck in park, he stepped out to check the damage. The austere concrete structure of the prison loomed ominously over the parking lot, casting deep shadows despite the afternoon sun.

The man unfolding himself from the sleek, dark-blue Lexus was six-two, maybe two hundred pounds, with jet-black hair worn straight back in a ponytail. He was dressed in a fancy Western-style suit, his expression hidden behind silver-framed glasses with dark-tinted lenses.

A high-priced lawyer type, Noah decided. Just what he

needed. "Sorry," he said, joining the man who stood beside his car's front bumper. "I never saw you."

The man regarded his bumper without a trace of expression. The Lexus didn't appear scratched. There was a small scrape on Noah's truck but that was all. He took in Noah's sheriff's uniform and nodded curtly.

"No harm done."

"Would you like my insurance information?"

The man gave a quick shake of his head. "That won't be necessary."

He turned, ponytail swinging, and returned to his car. Noah frowned. At a guess, the man had a Mexican background that he went to great lengths to hide. Noah wondered if he was effective in front of a jury. There was something cold, almost menacing, about his arrogance.

Noah returned to his truck, fastened his seat belt, and finished backing out. The stranger waited, taking the vacated parking place. In the rearview mirror, Noah watched him step from his car, place a Stetson firmly on his head, and stride purposefully toward the prison entrance.

With a frown, Noah dismissed the man and glanced at the clock. He had several errands to run, but if he hurried he could still make it home in time for his daughter's phone call. He was anxious to hear how a sheriff's daughter was making out in the high-society world of her fiancé's family.

Noah liked Doug Rossiter. The strapping young man with his dark good looks was serious, levelheaded, and unpretentious. More important, he adored Lauren and balanced her enthusiasm for life with a practical side that kept her grounded. Noah was pleased by their engagement, even if his daughter was awfully young.

Maybe he was simply getting old—or feeling a tad overprotective. He dismissed the thought wryly. He didn't feel old, and if he was overprotective, well, he'd been that way from the moment he and Beth had brought Lauren home. He'd taken one look at that tiny, sweet face staring up at him with large, unfocused eyes and had known he'd move mountains to protect that little baby.

Besides, they'd only had each other since his wife died when Lauren was five years old. Things hadn't been easy at first, but he hadn't done so badly. Lauren had grown, becoming a beautiful, intelligent young woman—even if he did say so himself! And he planned to enjoy what was left of their father-daughter time together.

"WHAT ARE YOU doing here?" J. B. Crowe barked.

Luke Silva let his boss's annoyance bounce off him. If there was one thing he'd learned over the years, it was how to handle the notorious gangster.

He flicked a bit of nonexistent lint from the fancy trim on his Western jacket and surveyed the prison's sterile environment. Guards were positioned strategically around the room. None paid him any more attention than they did the other friends and loved ones sitting in front of the glass wall that separated guests from inmates in the open, narrow room.

"It's Cooper," he said softly into the phone. "He's out of control, J.B. He's decided with you in here, maybe he should be the one running things. He sure doesn't intend taking orders."

And that rankled. How it rankled. With J.B. in prison, keeping things running was Luke's job. Everyone knew it. Everyone except Sebastian Cooper. Luke didn't intend to tolerate upstarts in his ranks. He wanted to nip this power play now. Permanently.

He'd tempered his urge until he spoke to J.B. It paid to move carefully. J.B. might have some future role in mind for Cooper Consulting Inc. He would be most unhappy if Luke screwed that up.

Though J.B. was in prison, he was still the titular head of the association of Texas "businessmen" they worked with and through. As long as so many of its members remained loyal, Luke wasn't about to make big waves. Oh, he intended to change the situation, but he knew how to bide his time. Right now it was wisest to move carefully—with J.B.'s sanction.

Prison hadn't altered the older man's glare one bit.

"We may want to use him later. Send him a warning," he barked.

"A warning?" Luke asked softly.

"One he can't misinterpret," J.B. said coldly.

Satisfaction rippled through Luke. "I can do that."

Luke forced himself to remain still, though he was anxious to be away now that he had what he wanted.

J.B. eyed him for a moment, then inclined his head. He set his phone down and stood abruptly, signaling the end of their session.

Luke rose as well, replacing his dark sunglasses. He was happy to be leaving the uncomfortable confines of the prison. Already, he was mentally planning the sort of warning that would get Sebastian Cooper's full attention.

Killing Cooper outright would have been preferable, but it was messy and there were certain risks involved. A warning lowered the risks.

Luke's lips edged upward. Perhaps a lesson would serve his purpose better after all. The message would have to be showy and effective in case there were others having visions of grandeur.

He paused by the bumper of his car and checked again to be certain there was no sign of the earlier, minor collision. An idea began to form. Cooper was a wheeler-dealer. He was very fond of money and things. Among the things he favored most was a customized green Jaguar.

Slowly, Luke began to smile. He wouldn't use one of the regulars on this. He couldn't afford anything being traced back to him if the job went wrong. Norman Smith was the answer. The mercenary always gave satisfaction and he was good with explosives. He was also totally anonymous.

Smith worked through intermediaries. He wouldn't know who hired him—or care.

He was expensive, and he demanded cash up front, but that was okay. He never screwed up and he never left witnesses. Luke hoped the man was still working out of New York. Importing the talent made things that much safer.

Luke flipped back his ponytail, set his Stetson on the passenger seat, and settled behind the wheel, planning the message he would send Mr. Sebastian Cooper.

# CHAPTER ONE

AFTER TWENTY YEARS it felt strange to be standing in the outskirts of the city she'd left behind. San Antonio, Texas didn't feel like home. Skylar Diamond was pretty sure it never had. She'd moved to New York City when she was only twenty and she'd never looked back. She'd embraced the New York high-fashion lifestyle completely, doing her best to erase any trace of her indigent Texas background.

Yet she'd never escaped the knowledge that here in this city she'd given away a vital part of herself.

Sky coolly surveyed the bustling airport. For weeks she'd been trying to convince herself that the past should stay that way. It wasn't too late. She could still turn back.

But she knew she wouldn't.

After all these years of wondering, she was about to find out what had become of the infant she'd given up at birth. Her breath caught as her heart rate speeded up. The concept was as frightening as it was exciting.

Gratefully, she handed her heavy laptop computer case to a skycap. He immediately offered to take her briefcase.

"No, thank you." She clutched the case a little tighter. "I'll hang on to this myself."

Inside were her working files for the new line. She'd already had one set of files disappear. Stolen most likely. Sky wasn't about to lose any more.

As she waited for the skycap to collect her bags, she noticed a man who'd been in coach on her flight eyeing her archly. Nice enough looking, but she recognized the type.

A ladies' man, probably married with children. He'd be in search of a little action to fill the evening hours before taking care of whatever had brought him to San Antonio. His winter suit was good quality, but off the rack and more suited to New York than Texas. She turned him off with a look Ted had claimed froze a man right down to the marrow.

The male of the species currently ranked right below cockroaches and fly larvae in her estimation. Too bad she hadn't used that look to intimidate her former lover when she first met him. She could have saved herself some trouble.

The stranger blinked and set his jaw. Obviously, he wasn't used to rejection. Too bad. She wasn't interested in anything he had to offer. The only thing of interest to her right now was the quest that had brought her back to Texas.

His lips tightened in a thin line and his eyes narrowed. He pivoted and headed for the men's room a short distance away. Good.

Sky glanced at the skycap. He reached out to snag yet another of the bags she'd indicated from the conveyor belt. She tried to relax, while mentally urging the luggage to hurry. A rising impatience beat at her soul as it had been doing since she got off the telephone with the woman from the Finders Keepers detective agency yesterday evening. It was still hard to believe that Lily Garrett Bishop had actually discovered what had become of her daughter in such a short time. The agency was as good as it was reputed to be.

Her daughter.

A shiver skimmed down her spine. She was actually going to see her only child. Excitement was tempered by anxiety and her emotions continued their roller-coaster ride. She wanted to shout at these people to hurry along so she could get going.

Sky found herself tapping her foot and stopped, annoyed by her outward sign of impatience. She needed to calm down. Nothing would happen tonight anyhow, beyond checking into a hotel. She hadn't expected to catch a plane to Texas this quickly. She'd thought she would need a couple of days to get things organized. Had she known how smoothly everything would fall into place, she would have arranged to meet Lily this week instead of next.

Sky told herself it didn't matter. While she didn't have any details, Lily had given her the essential information. Once Sky knew where her daughter now lived with her widowed father, she hadn't been able to rest until she finally located Darwin Crossing, Texas. The search had taken perseverance. Darwin Crossing appeared to be a one-street town in the middle of nowhere. The place wasn't even on most maps. The nearest marked town was a small place called Bitterwater, and even that didn't have a hotel. What it had was a rooming house. Sky promptly made a reservation.

Tomorrow morning she would drive into Bitterwater, check into the rooming house, and search out Darwin Crossing. If the town was as small as it looked, she should have no problem locating her daughter.

Sky ignored the bustle of people around her while she waited for her bags to be collected. Dressed as always in New-York-style chic, she knew she stood out in the crowd. Her transformation over the years had been so successful that no one gave her a second look in New York—unless it was admiring.

With a sigh she kept an eye on her laptop computer case as people jostled and shoved, vying for luggage on the spinning carousels. Her matched set was distinctive, but there was quite a bit of it. Five bags, to be precise—not including her computer and the briefcase. Since she didn't know how long she'd be staying, she'd packed nearly everything she owned when she walked out of her pricey co-op in Manhattan.

Vaguely, she wondered if she would ever return. She

would finish the winter line, of course, but she was burned out and stressed to the max, as Ted was fond of saying. Her entire life hinged on the outcome of the step she was about to take.

She was in a strange mood, she admitted. Even for her. Maybe finding Ted in her bed with their next-door neighbor's twenty-three-year-old daughter had caused her brain to short-circuit. It had certainly made her angry enough to finally kick him out of her home and her life for good. She should have done it a long time ago. Habit had kept them together. Habit, and the fact that he was a perfect social escort whenever she needed one. No doubt he viewed her much the same way. He could hardly escort the little Lolita to his business functions.

Sky frowned. Other than making her feel annoyed, Ted's behavior didn't really matter to her anymore. Maybe her mood was due to the uncertainty of her quest. Finding the daughter she'd given up at birth twenty years ago was stressful enough to put a person in a strange mood.

Sky had no idea what she would do or say once she met her daughter face-to-face. And for someone as disciplined as she was, this uncertainty was a weakness that made her uneasy. Would her daughter hate her—or welcome her?

She looked around for a new place to direct her thoughts as a ruggedly handsome man in a sheriff's uniform strolled past. Diverted, Sky found herself staring. Now, that was a man worth paying attention to. He carried himself with unconscious grace, radiating self-confidence and easy assurance—a man who was comfortable with himself and the world around him.

Then she caught a brief glimpse of the vivacious young blonde on his arm. His large, well-formed body blocked the girl's features completely, but that hardly mattered, since he was the one who compelled her attention. He grinned down at his companion affectionately. Sky turned away.

What was it with older men and blond girls young enough

to be their daughters? She found her perfectly manicured nails digging into the leather strap on her briefcase and forced her fingers to relax.

Another jerk. An extremely compelling-looking jerk, but a jerk nonetheless.

Unless the girl *was* his daughter. Sky froze at the thought. *Good news, Ms. Diamond,* the woman from Finders Keepers had said. *We located your daughter in a tiny town called Darwin Crossing. She lives there with her father, the town sheriff.*

An eerie expectancy settled over her, leaving her momentarily deaf and unable to draw a breath. It couldn't be. Sky took a grip on her vacillating emotions and strained for a clear view, but too many people stood between her and the young woman.

Blood thundered in her head. She was shaking. Visibly shaking! This would never do. It couldn't be her daughter. Sky would look like an absolute fool if she went charging over there.

But what if it was? What if that was her daughter standing there only a few yards away?

Sky stepped forward, trying to follow their progress through the crowds. She felt hot and cold at the same time. If it was her daughter, what would she do? Oh, God, she wasn't ready for this. Her gaze flew to the man's features. Smile lines crinkled the corners of his eyes and bracketed his mouth. They softened the strong planes of his face as he leaned into the young woman, intent on what she was saying.

He really was an extremely good-looking man. More important, he didn't touch the girl like a lover, but rather the way she thought a caring father would do. Not that she had any experience of her own to base that judgment on. Still, her daughter had a man she called her father. This could be them.

But what if her daughter didn't know she'd been adopted?

Sky's heart continued its erratic thumping as she moved again, trying for a view of the girl's face, silently urging her to turn around.

But the girl turned in the opposite direction to speak to another young woman standing there. Sky watched the sheriff as he hoisted a heavy-looking bag without effort from the carousel. Unlike her former lover Ted, of the sagging middle and soon-to-be flabby forearms, this man had a lean, sleek grace and easy strength that hadn't come from any gym. He moved with the suppleness of someone who used his body in physical ways.

What would he do if she approached them? What if he denied her claim? What if this wasn't her daughter?

A large family group walked in front of Sky and came to a halt. Quickly, Sky moved around them, walking closer to where the couple stood. But other than the mass of long, shimmery blond hair, she still didn't have a view of the girl's face.

Sky's body felt brittle from the tension of not knowing.

A little boy broke away from his sister's hand and darted in front of Sky. The stroller he'd been pushing would have hit her if she hadn't jumped back in time. The boy's older sister screamed at him. The child screamed back. An adult stepped into the fray, scolding both children.

Sky tried to move around the group and found her path blocked momentarily. When she looked toward the sheriff and the girl, they were heading down the concourse, away from her. Sky nearly cried out in protest. The girl still had her back to Sky. She flipped her long straight hair over her shoulder and kept up a steady monologue of chatter.

"Ma'am? I think I got them all."

"What?" She stared blankly at the skycap who'd tapped her shoulder.

"Your suitcases. Is this all of them?"

Reluctantly, impatience beating at her soul, she glanced over the contents of the skycap's long, flat cart. Her computer case now rested precariously on top and she mentally ticked off the seven bags.

"Yes. That's all of them."

The girl and the sheriff were well down the concourse, moving briskly. The family was also on the move. The sister gave her little brother a smack when she thought no one would see. The tyke let out a wail and the group came to a halt again.

Sky exhaled a shaky breath of disappointment and turned away. Maybe it was just as well. This crowded, noisy airport was hardly the best place to meet her daughter for the very first time. Besides, it probably hadn't been her daughter. The coincidence would be far too incredible.

"You must be plannin' to stay awhile."

Looking at the skycap's pleasant face, she forced a smile in return. "Perhaps."

She followed him outside, breathing deeply of the temperate weather while she tried to calm her jangled nerves. If only she'd gotten a decent look at the girl's face.

"Imagine our weather is a nice change after that cold, rainy slush they've been saying you New Yorkers are having."

"What? Oh. Yes." She tried to focus on her companion instead of the rushing thoughts filling her head. "They are predicting snow for New York City this week."

He shook his head. "I'll take Texas weather any day. Taxi, ma'am?"

His warm Texas drawl was a pleasant change from the frequent nasal snarls of busy New Yorkers. Her own voice held almost no hint of the twang she'd grown up with.

"Yes, thank you."

The car company had suggested she check with them again once she landed, but even if they did have a luxury car available now, she wasn't up to dealing with driving at the moment. They could just deliver the car as promised in the morning.

"The Grand Hotel, overlooking the River Walk," she told the cabbie who leaped forward to claim her as a passenger.

The sidewalk was jammed with people and someone jostled her with force. She hit the cart full of suitcases, which were already shifting. Turning indignantly, Sky glared at the offender.

For an instant, her gaze locked with pale-blue eyes spaced too close together. The handsome man from the plane swept her with a chilling stare. Without a word of apology, he strode past clutching a black laptop computer case.

A ghost of unease made her watch as he hurried away. From out of the crowd, a uniformed security person followed quickly in his wake. The two were swallowed by a throng of people intent on their own goals.

Was security chasing the man from her plane? Come to think of it, she didn't remember him holding a computer case earlier when he'd offered her that come-on smile. Of course, she hadn't really paid him that much attention but...no, she was pretty sure his hands had been empty. Suddenly, edgy, she turned back toward her own computer case, only to see the black bag being lifted by the driver.

"Did you want this up front with you, ma'am?"

Sky forced herself to relax and shook her head. "No. You can put it in with the other luggage." She wouldn't be working tonight.

She turned back to the skycap, tipping him generously. She allowed him to open the taxi door for her and slipped inside. The unpleasant scent of stale food lingered in the air. Obviously the driver had eaten in here recently. Her stomach rumbled, reminding her that she was hungry, too. Well, the hotel boasted a five-star restaurant so she wouldn't have far to go once she checked in.

As she settled back into the seat, attempting to maintain the cool facade she'd perfected over the years, she decided what she needed was a long soak in the room's Jacuzzi tub to unwind and see if she could get her nerves to calm down. Maybe then she would enjoy room service overlooking the River Walk.

Very soon now, she'd learn what her actions all those years ago had wrought. She needed to stay calm and in control before meeting her daughter for the first time. It would never do to give in to the rising excitement bubbling inside her.

Staying calm and in control soon became her mantra because the hotel was a worse mob scene than the airport had been. The timing of her arrival couldn't have been worse. Some sort of large business conference was in the process of registering. The place literally swarmed with frenzied people. Sky waited at the curb with false patience for a bellman with a cart to load her baggage and write her a receipt.

"Is it always like this?" she asked him.

"No, ma'am. This is nuts right now. If you need your luggage right away, you'll have to call down to the bell captain's desk after you get your room assignment. Give them this number and we'll send the luggage right up, but we'd appreciate your patience. As you can see, we're going to be running a little behind."

Sky tipped the man and nodded, then walked into the lobby to check in. The front desk was efficient, but understaffed for this sort of a rush. Sky waited her turn, accepted the key card, and went straight to her room.

She got through to the bell desk with no problem. They promised her luggage would be sent up as soon as possible. Resigned, she headed for the bathroom, only to discover the toilet hopelessly stopped up. When her call to housekeeping rang unanswered, her calm disintegrated.

Living in New York had taught her many things—including how to get what she needed. Sky took the elevator back down and strode across the lobby, cutting past people still waiting to check in. Politely, but firmly, she expressed her displeasure.

"I'm Skylar Diamond in room 1217. The toilet is unusable and housekeeping isn't answering their phone."

The harried clerk grimaced.

"I'm terribly sorry, Ms. Diamond. I'll call maintenance to your room right away."

"I would appreciate that."

As she turned from the desk, her stomach knotted. Despite the crowd, she spotted him at once. The good-looking man from the plane stood to one side, openly watching her. He no longer clutched the computer case, and gone was the male perusal. This was a far different expression altogether. Cold. Hard. Calculating.

Before she could move or speak, he spun and strode across the lobby toward the main entrance. A shudder traveled up her spine. She felt as if she'd just had a close call with danger. Was he stalking her? Sky was certain she'd never seen the man before today. Was it mere coincidence that he'd chosen this hotel, or was he part of this conference checking in?

Feeling paranoid, she considered that he could have overheard her destination when she'd given it to the taxi driver outside the airport. Her apprehension escalated as she realized it was also possible that he'd heard both her name and her room number just now.

Apprehension changed to budding fear. The Grand was by far the most exclusive hotel in downtown San Antonio. The man had flown tourist. While it didn't automatically mean he couldn't be staying here, Sky had a bad feeling. Hadn't security been chasing him at the airport? She was wearing quite a bit of gold and precious stones on her wrist and at her neck and ears. Jewelry was a new passion of hers. Perhaps she should report the man to hotel security.

"And tell them what?" she muttered to herself. "All he's done so far is glare at me."

Still trying to decide what to do, she rode back up to her floor. The telephone was ringing when she stepped inside her room.

Genuine alarm flashed through her. No one knew where she was staying. She hadn't even told her office yet. She'd made all the arrangements herself at the very last moment after speaking with Lily Garrett Bishop yesterday.

Probably the hotel desk was phoning about the toilet. Taking a deep breath, she lifted the receiver. Her hand was steady enough, though her heart thudded more quickly than normal. "Hello?"

A second of staticky silence filled her ear. There was a decisive click as someone hung up.

Sky held the telephone for several long minutes before replacing the instrument on the nightstand. There was no reason to believe the call had come from the stranger downstairs, but she couldn't stop the apprehension from slithering up her spine.

A loud knock on her door made her jump, her hand hovering over the telephone.

"Who is it?"

"Bellman."

Unnerved, she crossed to the door and peered through the peephole. She was only slightly reassured by the sight of the smiling young face on the other side.

Taking a calming breath, she opened the door.

"Hold on a second, there!"

A portly man in a maintenance uniform rushed forward before the bellman could step inside.

"Don't unload the lady's bags until I have a look. We've been having problems with the commode in this room for days. I suspect we're going to need to move her to another room."

"Should I take her things back downstairs?"

"Give me a minute first."

The maintenance man apologized profusely on behalf of the hotel, surveyed her bathroom, tsked once or twice and asked permission to use her telephone.

Sky waited, oddly comforted by the presence of the two men.

He hung up and turned around, shaking his head. "Nobody ever listens. We're going to be moving Ms. Diamond to another room. Take her stuff back downstairs until they reassign her. I'm real sorry for the inconvenience, Ms. Diamond. I told them there was a problem in here, but someone didn't relay the information to reservations. We'll have you resituated immediately."

Sky sighed. There wasn't much point in berating either of these two men. And if they switched her room, the man from the plane would no longer know her room number.

The crowd had thinned substantially by the time they got to the main lobby, but luggage was stacked on carts all over. Hers rejoined the others sitting to one side while she waited for the hotel to process a new room.

Sky clutched her briefcase, her gaze constantly roving over the crowd. There was no sign of the man from the plane. In minutes she'd been upgraded, at no additional cost, to a far more luxurious suite on the floor above the original one, with profuse apologies ringing in her ears.

Still, Sky didn't relax until the bellman stacked her bags inside, set the computer case on the desk, and departed with a smile and a good tip. With a profound sigh of relief, she settled into the spacious new accommodations. She'd requested privacy this time so her dilemma had been solved. The man with the menacing eyes would have no way of tracking her down.

She'd be leaving the hotel before most people were up and about in the morning. Since she planned to have dinner in her room, odds were, she would never see the stranger again.

IT WAS THE stupid little things that could ruin a perfect reputation after years of work. A guilty conscience made a man foolish.

The man sometimes known as Norman Smith had been so certain that airport security guard was stalking him that he'd switched the computer case with the blonde's. And all for nothing. The weaselly bastard had been going after a mundane pickpocket, not him.

He needed better control. Much better control. Maybe he was getting too old for this business. Maybe it was time to think about retiring. He had a tidy sum resting in an offshore bank. Not enough to buy him an island perhaps, but there was a location in Hawaii that looked promising, plenty of space and white sandy beaches. He could share an island paradise like that.

Maybe after he completed this assignment, he'd hop a plane to the Islands and have another look around. He could rent a place for a year or so to see how he liked living there. He could still do the odd job or two—unless he was suddenly going to start jumping every time someone looked at him funny.

Business had been brisk of late and he'd grown unaccountably tense. The last two jobs hadn't gone well. In fact, the last hit had nearly gotten him caught despite all his careful planning. He definitely needed a vacation. Today was a prime example. He shouldn't have let himself be sidetracked by that blonde. Normally he had better control.

But God, she was something. She carried herself like a movie star. He'd always been drawn to the classy type. They didn't usually come with such a cold put-down, either.

Anger churned in his gut. Who did she think she was? He could buy and sell her a million times over.

The thought made him smile. The smile turned into a chuckle. Then he scowled, emerging from the stairwell where he'd donned the stolen, protective camouflage. He started down the hall, his senses alert while his mind probed her reaction to him at the airport.

Cold, snobbish piece of tail. She'd looked at him like he was dirt. Well, he'd teach her some manners. Too bad it was the last lesson she'd ever learn.

He chuckled again, then he quickly looked around to see if anyone had heard him. No, he was still alone in the hallway. The maintenance uniform was a loose fit on his lean frame, but it would serve the purpose. She would see only the uniform and let him in.

He nodded to a couple leaving their room and they nodded back. Emboldened, he lengthened his stride. No one would question his right to be walking around in this outfit. Hadn't he learned it was all a matter of acting as if you belonged? People always saw what they expected.

He started paying attention to the room numbers: 1213, 1215, 1217. Perfect. He knocked once and called out.

"Maintenance."

Nothing happened. There was no stir of sound from inside. She'd probably gone out to eat. Or maybe she'd fallen asleep on the bed. That would be even better. He pulled on a pair of thin latex gloves. Removing a set of tools from his pocket, he set to work on the lock.

Inside the darkened room a minute later, he hit the light switch. His gaze swept the place. Instead of the jumble of luggage he'd expected to see, the room was completely empty.

Gone. She was gone!

Fear and fury mingled. Where had she gone? She'd been here when he'd called her room a short while ago.

There was only one reason for her to take off like that. She must have opened the computer case!

Fury all but choked him. Damn her! She'd taken off with his money. She must have thought she'd struck it rich. He'd teach her. He'd teach her good. Snooty Ms. Diamond would pay and pay for this inconvenience. Because that was all he would let it be. He'd get the money back and the C4 explosive as well.

He cursed viciously. Stupid! One stupid moment of panic and his reputation hung in the balance. His fingerprints were all over that case. If she'd taken it to the police—

He calmed his momentary panic. Even if she had, they couldn't touch him. They wouldn't have a name to go with those prints, nor would they know where to look. And his career wasn't ruined yet. Fortunately, he'd removed the client's instructions in the rest room when he'd picked up the case from the unseen courier.

He patted his hip pocket, satisfied by the crinkle of paper. Unfortunately, now he would have to purchase or steal some explosives himself. Risky. He could make a couple of bombs from scratch of course, but they wouldn't be as professional as the C4. And this job needed to go right. He pounded his fist in his hand. He had some time. Maybe he could find the bitch and get his case back again. Damn her!

He lifted the lamp from the dresser, yanking the cord from the socket. The lamp shattered satisfactorily against the wall over the king-size bed where he hurled it. Where had she gone? When he'd searched her computer case at the airport, all he'd found was her business address inside. Would she go back to New York once she realized what she had?

Not likely. She'd had too much luggage with her. Hell, with his recent luck she was relocating here in Texas. How was he going to find her? Texas was one big mother of a state. She could have gone anywhere. If he started asking questions, people would remember him. There had to be a way to figure out where she went.

A noise at the door sent him spinning around. There was no time to move out of sight and nowhere to hide. Another man in a maintenance uniform stepped inside, a rack of tools in his hand. His friendly face registered startled shock, then moved to puzzled surprise.

The man sometimes known as Norman Smith smiled at the newcomer coldly.

"Uh, who are you?" Dark features pleated in puzzlement, not yet alarmed. "I was told we've got a problem here."

He waited for the man to close the door to the hall. His fingers wormed their way inside his pocket to the comforting hard steel of the knife that rested there.

He liked knives. They were much quieter than guns.

"It's unfortunate, but it looks like I'm the man who's going to make all your problems disappear."

## CHAPTER TWO

THE SUN WASN'T even up when Sky finished dressing, checked her watch, and decided she had time to send her assistant a quick e-mail before she hit the road. The computer case still sat on the desk where the bellman had set it the night before. Spinning it around to open it, she stopped, her heart pounding loud enough to be audible.

"This isn't my case!"

While similar, the case was too light and had some sort of fancy lock on the front. Anger and panic warred within her even as she reached for her briefcase to check on her files. The machine's files weren't irreplaceable, the ones in her briefcase were. She breathed again when she found everything where it should be. Then she reached for the telephone.

"I suspect this is a simple mix-up," the hotel security man told her a short time later. "There's no identification on the outside, but this is an expensive lock. Someone is going to want this case back."

"Can't you open it?"

"No, ma'am. Not with this lock on it."

"Mr. Ellenshaw, I need my computer. Can't you break the lock and find out who this case belongs to?"

The earnest young man shook his head. "Sorry, Ms. Diamond, I can't do that. Believe me, whoever got your computer is going to be as upset as you are over this mistake."

"I doubt it."

Especially if that person was from a rival designer's

house. This wouldn't be the first time another designer had gone to extreme lengths to steal an upcoming series of designs. Sky had been a recent target so she knew firsthand. There was big money in the world of fashion. Theft happened more often than people realized. And there wasn't a thing she could do about it.

"I'm certain we'll hear from the owner this morning," he assured her earnestly.

"That's all very well, but my car is being delivered in fifteen minutes. I have to leave. What am I supposed to do?"

"As soon as your computer is located we'll have it delivered to you. In the meantime, I have some forms for you to fill out."

"Of course you do."

Arguing was pointless. If the competition had her computer, they already had everything on it. Recriminations were useless. She could only hope Mr. Ellenshaw was correct, that in all the confusion yesterday, the bags had been switched by mistake.

"And if no one does complain about having the wrong computer?" she asked as she finished filling out the requisite paperwork to get her laptop computer returned in the event they recovered it.

"Er, then you'll have to file a claim through the insurance company."

"Naturally. And what happens to this one?"

"Oh, we'll hold on to it. It's possible a guest who checked out might not discover the switch for several days." At her raised eyebrows he hastened to add, "But I really don't think that's going to be an issue here, Ms. Diamond."

The door flew open. A young woman in a security uniform stood there, a peculiar expression on her face. "Ray, I need to talk to you right away."

"I'll be with you in a min—"

"Now! This won't wait!"

"Excuse me a moment, Ms. Diamond."

He walked to the door and stepped into the corridor with the agitated woman. The door didn't close all the way and the woman's frantically whispered words floated into the room.

"One of the maids just found a maintenance worker downstairs in an empty room. He's dead. She says his throat was slit. There's blood all over the place."

The security man uttered an oath. "Follow procedure. I'll be right there."

Sky wasn't surprised when she was hustled to the front desk. A bellman was summoned to collect her bags and bring them downstairs. By the time she finished filling out the paperwork for the car that was delivered, a surprising number of uniformed police officers were trooping through the lobby. At 5:33 a.m. it seemed highly unlikely the early risers were going to believe the police were here for a conference.

Not her problem. Sky tipped the deliveryman and walked outside, her briefcase firmly under her arm. This time she checked each piece of luggage carefully as it was being loaded into the trunk of the luxury car. Two men she'd bet were plainclothes policemen strode past the unfazed doorman.

"All set, ma'am. Come back and see us."

Not if she could help it. In her opinion, the Grand's reputation was highly overrated.

Only after she was inside the car with the engine running did she shrug off the morning's frustration and allow anticipation to hum through her body. There was nothing she could do about the computer right now. The loss couldn't override her main reason for being here in Texas.

Somewhere down the road her daughter was waiting, even if the girl wasn't aware of that fact. In her mind, Sky had held countless conversations with the faceless young woman. She'd rehearsed all sorts of opening gambits. Yet she still didn't know what she was going to say when the time finally came. More and more she wondered if she was doing the right thing at all. She had no rights here. But even if she didn't tell her daughter who she was, Sky needed to see her, maybe watch her and hear her speak. It was that simple and that complicated.

She opened her map, took a quick look at the printed directions she'd made for herself, and set out into the early-morning traffic.

Finally, after all these years, maybe—just maybe—she could convince herself that she'd done the right thing after all.

DINNER WAS nearly ready. His daughter would be home from work soon, Noah thought in satisfaction. Having Lauren around always brought the tiny ranch to life. The place was going to feel so empty once she moved away for good. Lauren had a way of comfortably filling even the silences with her good-natured presence. It had been bad enough this past year and a half with her away at school most of the time, but at least there had been vacations and semester breaks to look forward to. Soon it would be periodic visits instead.

Letting go might be part of the parenting process, but he didn't have to like it.

The telephone rang, pulling Noah from his introspection. He rinsed his hands and reached for the instrument.

"Hello?"

"Noah? Zach Logan."

The name from his past raised his eyebrows. Zach Logan had been his boss when he worked for the Dallas Police Department fifteen years ago. He hadn't seen the man since last April when one of Zach's cases had reached into this part of Texas and Noah lost a deputy.

"Hey, Zach, what's new?" Noah cupped the phone under

his chin and finished drying his hands on the dish towel as he checked the water boiling on the stove.

"I called to give you a heads-up."

Noah turned down the heat as he slid the pasta into the boiling water. "On Francis Hartman?"

"You heard they released him?"

"I dropped a prisoner off last week. The warden told me."

"Then do you know Hartman disappeared from view yesterday?"

Noah's muscles tensed then relaxed. "Francis Hartman is a brainless thug."

"Who apparently carries a mean grudge."

Noah swore.

"Yeah. While I agree he doesn't have the brains God gave rodent dung, it's a good idea to watch your back all the same. The brainless ones are often more dangerous than we expect."

"Point taken. Thanks for the warning, Zach. I'll alert my people. Any wants or warrants?"

"Not yet."

"Well, I'm not overly worried. Hartman will stand out if he makes the mistake of showing up here in Darwin Crossing. I think he's just barely smart enough to recognize that."

"Good point. You aren't exactly a bustling metropolis out there, are you?"

"We like it that way."

"Uh-huh. Guess that means coming back to work for me again is out of the question, huh?"

For one tiny second, Noah hesitated before rejecting the offer. Once Lauren was happily married, his initial reason for leaving Dallas was gone. He'd loved the undercover work he'd done for the Dallas P.D. On the other hand, he was older now. Old enough to know it was a young man's game.

"Thanks anyhow, Zach."

"Just remember, the offer stands anytime you want. How's your daughter doing? I hear she's engaged."

Noah smiled. "She picked herself a nice guy. He's about to graduate from veterinary school."

"Isn't that what Lauren is studying?"

"Yeah. She intends to go into partnership with him. They've already talked to the vet over in Trueblood about buying into his practice in a couple of years. He's getting ready to retire."

"That's terrific. So Lauren's away at school right now?"

"No, actually, she's doing this semester via some new computer courses. She's determined to save money before the wedding and this lets her work part-time as a veterinary assistant for our vet here in Bitterwater."

"Independent as ever, huh?"

Noah's grin widened. "That's Lauren."

"Still bringing home strays?"

"Afraid so." He eyed the three dogs and one battered old cat sprawled on the kitchen floor. Each one had been a rescue that had ended up costing him a fortune in vet bills. Lauren was always bringing home strays of one sort or another. Long ago, he'd accepted the defeat of that particular battle.

Zach chuckled. "Glad to hear she's doing so well. Just to be on the safe side, you should probably warn her to be careful. Listen, Noah, there was another reason I called."

"Figured as much."

"Could I use your office to set up a meeting? We've got an undercover operation that I don't want to see compromised. I figure you're far enough from anywhere that we can make sure no one sees the meet."

Noah ran a knuckle across his jaw, remembering what had happened the last time he'd gotten involved in one of Zach's operations. His deputy had been a year from retirement when a pair of thugs from a baby ring ran him down. It hadn't been Zach's fault, but Noah still felt the loss.

"I guess I can arrange that."

"Good. I'll let you know the particulars as soon as I do."

"All right." The dogs suddenly scrambled to their feet and dashed down the hall. Lauren was home. "I've gotta run before I burn dinner, but thanks for the call. It was good to talk with you again."

Joyous barks greeted the arrival of his daughter. Noah smiled in satisfaction as he hung up. He grabbed the salad from the refrigerator and set it on the table, then he pulled out the colander. The clicking of paws preceded his daughter into the kitchen.

"Hi, Dad! Dinner smells great. I'm starving."

The animals collapsed in a boneless pile inside the door, watching Lauren with canine adoration as she gave him a quick hug and headed for the stove to check on the garlic bread he had warming.

"Yum."

"Go wash up. Dinner in five."

When Lauren returned from the bathroom, they fell into their usual dinnertime routine. The dogs waited hopefully for something to fall in their direction, but were quickly distracted by their own food bowls so he and Lauren could eat in peace. The cat disappeared with a haughty flick of her tail. As he ate, Noah listened to Lauren describe her day with her usual cheerful enthusiasm.

"Oh, and Doug's coming to spend this weekend if that's okay, Dad."

"Anytime." He swallowed a mouthful of pasta and regarded his daughter. "He's not going to drive, is he?"

"No. He's flying into San Antonio and renting a car."

Noah raised his eyebrows. "Pretty expensive for a weekend."

"I know, but he can afford it. And he says I'm worth it."

He shared her grin. "He's right. Listen, there's something

we need to discuss. You know that snub-nosed .38 I gave you?''

Her eyes went from blue to gray as she studied him seriously. ''Uh-huh.''

''Start carrying it for a while.''

''Uh-oh. What's happened?''

His daughter never failed to amaze him. He thanked God every day for the miracle of Lauren. If only Beth had lived to see what a strong, beautiful, levelheaded woman they had raised. He took a bite of salad, chewed, swallowed past the lump in his throat and proceeded to explain about Francis Hartman.

''Okay, Dad, I'll stay alert.''

''The odds of Hartman actually coming here are pretty small,'' he assured her. ''If he holds to his usual routine, he'll be back in jail in a matter of days.''

For Noah and Lauren the following day was life as normal with some heightened caution and awareness. In the afternoon, Noah spent several frustrating hours trying to track down an oil leak in his truck before he gave up and drove into town. He groaned at the sight of Alma Underwood pumping gas into her sports utility, but there was no avoiding the woman unless he drove all the way over to Bitterwater. He brought his truck to a halt and looked around for Marvin Gates. Old Man Lacy had the hapless mechanic cornered inside the garage, garrulously complaining about something under the hood of his ancient pickup.

''Noah! I was just heading home to give you a call,'' Alma said. ''You have to do something.''

Too late to hide, he thought ruefully, and strode over to Alma. ''Afternoon, Alma. What do I have to do something about? I'm not even on duty right now.''

She finished filling her gas tank and began screwing the cap back in place while Noah rested a foot against her front fender.

''Ha! You're the county sheriff, you're always on duty.

Besides, you know young Terry's still wet behind the ears. This woman would chew him into little pieces.''

The idea of anyone chewing his six-foot-three inch, 220-pound muscled deputy into little pieces made Noah smile. Terry Gooding might be young and inexperienced, but he wasn't stupid or Noah wouldn't have hired him.

"What woman, Alma?"

"The one over in my café. She's been hanging around Darwin Crossing for two days now. She doesn't belong here." Alma's seamed face creased even further.

"Where does she belong, Alma?" Over her shoulder, Noah saw that rescue wasn't imminent. Marvin was still busy.

The older woman sniffed. "City woman. Now, I ask you, what business could she possibly have here in Darwin Crossing? As the sheriff, you should talk to her. Find out what she's up to."

He tried to keep amusement out of his voice as he tipped back the brim of his Stetson and tilted his head.

"You mean you haven't pumped her for information already?" There was no better source of information in town than Alma Underwood. The woman lived for gossip.

"Humph. Not that one. You can't pump her with a twelve-gauge. She's real cool-like. Cuts you dead with a look. Good-lookin' broad, I'll give her that, but only if you like the snooty type. She comes into my place and just sits there watching."

"Sitting's not illegal, Alma. Neither is watching. And you do own the only café in town."

The older woman scowled. "She doesn't come there to eat. She orders perfectly good food and then sits there playing with it while she looks out the window or scribbles away on this pad she carries."

Alma took her food seriously. Noah kept his grin inside and glanced over at his pickup to be sure it wasn't blocking anyone. Marvin was still occupied.

"I guess city women are picky eaters, but I'm afraid that isn't illegal, either."

Alma set her jaw and eyed him from beneath thick round glasses. "Okay, I didn't want to say this right out, Noah, but if you're gonna take that attitude, now I will. She seems to be watchin' your Lauren."

"What?"

Amusement vanished at the mention of his daughter's name. Noah came away from the fender of her SUV. Tension took a two-fisted grip on the base of his stomach.

For an instant, he thought about Francis Hartman, then discarded the idea of a connection. But a much older fear reared its ugly head.

"Thought that might get your attention."

Beth had laughed at him, told him his worry was foolish. But while she was a cop's wife, she didn't see and hear all the things he did. From the day they adopted Lauren, he'd always secretly feared that one day Lauren's birth mother would come and try to take their little girl away.

"Are you sure about this, Alma?"

"Course I'm sure."

Who would be watching his daughter?

"A woman," he said almost to himself. The adoption had been perfectly legal and nearly twenty years ago. Still, Beth's death had strengthened the fear. What if Lauren's biological parents learned that Beth was dead? What if they decided they'd made a terrible mistake? He'd never understood how anyone could give up a precious baby like Lauren in the first place. His fear had not abated after Beth's funeral. It had even played a small role in his moving out here in the middle of nowhere after he found himself a widower. Strangers were always noticed here in Darwin Crossing.

"Course she's a woman, didn't I say as much?"

"Who is she?" he demanded.

"That's what you need to find out," Alma said, sounding exasperated. "The woman has a file in that briefcase she carries around and your Lauren's name is scrawled on the face of it.''

The tension building inside him coiled itself into a tight knot.

Alma bobbed her head as if she knew the impact her words were having. ''If someone is checking on your daughter, maybe it's time to make sitting and watching illegal here in Darwin Crossing.''

''Where is this woman now?''

''In my café,'' Alma said with satisfaction.

Noah battled his spreading tension.

''You know, it occurred to me to wonder if that high-society boyfriend of your daughter's might have gone and hired himself a fancy private investigator to keep an eye on his fiancée,'' she added.

Alma's suggestion stopped him cold, changing the direction of Noah's thoughts. Douglas Rossiter came from a wealthy background. In fact, the Rossiter family was well-known amid the Dallas elite. While Doug didn't strike him as the jealous type, it was barely possible that he was having some sort of check run on Lauren. Lauren had just returned from a visit with the Rossiter family, relating amusing tales about their lifestyle, which was so different from her own. Did they think she hadn't fit in?

''You can't trust them society people,'' Alma insisted. ''They're always lookin' down on hardworking folk like us. I told you it was a bad idea to let your Lauren marry outside her class.''

Noah brushed that aside, but he couldn't dismiss the assumption that this new stranger was a private investigator. It was within the realm of possibility that someone in the Rossiter family was checking on Lauren. That made more sense than a relative suddenly trying to make contact after all these years.

The investigator would find absolutely nothing, of course, but the idea of the whole thing made Noah angry. If this woman started probing around in Lauren's background, she could stir her unknown birth mother into taking some sort of action. After all, Lauren was marrying into a wealthy family.

"I called Terry," Alma continued, "but he says he can't do anything unless she breaks the law."

True enough. "I'll go over and have a talk with the woman."

Alma's eyes lit victoriously.

"You do that," she called to his retreating back. "That woman's up to no good."

Noah waved to Marvin as he left his truck where he'd parked it and started down the street. The mechanic could look for the oil leak later. Noah strolled toward the café with deceptive speed. The stranger's sleek silver luxury car was parked out in front, looking mildly intimidated by the much larger vehicles that surrounded it. A rental out of San Antonio, Noah noted.

His stomach tightened another notch as he realized where he'd seen the car before. Yesterday, it had been parked in Bitterwater not far from the vet's office where Lauren was working.

Noah hadn't paid the car any attention when he'd driven past, other than to note how out of place it looked. He hadn't seen anyone inside and assumed the driver was with the vet. Now the tension inside him began to unfurl. Thank God for Alma's warning.

While he doubted a private investigator would spring for an expensive luxury car to drive around in, one never knew. As soon as he was close enough, he made a mental note of the plate number. Then he walked up beside the car and peered inside.

"May I help you with something?"

Her sultry voice did a slow crawl up his spine. He lifted his head and drank in the view of the woman standing behind him. She was gorgeous. Absolutely gorgeous. There was no mistaking her for a resident even if he hadn't known everyone by name in a hundred-mile radius. The woman looked more out of place than her car. Five-seven, he'd estimate, slender, but not without some nicely placed curves. Grace Kelly came to mind with those cheekbones and that glowing skin. The woman's hair was cut to her chin in a style that looked expensively chic, yet artfully simple. The style suited her.

"Just looking," he told her as he adjusted the brim of his hat and watched in puzzlement as her body seemed to tighten in recognition. He'd swear she was a total stranger, yet her body language said otherwise.

The shaft of unexpected and unwanted desire caught him unprepared. He wondered if she felt the pull of this sudden chemistry, as well. Dressed in a navy pantsuit that fit as if it had been designed just for her, she managed to look completely feminine, yet at the same time conveyed a sense of professionalism. His gaze was drawn to the V of her open-necked, white silk shirt, which stopped just short of the nicely rounded curves of her breasts.

"Like it?" she asked coolly.

Her voice was soft velvet wrapped around spikes of steel. The voice made him think of other soft things he'd like to wrap around steel. Uncomfortably embarrassed to be caught staring, he tried for a smile. "What's not to like?"

Spots of color appeared on her cheeks. "I meant the car."

He tipped his head to one side and let his smile widen. "So did I."

For a moment, she seemed disconcerted, but her cool mask quickly settled back into place. No wonder Alma didn't like her. Few women would. And most men would feel intimidated—the ones who didn't see her as prey. He had to rein in a pretty strong predatory feeling of his own. The woman was class, yet she gave off an aura of sensuality that reached inside him and grabbed him where he lived. And all with no effort on her part.

Behind the dark lenses of her glasses, he sensed her assessing his faded work jeans, matching jacket, boots and plaid shirt. Fingering the brim of his hat, Noah figured he failed her fashion test hands-down. He'd spent the past few hours under the hood of his truck. Fashion hadn't come into his choice of clothing, and it didn't worry him now.

"We don't see many cars like this one around here," he said.

Her head inclined toward the line of pickup trucks dwarfing the car. "I've noticed."

"We don't see many strangers in town, either," he said, inviting her to share her reasons for being here.

"Don't tell me you're the welcoming committee."

Strands of soft blond hair shimmered in the sunlight as she tossed her head. He found himself watching with interest as each lock fell smoothly back into place as though well trained.

"Nope, but I admit I'm curious. There isn't much to lure visitors to Darwin Crossing."

"You might be surprised." Her words seemed to startle her. She started forward briskly. "Now, if you'll excuse me…"

He blocked her by the simple expedient of turning around directly into her path. She bumped his shoulder and jumped back as if scalded.

"Is there a problem here, Sheriff?"

As a law enforcement official, he'd met this sort of defensiveness before. Lots of people didn't like cops for all sorts of reasons. Problem was, she shouldn't know his occupation. He wasn't wearing his uniform.

"Now, how could you know I'm the sheriff?"

He watched with interest as the color faded from her cheeks. He fought down an urge to remove those dark sunglasses so he could see the eyes beneath. What color would they be? And what would they reveal?

"I saw you in uniform the other day."

The keen anticipation that had been building inside him shut down instantly at those words. He hadn't been in uniform since he picked Lauren up at the airport a couple of days ago. At least a full day before Alma said the stranger had come to town. He leaned back against the door to her car. "Is that right? Which day would that be, exactly?"

"I'm not… Does it matter?"

"I'm afraid so."

"Why?"

"Alma tells me you've been hanging around the past couple of days."

"Alma being…?"

"The woman who runs the café."

"Ah. That Alma."

She'd regained her composure, and this time her look was designed to reduce a man to the level of cow manure.

"So what seems to be the problem, Sheriff? Tips not generous enough?"

"I wouldn't know." He came off the car and closed the distance between them, deliberately using his body to intimidate her. "But I would like to know why you're here in town and how you know who I am," he said with deceptive softness.

He was unaccountably pleased that she held her ground. This was not a woman who would be easily intimidated. His reflection stared back at him from the mirrored sunglasses. He had a feeling he'd be seeing sparks flashing if he could see her eyes.

If she was a private investigator for the Rossiters, they were obviously hiring unusual new talent. No surprise there. They had plenty of money.

Noah put her age somewhere near thirty. Up close, her skin was flawless, her makeup so carefully applied as to appear nonexistent. And as the breeze shifted direction, the air carried a subtle hint of fragrance—something delicately feminine. Soft. Unobtrusive. Almost elusively compelling.

Just like the woman herself.

He found himself relaxing despite his instincts to the contrary. He didn't want to like her, even if he admired her spunk. And he sure didn't want to be attracted to her, yet it was hard to prevent. Noah chided himself for being mildly distracted by the rise and fall of her chest. She'd gone back to looking unruffled, but he could almost hear her thoughts whirling.

"If you must know, Sheriff, I'm here sketching."

He'd give her points for originality, but she'd lose on the delivery. He didn't have to see her eyes to know they'd be shifting away on that answer.

"Not much scenery here in town," he said mildly.

"You'd be surprised."

Her tone was dry, but her meaning unmistakable. He was the scenery she was talking about.

He knew women found him attractive. His daughter had once come home after a dance to gleefully inform him that he was considered the catch of the county. Now that same sense of embarrassment crawled over his skin at her deliberate stare.

She lifted her chin and her expression became serious. "I'm not sketching scenery, Sheriff," she said. "I'm a clothing designer. I came here to soak up some atmosphere for a new winter line."

Noah didn't have to ponder that one. "This is February."

Sky found herself on the verge of smiling. She caught herself in the nick of time. This strangely compelling attraction she felt was dangerous. The sheriff was the sort of man a woman spun fantasies about, the kind of man they put on billboards to convince men—and the women in their lives—that some product could make them look like him.

It was a delicious fantasy. *He* was a delicious fantasy.

Too bad he was her daughter's adoptive father.

# CHAPTER THREE

SKY TRIED to steady the erratic beat of her heart.

When she'd asked the man at the gas station about Lauren, he'd casually pointed her out. Sky hadn't seen her daughter up close yet, but she'd been following her, trying to learn all she could while remaining unobtrusive. She hadn't yet decided on an approach.

The moment she saw the sheriff looking over her car, she recognized him from the airport. There was no mistaking the sexy stranger in uniform or not. To think she'd come so close to meeting her daughter within minutes of landing here in Texas. This had to be some sort of fate at work. For a second she was tempted to tell this incredibly handsome man who she really was. Fortunately, caution prevailed.

"Designers have to work well ahead of the calendar year, Sheriff," Sky said, stalling as she tried to decide the best tactic to take. "The designs I'm sketching right now are for next winter," she explained.

The sheriff had a devastating smile that invited a person to smile back. Sky ordered her pulse to behave. She wasn't here to have a flirtation, and based on her observations, Lauren would drive past any minute now. Sky had hoped to arrange an "accidental" meeting of some sort today, but she could hardly do that under the watchful eyes of Lauren's adoptive father. Sky had to get rid of the man somehow.

"I don't suppose you would have some identification I could see," she asked, trying to reassert control of the situation.

His eyes glinted.

"I think that's supposed to be my line."

"You aren't in uniform," she pointed out.

"But you're the one who called me sheriff."

"I might have made a mistake." A big one. She had no business baiting the one man who could ruin everything.

He surprised them both by chuckling. The deep sound rippled over her nerve endings, bringing an inadvertent smile to her lips. But when he slid his fingers deep into the front pocket at his hip, her mouth went dry. She followed his fingers, drawn to the fit of his jeans over that nicely muscled form.

Good grief, what was wrong with her? She never stared at a man like this. She was too old to be gawking at him like some virginal schoolgirl even if he was as tempting as sin itself.

He smiled with chocolatey rich brown eyes and she knew he'd noticed her watching him. Warmth bathed her cheeks and she forced herself to look away. A woman could lose all coherent thought staring into eyes like those.

He withdrew a folder and flipped it open. Sky barely glanced at the badge inside. She already knew what it said and she was busy being irked by the chemical rush feeding her hormones.

"Now that I showed you mine," he said softly, "how about a peek at yours?"

She could actually feel her blush growing brighter. Not for the first time she cursed her porcelain skin, which made blushing an uncontrollable fact of life. That was bad enough, but for some stupid reason she couldn't seem to catch her breath. The lines beside his mouth and eyes deepened. Another smile edged up the corners of his lips as he slipped the folder back inside his front pocket.

She should be striving to convey her annoyance. Instead, his expression made her feel vividly alive and totally female. The heady rush made it impossible to dislike the man. Still, she'd better get the upper hand fast.

"A quick peek like that hardly merits a full display on my part," she said tartly. "I haven't broken any laws."

"None that I know about, anyhow."

God, but he had a killer smile. The perfect accompaniment for that deep sexy voice and those seriously dangerous bedroom eyes. Madison Avenue would kill to have him.

"You really are the local sheriff?" she asked, stalling.

He tipped back the brim of his hat, watching her steadily. "Duly elected and everything."

She'd bet every female in the county had voted for him just to catch a glimpse of that smile.

The abrupt sound of a car horn made them both jump. Sky's mouth turned into a desert when she realized she was about to have her "accidental" meeting after all. Her daughter was right on schedule and Sky still wasn't prepared.

Her knees threatened to buckle. She wanted to wipe away the sudden dampness from hands that were visibly trembling. Instead, she clutched her bag more firmly, drawing it against her like a shield. This was her daughter, a piece of her very being that no one and nothing could deny. And not a sound issued past her dry, parted lips.

The sheriff had spun to face the vehicle behind him. The functioning portion of Sky's mind told her he was cursing under his breath as he hurried forward. He wasn't going to want to learn why she was here. Her worst-case scenario would come true if she didn't handle this perfectly.

But that was her daughter sitting there!

"Hey, Dad!" Lauren called through the open window on the passenger's side of her car. "Marvin wants to know what you want done with the truck. He said you just walked off and left it there. I told him that oil leak must have gotten the best of you."

"Lauren, I'm busy right now."

Instantly, her eyes darkened in concern. Sky wanted to

protest. She wanted to come forward. Yet she stood mute as stone, emotion obstructing the words clogging her throat.

This was her daughter. That small, precious life she'd carried inside her body for nine long months, the infant she had never seen, was now a grown woman staring back at her with eyes so like her own. Sky felt numb.

"Sorry, Dad."

The sheriff's shoulders relaxed, but he kept his back turned to Sky, deliberately not introducing them.

"That's okay. I'll talk to Marvin when I'm through here."

"Need a lift home?"

He shook his head and his tone gentled. "No, thanks. The truck got me here, it will get me back. I've got chili in the slow cooker. You can do the salad, but don't let Limpet con you into any more green pepper. It gives him gas."

She grinned impishly. Sky's heart turned over as she recognized the look. Her own mother had often given it to Sky many times over the years.

"I won't, Dad."

"I should be home in an hour."

"Okay." With a curious glance at Sky, she pulled away.

Sky drew in a jagged breath, breaking the stasis that had held her so silent. In that brief exchange, she had learned everything she'd wanted to know about her daughter's relationship with her adoptive father. Their loving bond was almost a tangible thing.

The jagged pain that razored its way through her had its roots sunk deep in jealousy. She stared after Lauren with a longing that brought the sting of tears to her eyes once more.

Noah turned to find the woman watching Lauren drive away with an expression he couldn't define, but one that instantly raised new alarms. He no longer felt indulgent, nor would he allow the chemistry between them to interfere any further.

"I'll see your identification now," he said briskly.

He sensed a moment of apprehension, then her hand slid quickly inside her briefcase. Belatedly, his training kicked in. He reached back toward his weapon.

"Hold it!"

She raised her face, the hair parting smoothly away from creamy smooth skin. "What?"

"Bring your hand back out real slow."

Her mouth opened in an O of surprise. With a jerky nod, she slowly withdrew her hand. Her fingers clutched a black leather wallet.

"Set the briefcase on the hood of your car."

She complied without a word, but she was trembling. He ignored a momentary desire to reassure her.

"Now take your driver's license from the wallet."

Her fingers shook just the tiniest bit as she fumbled to remove the license. A business card fell to the ground at his feet. With a darting movement, she scooped it quickly, but he glimpsed the gilt lettering on the front and made out the word *investigator*. His chest felt hollow as she stuffed the card back inside the wallet, looking guilty as sin.

"Here, Sheriff."

She was careful not to touch him as she handed him her driver's license. Noah scanned the plastic card while keeping part of his attention on her. He wished he had his radio. He had no way to run her license. And he was definitely going to run it.

"Skylar Diamond?" he asked suspiciously. The picture wasn't flattering, but it was her. The name sounded as phony as her story about being a fashion designer.

"My mother thought it had a dramatic ring to it."

"What did your father think?"

Her shoulders lifted and fell. "I have no idea. He didn't stick around long enough for me to meet him."

Chagrined, he couldn't think of an answer to that. He wished she'd take off those glasses. You could tell a lot about a person from their eyes. Noah studied the New York address. He wasn't familiar with the city, but he thought the location sounded uptown. The high-rent district would certainly go with her outfit, which was as out of place here in Darwin Crossing as the woman herself.

"Is this your current residence?"

"Yes."

But he'd caught her momentary hesitation. Was she lying? Or did she simply not want to answer his questions?

"Where are you staying here in Texas?"

"A rooming house in Bitterwater."

"Why?"

She cocked her head to the side. "Why what?"

"What are you doing in this part of Texas, Ms. Diamond?"

"I told you. I'm here to—"

"Get inspiration for a winter line of clothing? I don't think so."

"It's the truth," she insisted stubbornly.

"Then what do you want with my daughter?"

She sucked in a startled breath. "I...don't know what you're talking about."

His jaw firmed. She was lying. That made it real easy for him to overlook her beauty and any attraction he felt toward her.

"According to my sources, you've been hanging around town for two days now, watching Lauren. I want to know why."

Instantly, she bristled. "I don't know who told you that...."

Her voice trailed off as her head turned. Alma stood against the nearby building watching them, hands crossed over her chest while she rocked back and forth on the heels of her boots.

"Ah. The town watchdog, I suppose."

Noah didn't respond. He could almost see the woman's

mind at work. He'd give a lot to be able to read the individual thoughts.

"All right, Sheriff. I was watching your daughter. But I didn't know she was your daughter."

Another lie? He couldn't be sure.

"I saw her in town the other day and wondered if she'd be interested in doing some modeling."

His gut tensed. The story was plausible given the way she dressed and acted, yet her body language was all wrong. One hand flexed nervously against her side. The other gripped her wallet tightly.

"Modeling," he said softly, as if he'd never heard the term before.

Her fingers stilled. She drew in a breath. "Yes, modeling. You know, where a person wears designer clothing for the purpose of displaying said clothing to others."

He'd give her points for a quick rally.

"Your daughter would be perfect for the line I have in mind."

"I thought you designed the clothing. Don't tell me you also hire your own models."

"I do when I see a young woman who would do justice to them," she argued. "She's tall, willowy, blond, the perfect image of a young, upcoming executive. She'd make an excellent model."

"Over my dead body."

Noah heard a murmur of assent. He glanced around and saw that Alma had been joined by two of her cronies. Great. They were starting to draw a small crowd.

"I'm going to ask you to step over to my office, Ms. Diamond. The red brick building across the street."

She tensed. "Am I under arrest?"

"Not yet."

"What's that supposed to mean?"

"It means I want to run your identification through the computer. I'm asking for your cooperation."

"And if I refuse?"

"Then I'll have to insist."

Her lips tightened. She tossed her head in the direction of the onlookers. Alma looked smugly satisfied.

"Very well, Sheriff." She reached for her briefcase.

"I'll get that," he told her quickly. "Head for that red brick building across the street."

"The one that says Sheriff on the window?"

Without waiting for a response, she strode across the street, head high, her spindly high heels clicking against the pavement. He picked up her briefcase and followed, refusing to be distracted by the subtle sway of her hips. Skylar Diamond moved like a queen.

Well, she should have stayed in her own little kingdom. Darwin Crossing was his town.

The slim briefcase had no betraying bulge and not enough weight for a gun. He didn't really think she was dangerous in a physical sense—unless he counted the sensual tug she created inside him without even trying.

Noah shook his head. The briefcase was unlatched. He hesitated only a second before lifting the flap. Papers, disks, files, notebooks. A manila file with some handwritten directions sticking out. Finders Keepers was written in a bold scrawl across one of them. Now, why did that have a familiar ring to it? He didn't have time to read more because she reached the office door and stood waiting expectantly.

His lips curved wryly. He held the door open for her and allowed her to precede him into the office. The dispatcher, Marissa Hurtado, looked up questioningly. Noah gave her an imperceptible nod.

"Go straight back to that first desk and have a seat, Ms. Diamond," he directed.

She paused to let her glance quickly scan the room, no doubt categorizing and dismissing the badly scarred furniture and the messy papers spread everywhere. He'd decided the papers bred in secret overnight just to frustrate him.

Paperwork was the bane of his life. He set his hat on top of the newest stack and walked around his desk.

"You might want to take off your sunglasses," he suggested as she perched stiffly on the edge of the visitor's chair.

"Why would I want to do that?"

He indicated the overhead fluorescent lights. "No sun?"

After a moment's hesitation, her hand reached for the glasses and slipped them off. Silvery-gray eyes met and held his gaze. "Happy?"

He tried not to smile at her sarcasm. "Ecstatic."

"I'm so glad."

Noah thought again that she was one of the most beautiful women he'd ever seen. Thick, dark lashes framed glittering eyes that held just the faintest trace of apprehension. But if she was nervous, it wasn't enough to stop her sassy mouth.

"So, now what?"

"Now I'll run your license and see if there are any wants or warrants."

She fidgeted and quickly stilled beneath his inquiring gaze.

"Is that a problem?"

"No. Of course not."

Her fingers tapped the edge of the armchair. She bit down on her lower lip in contemplation, drawing his attention to their fullness and the soft curve of her mouth.

"I'm fairly sure I paid that overdue parking ticket," she muttered.

Noah didn't want to like her. Especially since he wasn't sure what sort of a threat she presented. But Ms. Skylar Diamond had a disarming way of draining the tension right out of him.

"I'll let you know if you did in just a minute."

She fidgeted some more as he waited for the connection. "Nope. No parking tickets. But you aren't much for stop signs or speed limits, are you?'' he asked when her information finally came up on screen.

She settled back in the hard wooden chair and regarded him coolly. The telephone rang and he heard Marissa answer.

''It's a matter of perception,'' she told him. ''The New York police department can be very rigid about some things.'' She sounded mildly aggrieved. ''And I *know* I paid all *those* fines.''

''So you did,'' he agreed. Behind her, Marissa was dispatching his deputy clear out near Butte Point. Noah frowned before returning his attention to Skylar Diamond. ''No wants or warrants came up.''

''You sound surprised.''

''You never know.''

Part of him wished something had come up so he'd have an excuse to hold her until he knew what was really behind her sudden appearance here in Darwin Crossing. Alma's suggestion coupled with the business card in her wallet brought back his earlier fears.

''So I can go now?''

The telephone rang again. He paid no attention. ''In a bit. Mind showing me that card you dropped earlier?''

Her silvery eyes darkened to gray-green while her nails bit into the wooden arm of the chair.

''Yes.''

''Why is that?''

She held his gaze without flinching. ''Because unless I'm under arrest, I'm going to leave now.''

''Noah,'' Marissa interrupted. ''I'm sorry, but Henry's bull just took down the fence again. Jackson called it in. He says he's going after the bull with a shotgun this time. I just sent Terry on another call out near Butte Point.''

Noah cursed. Knowing Jackson's temper as he did, his darn fool neighbor wasn't making idle threats. The man had no patience left when it came to Henry's bull. If Noah didn't want the Hatfields and McCoys reenacted in his own back-yard, he was going to have to do something about that blasted animal.

"Call Jackson back. Tell him to stay put until I get there. If he fires that shotgun I'll arrest him for disturbing the peace. I'm on my way."

He didn't want to let Skylar Diamond go, but he had no valid reason to hold her.

"You're free to go, Ms. Diamond, but stay away from Lauren. My daughter is engaged to be married this summer. The last thing she needs or wants is a career in modeling."

Her composure slipped when he mentioned the engage-ment. He saw an instant of shock before she rallied, blank-ing her expression completely. Now why should she care one way or another? The phone rang again as she came to her feet. Noah rose, as well.

"Isn't that for her to decide, Sheriff?"

"You don't know when to quit, do you?" But she defi-nitely had spunk, he'd give her that.

"This isn't the middle ages, you know. Women do have choices."

"Noah," Marissa called out, "that was Henry's wife. Henry went after the bull and Jackson. She said he took his rifle with him."

"Damn!" He didn't have time for this, but it looked like he'd have to make time. "I'm on my way."

He grabbed his hat, closing the distance between him and the woman. Flecks of blue and green shimmered in her eyes as excitement warred with apprehension. While she flinched slightly, she didn't back up or lower her gaze.

"Go back to New York, Ms. Diamond. You've over-stayed your welcome in Darwin Crossing. If I find you around town again I'll arrest you for loitering."

Her lips parted. For just an instant, he had the strongest impulse to taste those lips. Then sanity reasserted itself and he put his hat on and strode out the door. He heard her address Marissa before the door swung shut.

"And I thought New Yorkers had a reputation for being cold."

Noah sprinted for the gas station and his leaky truck. So she thought he was cold, did she? Well, cold was the one way Skylar Diamond definitely didn't leave him.

THE MAN sometimes known as Norman Smith worked the locks, cursing under his breath until he got past the last one. He had a feeling this wild-goose chase wasn't going to be any more productive than his search of her office had been. Coming to New York had been a mistake. She'd covered her tracks well.

He'd called her office, looking for her, but her well-trained staff refused to give him any information. He'd hoped she'd left a record of her plans somewhere in her office. Unfortunately, that hadn't proved to be the case. Getting inside the well-protected building had taken time and ingenuity, but all he'd learned for his efforts was her home address.

He'd let the rising tide of his anger get the best of him. Probably, he shouldn't have given vent to his frustration by tearing up her office. When she found out, it would just send her deeper into whatever hole she'd found for herself. But she had to know he'd be coming after her. Surely she wasn't so stupid she'd think he didn't want his money back.

She had good locks, he admitted as the last one gave. And the security in her building was pretty good, as well. Not as good as he was, of course, but she was going to pay for this inconvenience. He was going to hurt her—badly. He'd already started planning all the ways he would make her pay.

He slipped silently inside her dark apartment, listening hard. There was no sound. He used his tiny pen flash to lead him to her pristine, empty bedroom. Damn it! He wanted that computer case! He needed that computer case! If she thought she was going to take his money and walk away without consequence...

He slipped the knife from its sheath and scored the fancy white bedspread viciously. Not bothering with stealth any longer, he flipped on the bedroom light and opened her closet. Too many empty hangers. Looked to him like she'd split for good. Remembering all that luggage she'd had with her, he wondered. Maybe she hadn't taken off with his money after all. Maybe she'd been planning from the start not to come back again. If she was on the run for some reason, she could be anywhere at all by now. He needed an address, a phone number. Something that would tell him where she'd gone.

Norman Smith was nothing if not thorough. He destroyed or damaged every inch of the apartment, pausing by the telephone and the blinking answering machine.

He listened and discarded the five messages from her friends and co-workers and concentrated on the memo pad beside the telephone. She'd written several messages on the top sheet of paper, but then she'd drawn stupid doodles over half of them. He couldn't make out all the words. The hotel name was clear enough, but he already knew she wasn't there any longer.

Bitterwater. What the hell was Bitterwater? At least it looked like Bitter something. A place? Or had she been drinking water that tasted bitter? He cursed again. Bitterwater could be one of those small Texas towns. There was a phone number below it with a Texas area code. Unfortunately, the phone number wasn't legible beyond the first few digits.

There was a dollar amount. A hotel fee?

He'd find out. He was very good at puzzles. Haughty Ms. Diamond was about to learn that fact. And then she'd discover some of the other things he was good at.

Especially murder.

# CHAPTER FOUR

SKY FACED the morning with a heavy heart. Rain beat a sympathetic tattoo against the windows. She had barely slept all night and it showed. Even a shower and makeup didn't help. What little sleep she'd managed to get had been haunted by conflicting emotions. And Sheriff Beaufort was at the center of the storm.

The handsome sheriff had to be the most intriguing man she'd ever met. Why did he have to be her daughter's adoptive father? She considered it luck that he hadn't recognized her name. Even though adoption records were supposed to be sealed, there was always the chance that someone in his position had learned the truth somehow.

She cringed when she remembered the ridiculous story she'd made up for being in Darwin Crossing and her interest in Lauren. He hadn't believed her, obviously. She should have told him the truth.

Only she hadn't wanted to see the condemnation in those chocolate eyes when he learned she'd given up her only child at birth.

Watching Lauren and the sheriff interact yesterday, Sky had felt a pang of envy for their easy camaraderie. It reminded Sky of her relationship with her mother. Lauren had grown up happy and loved—without the poverty. Wasn't that why Sky had come all this way? She'd wanted to know if she'd made the right choice all those years ago. She had.

So why did she feel so empty inside?

Sky shut her eyes. At thirty-nine, she didn't feel like a

mother, much less the mother of the bride. But at least technically, that's what she was. Last night she'd concluded that the only right thing to do was to go back to New York without saying anything to Lauren. Her daughter needed nothing from the birth mother she'd never known. Sky's presence here would only cause trouble. The sheriff had done a fabulous job raising her daughter. Sky had no right to interfere.

Taking a deep breath, she looked around at the fussy little room and decided she would drive back to San Antonio this afternoon. She'd come looking for her past and she'd found it. Time to get on with her life.

If she could get a booking at the Grand Hotel again, she could talk with that security officer she'd dealt with the morning she'd discovered her missing laptop. Ray Ellenshaw never seemed to be available when she called to check on its status. The three different people she'd spoken with all claimed her computer case hadn't been turned in yet and no one had come forward to claim the switched case.

Maybe if she showed up at the hotel in person, she could convince the manager to open the case and check for identification inside. While it wasn't critical, she'd really like to have her computer back. She had the whole weekend before her meeting with Lily Garrett Bishop and she'd like to get some work done.

As tempting as it was to simply board a plane and go home, Sky decided to attend the scheduled meeting with the detective agency. She wanted whatever background information they had compiled on her daughter. It was all she would ever have of Lauren.

To add to her misery this morning, she'd awakened with a dull headache and she didn't have any aspirin with her. She might as well buy a few sundries here in town before she left. This headache didn't feel like it was going away anytime soon.

Sky went downstairs to tell the nice couple who ran the

boardinghouse that her plans had changed. She'd be checking out as soon as she got back from the store.

But on leaving the store she discovered the wind had picked up, giving the rain some added emphasis. The dismal day suited her mood perfectly. She hurried to her car and sat there listening to the rain whip against the rooftop. The return trip to San Antonio would be a long one, especially since visibility wasn't all that good. She hated driving at the best of times. Sky wasn't looking forward to this drive with depression and a headache for passengers.

Glancing at the bag on the seat beside her, she debated about swallowing a couple of aspirin now, but she hadn't bought anything to drink. The headache could wait until she got back to the boardinghouse. Obviously, it had nowhere else it wanted to be.

The veterinary clinic where Lauren worked was in the opposite direction, but despite her headache, Sky found the temptation to drive past it one more time irresistible.

She wouldn't stop. She just wanted to drive past and silently wish her daughter a happy life.

The wind continued to push sheets of rain at her car, giving her windshield wipers a frantic workout. At times she could barely see the road. Maybe she'd better wait until the storm slowed before setting out for San Antonio. Sky rounded the tree-shrouded corner near the clinic slowly, thankful for the lack of traffic.

Without warning, a large black shape bounded across the road directly in her path. Sky tromped on the brake. The car skidded, seeking traction on the wet pavement. She felt a thump and her heart slid into her throat. The ghostly shape of a vehicle suddenly loomed in front of her but there was no time to react.

The air bag deployed with a shock of sound and a burst of white powder. Stunned, she sat there while the bag deflated. Her eyes gradually focused on the writing across the back of the large sports utility vehicle.

*County Sheriff.*

"Oh, no."

Fate couldn't be that cruel. Sky struggled to open her jammed door without success. Glancing out the window, she saw a large shape in a bright-yellow slicker descend from the driver's side of the sheriff's car and start back toward her.

Since her door wouldn't budge, she climbed across the seat to go out the passenger side, but that door was stuck as well. She pushed with all her might, trying to force it open. By then, he was there to help.

She stepped on the pavement and staggered. Large, capable hands gripped her upper arms to steady her. She ignored the cold rain that slapped at her face and looked up.

"I don't believe it," he said.

"Me, either. Are you hurt?"

Brown eyes surveyed her from under the brim of his Stetson. "No. What about you?"

She ignored the trembling that had started somewhere in her middle and spread in all directions. The animal.

"I'm okay, but we have to find it!"

She tugged free of his hands and plunged unsteadily toward the stand of trees at the side of the road.

"Wait a minute. Come back here. What are you doing? Find what?"

"The bear. He ran right out in front of me," she said, tossing the words over her shoulder. She reached the edge of the road where she thought she'd seen the animal disappear. The sheriff grabbed her arm again, preventing her from stepping into the overgrown thicket.

"Did you say bear?"

Sky wiped at the water streaming down her face. The shaking was worse now. To top it off, her stomach had gotten into the act. She had a strong desire to throw up.

"A bear cub, I think. I tried to miss it." Tears suddenly lodged in the back of her throat as she remembered the thump. She swallowed hard. "But I didn't. We have to find it."

She pulled loose again and started for the trees.

"Get back here!"

"But it's hurt! It could be dying."

"Better it than you. Stop!"

Those incredibly capable hands had a firm grip on her shoulders now. She blinked water from her eyes in an attempt to see his face.

"Where's your common sense?" he demanded.

A sudden thrashing sound held them both riveted. Then the sheriff yanked her behind him as his gaze swept the overgrown brush. Sky spotted the dark shaggy shape in the darker shadows near a large tree.

"There! He's right over there."

The sheriff turned her, roughly shoving her back toward the road. Sky stumbled and almost fell.

"Get back!"

It took her sluggish brain a second to realize he was holding a gun. He suddenly looked a lot larger and more dangerous than any bear could ever be.

"Don't shoot him!"

The animal was struggling to crawl toward them out of the brush, making pitiful yelping sounds of distress. The sheriff cursed. He holstered his gun without looking at her. Stepping forward, he began talking in a low voice.

Sky nearly screamed in tension. What was he doing? That beast could attack him. What had *she* been doing?

"Go alert the vet," he called to her. "Tell him I'm bringing in a wounded dog."

"That can't be a dog. It's too big."

"Go! Hurry up. He's bleeding badly."

"Oh, God."

Sky pivoted and ran. She burst into the waiting room, dripping wet and out of breath even though she hadn't had far to run. Her pulse hammered so loudly she felt deaf.

"We need the vet," she told the startled young woman behind the desk. Her voice sounded unnaturally shrill, but she couldn't seem to control the pitch. "I thought it was a bear, but the sheriff says it's a dog. Only it's too big to be a dog. Please, get the vet. He's hurt."

The woman gaped at her. "The sheriff's hurt?"

"Not the sheriff, the animal."

"What animal?"

"The one I just hit!"

The woman blinked in confusion. She didn't move. Frantically, Sky searched for someone else. She spotted a familiar face shutting a door down the hall. Relief made her giddy.

"Lauren! Your dad needs help. He says the animal is bleeding bad. It ran out in front of me. I tried, but I couldn't stop. I'm afraid...it might die."

A tear escaped the corner of her eye and trickled down her cheek, mingling with the water streaming from her hair.

If Lauren was surprised by the fact that Sky had called her by name, she didn't waste time on questions. "I'll be right there."

Lauren disappeared to reappear a second later with a man in a white lab coat.

"Where's the animal?" the vet asked her.

"Over that way in some trees off the road." Sky swept her arm in the general direction. Before the vet reached her, the front door slammed open. The sheriff stood there, a huge, black, dripping beast draped across his arms.

"This way," the vet ordered.

Sky swayed. The sheriff had left a trail of bright-red blood splatters across the tile floor. She shivered hard. Someone touched her arm.

"Are you all right?" Lauren asked.

"I think—" Sky swallowed hard as her stomach suddenly launched an all-out revolt. "I need your bathroom."

"Come with me."

In the end, Sky decided that losing the contents of her stomach helped steady her nerves. Her knees were weak and she still felt shaky, but the shock was fading. She cupped her hands under the faucet and rinsed her mouth, splashing her already dripping face with water. She tried not to look in the mirror over the sink. Her one glimpse had made an indelible impression. Her eyes were wide and dark, and her face was so pale her makeup stood out in stark relief. Her sopping wet hair lay plastered against her head. And she'd left her purse in the car on the road!

She threw open the door, startling a gasp out of Lauren. Her daughter stood on the other side, poised to knock. In her other hand was Sky's purse and the plastic shopping bag.

"Dad thought you might want these out of your car."

"Yes. Thank you. I was just going to look for them. I think it's probably a good thing I didn't take those aspirins earlier. They wouldn't even have had time to dissolve." Sky realized she was babbling.

"You need to sit down," Lauren told her calmly. "The ambulance will be here shortly."

She followed her daughter to a small, cramped office. "I don't need an ambulance."

"You should let them check you out."

Sky shook her head. "I'm okay, just a little punchy. How bad is the animal hurt?"

"I'll find out. It was the Montgomerys' Newfoundland puppy."

"That couldn't have been a puppy. The animal was huge."

Lauren smiled kindly. She had her grandmother's comforting smile, Sky realized with a wrenching pang.

"He certainly is. Sit over here. Let's get your suit coat off. You're soaking wet. You can use this towel to dry your hair and I'll hang your jacket over here."

Lauren kept up a steady stream of chatter. Somehow, that reassured Sky, helping to steady her.

"Newfoundlands are big dogs. I'm not surprised you thought he was a bear. Actually, Clancy is only about eight months old."

"Oh, God. That makes it even worse. I hit a puppy. I really tried to miss him, honest. Is he going to be okay?"

Lauren took her hand, her face wreathed in understanding and sympathy. "He's going to be fine. We'll set his fractures and he'll live to cause more trouble, you'll see. The accident wasn't your fault. Clancy's a big bumbling oaf of a dog. He's always in some sort of mischief. Your hand is freezing. I'll get you a blanket to wrap up in."

"Thank you." Her teeth were starting to chatter. "I think you might be right. Maybe I am in shock."

Lauren stood. "I'll send the receptionist in with some coffee. You need to warm up. I have to go help the doctor with Clancy right now so I want you to wait right here until my dad comes back in, all right?"

Sky managed a nod, even though the thought of waiting for Sheriff Noah Beaufort was not a comforting one. She'd been so worried about the animal, she'd almost forgotten she'd hit his police car. He'd probably lock her up and throw away the key.

The receptionist brought her a thick fuzzy sweater instead of a blanket, and a cup of sugary hot tea instead of coffee. Sky hated tea, but she sipped it gratefully anyhow. The soothing warmth helped ward off her chills.

She toweled her hair dry as best she could between shivers and was just fishing through her purse for a comb when the paramedics arrived. They were very nice, very thorough, and not much older than her daughter.

"Are you sure you didn't hit your head, ma'am?"

"No. I had a headache before the accident. I really didn't get hurt at all. The car had an air bag, you know."

"Yes, ma'am. And you were wearing your seat belt."

"Of course."

The pair agreed she seemed to be okay, but recommended she see her family doctor to be safe. Sky didn't bother telling them her doctor was several hundred miles away. Her control was returning along with acute embarrassment.

Wait until her insurance company heard she rear-ended a police car. Her rates were going to triple. She contemplated that dire thought as time ticked away slowly. Just as she decided to go in search of someone, a nice-looking man in the requisite jeans, jacket, Stetson and boots arrived. He introduced himself as Lieutenant Bateman with the Bitterwater Police Department.

"Don't the police wear uniforms here in Texas?"

His grin was infectious. "I'm not on duty. It happened I was nearby when I heard Noah's call so I offered to take it."

"Oh."

"Why don't you tell me what happened?" the officer said.

"It will take all of two seconds."

As Sky was relating the events of the accident, a shadow filled the open doorway. She didn't have to look up to know Sheriff Noah Beaufort stood there listening. He was leaning back against the doorjamb, his head cocked, an enigmatic expression on his face.

"She tends to have a heavy foot," he inserted when she paused.

"I was not speeding," she protested. "It was raining too hard to drive fast. Besides, you're partly at fault in this accident anyhow."

His eyebrows disappeared beneath the brim of his very wet hat. "Now how do you figure that?"

If he thought he was going to intimidate her just because he was a sheriff, he had another thought coming. Sky rose to her feet.

"You weren't in front of me before I came around that

curve. That means you must have just pulled out. You should have seen me coming and waited. If you had, I wouldn't have rear-ended you.''

"No, then you would have hit me broadside.''

"What?''

He stepped into the room, striding right up to her, shrinking the small space even further.

"You were sliding across the road coming right at me. I was trying to get out of the way.''

"Well, you didn't do a very good job of it.''

There was a snort of laughter from the lieutenant. Sky ignored him, amazed to see a flash of humor in the sheriff's expression, as well.

"I ought to have Devlin here arrest you on charges of assaulting a police officer.''

Water dripped off his yellow slicker onto the floor and formed a puddle at her feet.

"Try it," she dared him. "I've got the bear to help make my case.''

"It was a dog and I don't think any testimony he gave would be in your favor.''

"If he hadn't—''

"You shouldn't—''

Lieutenant Bateman cleared his throat on a chuckle. They both stopped speaking to glare at him. He spread his hands, a wide grin on his face.

"I'll leave you two to sort this out or I'm going to be late. I'm not going to write you a ticket, Ms. Diamond—''

"It wouldn't be her first one," the sheriff muttered, slipping out of the wet rain slicker.

"Thank you," she told the lieutenant, pointedly ignoring the sheriff.

"—but the car rental place will need to be notified to pick up the car. We're towing it to the local garage.''

"Towing it?''

"The radiator is hosed. You won't be able to drive it, I'm afraid."

"Oh, no. What about the police car?"

"You dented my bumper," the sheriff said smugly. "Which reminds me, I'll need to see your insurance papers."

"Don't worry, I have my insurance card right here in my wallet."

"Good."

The lieutenant shook his head, still grinning. "I'd love to stay and hear how this is resolved, but I've really got to run. Talk with you later, Noah."

"Thanks again for responding, Devlin."

As the lieutenant left, the sheriff set his coat over the back of a chair and walked over to perch on the edge of the desk. Sky was very conscious of the fact that combing her wet hair had done little to improve her drowned-rat appearance, while he had the effrontery to sit there looking none the worse for standing around in the rain. She struggled out of the bulky sweater, no longer the least bit cold.

"Why don't you tell me what you were doing over here after I told you to stay away from my daughter," he said softly.

The words surprised her in the act of setting down the sweater. She rallied quickly. "Driving down a public road."

If only he didn't look quite so appealing as he leaned back and regarded her. He filled that sheriff's uniform quite nicely. He was nothing like Ted or the other men she had known in New York. Despite his mild manner, she sensed the leashed power lying beneath the surface of his calm. He was attracted to her, but that wouldn't help her one bit if he decided she was a threat to his daughter.

*Her daughter!*

"So you were simply driving down the road."

Abruptly she realized she didn't want to spar with him

over this. He was doing his best to protect Lauren from what he perceived as a threat. How could she fault him for that?

"I ran to the store to pick up a couple of things."

"Store's back that way."

She shrugged. "Believe it or not, I had no intention of stopping here today. This was a total accident—"

"No pun intended?"

"What? Oh. No. As I said, it was an accident unless you think I arranged to have that bear of a dog run out in front of my car so I could ram into the back of your police car, thus giving me an excuse to come inside and meet Lauren."

The tension eased from his body. After a moment his lips twitched. "Sounds pretty far-fetched when you put it that way."

"Uh-huh. And you'll note that we did meet, but I didn't offer her the job. I decided to respect your wishes. New York is filled with models. I was planning to go back and find one. As a matter of fact, I was on my way back to the boardinghouse to check out."

"Boardinghouse is the other direction, too," he said mildly.

"So sue me. The nice couple who run the place will confirm my intention to leave as soon as I returned."

"What about your search for inspiration?"

"I don't think haute couture is ready for the sort of designs this part of Texas is inspiring in me right now."

The twitch became a small smile. "Is that right?"

"Definitely. If you'll let me use the telephone, I'll call the leasing company and have them send out another car right away. I'll be in San Antonio in time for dinner."

"I don't think so."

He came off the desk. Her breathing quickened in immediate response. What was it about this man that made her think things she had no business thinking? She kept wondering what his mouth would feel like on hers. He wouldn't be a wimpy kisser, she was certain of that. Her reaction to him was all out of proportion to anything she had ever felt before. He was her daughter's adoptive father, yet that thought was hard to keep in mind when the air seemed charged with such physical awareness.

"Why don't you think so?" she asked.

"This is Bitterwater, not San Antonio."

"So?"

He stepped in front of her. His eyes were dark liquid pools. She hadn't been mistaken. Desire lurked just below the surface. No man had ever looked at her quite like that, as if she were some special treat he couldn't wait to sample. Her stomach did a funny little flip-flop.

"Even if they have a car and a driver available this late in the day, it's going to take them several hours to drive a replacement car clear out here from San Antonio," he said softly. "Especially in this weather."

"So I'll get there after dinner." Her voice sounded breathless. Her heart began to pound.

His gaze fastened on her mouth. She resisted an urge to moisten suddenly dry lips, while her body quickened with answering desire.

"You're in an awfully big rush to leave all of a sudden."

Her body hummed in anticipation. All her senses were alert to him. Her fingers itched to slide their way across that broad chest.

"You told me to go."

"So I did."

His gaze deepened. He closed the gap between them.

"What are you doing?" she whispered.

"Damned if I know."

## CHAPTER FIVE

"YOU CAN'T kiss me!"

Noah stroked back the silky damp strands of her hair. "I shouldn't. But I want to," he said quietly.

"Oh."

She seemed to stop breathing. His own breath was coming much too fast. He knew it was crazy but he needed to taste her. He ran his thumb across her bottom lip and it quivered provocatively. The sweep of her long sooty lashes hid her response, but she lifted her face as he lowered his head.

A door closed down the hall. Footsteps started in their direction. Noah jerked back only seconds before Lauren appeared in the doorway. Sky lowered her upraised face quickly as pink surged into her cheeks.

"Da— Oh. Am I interrupting?"

"No," he said tersely. "What is it, Lauren?"

His daughter gazed from one face to the other uncertainly. "I came to tell you that Clancy is out of surgery. He's going to be fine. I knew you wanted to know," she told Sky sympathetically.

"Yes. Thank you."

Noah glanced at his watch, surprised to see how much time had elapsed since the accident. "You were supposed to close at noon today."

"We did, right after you brought Clancy in. I stayed to help with the surgery."

"Didn't I see Doug's car outside?"

"Uh-huh. He got here in time to watch. You were talking with Lieutenant Bateman when he arrived. He's waiting for me up front. I have to put a couple of things away and then we're going to leave."

"All right. We'll be out of your hair in a minute."

"That's okay. Take your time."

An oddly wistful expression crossed Sky's face as his daughter left. It dissolved the instant she saw him watching, and was replaced by a look of challenge as she squared off to face him. He buried his unease to concentrate on his response. Skylar Diamond intrigued him, infuriated him, and stirred a basic need in him all at the same time. He hadn't wanted a woman like this in a very long time. Maybe never. The thought was like the woman—completely unsettling.

"I'll call a cab," she stated.

Noah shook his head. He realized she used hauteur as a cover-up, trying to hide her response to their physical attraction. The knowledge was comforting.

"Bitterwater doesn't have any cabs. I'll run you back to the rooming house."

"I don't think that's such a good idea."

"Nervous?"

Her chin lifted. "Of course not."

He smiled, glad to find himself in control of the situation and his emotions once more. "Good. Because what just happened won't happen again."

"Nothing happened," she said quickly.

"But we both wanted it to."

He loved the way color sprang so easily to her cheeks. She looked away.

"You're wrong."

"You didn't want me to kiss you?"

"I don't want to talk about this."

"I don't want to talk about it, either," he said huskily. "But talk is about all we can do right now."

"Ever," she said quickly.

"Did you know the pulse in your neck is racing? Just like mine."

Her eyes flashed to his face. "You're imagining things."

"Yeah. I certainly am."

He saw her imagination vault right there with him. Her body revealed the truth. Her lips parted, her flush heightened, and her eyes sparkled, changing color so they looked almost deep blue in this light.

Coldness settled in the pit of his stomach. Noah stopped in the act of reaching for her. Lauren had exotic eyes like those. They changed from gray to blue when she was excited, almost green when she was angry. He'd never seen anyone else with eyes like hers. Until now.

"Who are you?" His voice came out ragged with suppressed anger and fear. "What do you really want with my daughter?"

"What?"

For a moment she appeared genuinely bewildered, then her expression shut down. As if she had turned a switch somewhere, all emotion faded. He couldn't tell what she was thinking. Her eyes went flat and gray.

"I don't want anything from you or your daughter, Sheriff."

And her voice was as toneless and empty as her expression. Frustration chewed on him. He couldn't compel her to tell him what he wanted to know, but if Doug was still here, maybe he could eliminate one possibility.

"Wait right here. I need to have a word with my daughter's fiancé."

Doug was in the waiting room. He smiled a greeting. "Hey, Sheriff!"

"Glad to see you made it in."

"There was hardly any traffic this morning and the plane ride was uneventful. I wanted to leave last night, only I had to get a paper done."

"Doug, I need to talk with you for a minute."

"Sure."

The smile faded at Noah's serious tone.

"Did you hire a private investigator to check up on Lauren?"

Slack-jawed, he stared at Noah. "Of course not! Why would you even ask such a thing?"

"A woman has been following Lauren around for a couple of days now. I'm going to check out her story, but there's a chance she's a private investigator—maybe out of New York. I wondered if you or your parents..." He let the rest trail expectantly.

Doug shook his head, his features a mix of shock, outrage and concern. "I have no reason to hire a detective, Sheriff. I know all I need to know about Lauren. I love your daughter." His eyebrows beetled in concern. "Do you think this woman is dangerous?"

Oh, yeah. Skylar Diamond was dangerous. The chemistry between the two of them was nothing short of combustible. But she wasn't dangerous in the way Doug meant.

"I don't think she means Lauren any harm, and I didn't really think you hired her, Doug, but I needed confirmation."

"I would never do such a thing." He hesitated, then blurted out, "But I have to be honest with you and say that it does sound like something my mother might do. She means well." He hurried to add, "And she likes Lauren. After we stayed with them, she indicated she really approved of the match, but..." He shrugged. "My mother tends to be... That is, she worries about..."

"The wrong sort of person marrying into the family?" Noah asked mildly.

"Uh, yeah. I hope you won't think badly of her. She isn't really a snob, but she's always been overprotective. Dad says she can't help herself."

"It's no problem, Doug. I just need to know for sure.

When you get back to the house, could you call your parents and check for me?''

''Of course. They're flying to Greece today, but I'll give it a try, sir.''

''Let's not mention this to Lauren.''

The youth met his gaze and nodded in understanding.

''There's one more thing.'' Briefly, he explained about Francis Hartman and the threat he had made against Noah. ''I don't anticipate a real problem here either, I just want you both to stay alert.''

''Could this woman be working for Francis Hartman?''

''I seriously doubt it, but we won't take any chances.''

''Yes, sir. I mean, no, sir. We won't.''

''I knew I could count on you, Doug.'' He glanced at his watch and frowned. He hadn't meant to leave Skylar alone this long.

''I wonder what's keeping Lauren,'' Doug said.

Noah suddenly thought he knew. He muttered an oath and set off down the hall at a trot. The office door stood open. Skylar Diamond was gone.

''Is something wrong?'' Doug asked.

His curse came from the heart as Noah spun around, nearly knocking Doug over as he grabbed the door leading to the surgery. Doug followed on his heels in silent concern. They startled the vet, who was putting supplies into a cupboard.

''Sheriff. I thought you'd gone some time ago.''

''Where's Lauren?'' he demanded.

''In the back. She took the woman who hit Clancy back to see him.''

Noah strode for that door before the vet finished speaking. He burst into the kennel area and came to a stop. Tension drained from him as the two women looked up in surprise. They were hunched over an open cage where the huge black dog lay inertly, his back hip and leg swaddled in bandages.

''Daddy? What's wrong?''

Noah took in a breath and released it. "Nothing, honey. Everything's fine. I didn't know where Ms. Diamond disappeared to. I told her to wait in the office for me."

Skylar rose, her face flushing. She recognized his words as the rebuke he'd meant them to be.

"It's my fault," Lauren said hurriedly. "I knew how upset she was over Clancy and I thought she'd feel better if she saw for herself that he's doing okay. Sorry, Doug. I didn't mean to keep you waiting."

Doug moved to Lauren's side. He touched her arm lightly in support as he looked from Sky to Noah and back again. Noah realized everyone was staring at him, waiting for whatever came next.

Gruffly, he softened his voice while the adrenaline rush drained from his system. "I'm sure Ms. Diamond appreciates your kindness, Lauren. I just didn't know where she'd gone."

"My coat and my purse are still in the office," Skylar told him. "I couldn't go far without them."

"I didn't think you'd gone far," he admitted, chagrined to realize he hadn't even noticed that the items were there.

Lauren's sunny smile instantly reappeared. "I invited Ms. Diamond to our place for dinner tonight, Dad. I hope that's okay. The rental company can't get another car here until tomorrow. Since she doesn't know anyone in town and doesn't have any transportation, I figured she could join us, all right?"

Doug watched alertly, taking his cues from Noah, but it was Skylar's wryly amused expression that hooked Noah's gaze and held it captive. Her lips were curved in a little smile. Lips he still wanted to kiss, damn it.

She waited in silence for his reaction to this new dilemma. Noah searched for a reason to object and came up empty.

Lauren started to frown, clearly puzzled. She was used to his ready acceptance whenever she dragged home strays, animals or people. She wouldn't understand a refusal without some sort of explanation—an explanation Noah could hardly give until he knew more about Skylar Diamond.

"Maybe Ms. Diamond would rather spend a quiet evening at the boardinghouse after all the excitement this afternoon," he suggested.

"Not really." Her smile was deliberate. "I'd be honored to join you and your family for dinner."

"You may feel stiff later on from the accident."

"I hit *you,* remember? I'd say you're the one who's apt to feel...uncomfortable."

The word *stiff* settled between them for a heartbeat. She was silently laughing at him, Noah realized. He could see the amusement dancing in her eyes.

"If you'd rather not have company tonight, I'll understand."

Noah shook his head. "You barely dented my bumper. I was worried about your comfort."

"Great," Lauren enthused, breaking the spell between them before Skylar could respond. "Then it's settled. Doug and I can drop you off so you can change into something dry, and Dad can pick you up on his way home after work. He was supposed to be off today, but one of his deputies called in sick," she added pointedly.

Noah knew when he was licked. He took what satisfaction he could from Skylar's expression of dismay when his daughter arranged for him to be the one picking her up. He had the entire afternoon to do more checking—and get over his strange infatuation with Skylar Diamond. And he had the drive out to his ranch to cross-examine her. He could lay down the ground rules for her visit then.

A FEW telephone calls verified that there really was a fashion designer by the name of Skylar Diamond working out of New York. So she hadn't lied. At least about that. He stared at the papers covering his desk. It was possible she was telling the truth. Lauren was beautiful, tall, elegant, definitely pretty enough to be a model.

Maybe he was letting old fears resurrect themselves. From the day they had brought Lauren home, he'd worried that one day her birth mother would come to reclaim her. This had happened to a fellow officer some years before. It had taken years of expensive legal wrangling for them to keep the child, and in the end, it had nearly destroyed everyone involved.

The truth was, Noah hadn't wanted to adopt. He would have been perfectly happy with just Beth. But he'd known how important a child was to her so he'd reluctantly agreed. And once he'd seen Lauren, all his doubts and reservations had flown right out the window. She'd wrapped that tiny fist around his finger and latched on to a piece of his heart he hadn't known existed. He would have fought the devil himself to protect their little girl. And that made his fear all that much stronger.

Only Lauren wasn't a tiny infant anymore. She was an adult woman and no one could take her away now.

Still, he wondered about the card Skylar had dropped. He'd seen the word *investigator* on it. Why hadn't she wanted him to see it if it wasn't important?

Finders Keepers had been scrawled on that folder with directions. There was an investigative agency with that name run by a former Dallas policeman and his sister. While he'd never worked with the man, Noah knew Dylan Garrett slightly. Dylan had once worked for Zach Logan just as Noah had.

He was already running late to pick up Skylar, but he took a couple of extra minutes to call Finders Keepers. The answering machine announced the office was closed for the weekend. The emergency number gave him another machine belonging to Dylan Garrett. That number rang unanswered.

Didn't anyone stay home these days?

Frustrated, Noah grabbed his hat and drove to Bitterwater to retrieve Skylar Diamond. At least the rain had finally stopped.

Skylar was waiting on the front porch looking cool and sophisticated in yet another fashionable pantsuit that settled over her body in graceful lines. The rich cranberry color was elegantly refined, yet pleasingly feminine. So much for his former prejudice against pantsuits. On her they looked just fine, even if a bit too New York for Texas.

Beneath her jacket Sky wore an old-fashioned, high-necked lace-and-silk blouse that accentuated the rounded curves beneath. Anticipation zinged right through him. There went his iron control. He itched to peel her out of that formal little pantsuit so he could explore the provocative woman underneath.

Noah walked around his vehicle and held open the passenger door. She sailed lightly down the steps, her high heels making sharp decisive little clicks. She paused, eyeing the distance from the ground to the front seat and raised expressive eyebrows at him.

"I'll give you a boost," he offered.

"I think I can manage."

Gamely, she turned her back and reached for the door frame. The light fragrance she wore skimmed over his senses. He wanted to draw in a deep lungful, but resisted the temptation. Instead, as she started to pull herself up, he reached out, his large hands settling over the gently rounded curves of her hips to lift her easily into the seat. His body reacted immediately.

"Thank you," she breathed.

"You're welcome."

He shut the door and took a deep, clearing breath. It had been a long time since he'd been with a woman. He tried to tell himself he'd react the same way to any attractive female. Too bad he couldn't buy into the lie.

She sat demurely beside him, her hands clasped in her

lap. It took him a second to notice the troubled expression on her face.

"I'm not going to jump you, you know."

That brought her head around. "I didn't think you would."

"Is something wrong? Would you rather not come? I can tell Lauren you weren't feeling well."

"If you'd prefer I not go to your house, I'll understand. Thank your daughter for her kindness."

She reached for the door handle and he grabbed her arm. The touch was electric. He didn't like the need that twisted through him. Her expression showed instant alarm. Noah released his hold, puzzled.

"What's going on?" he asked gently.

"What do you mean?"

"Something's wrong. Your whole mood has changed since I last saw you."

For a moment he thought she wasn't going to answer. Then she gave a small shrug. "I spent the afternoon on the telephone with the New York Police Department. It seems my office was broken into last night. Someone all but destroyed the place," she said bleakly.

A cold knot of worry beaded at the base of his stomach. "Do they know who did it?"

"No."

"No suspects?"

She laughed mirthlessly. "Any and all of my competitors. At a guess, someone was looking for the new designs we're working up. When they didn't find them, they wreaked havoc."

"Seems a bit extreme."

"It's a cutthroat industry, Sheriff. There's big money to be made if you're lucky and successful. I've been both. That makes me a target. Fortunately, they didn't get into the safe."

"Do you want to go straight to the airport?"

"Thanks, but Detective Huang assures me there's no hurry. My capable assistant is handling things. I'll need to replace some furniture and all of the paintings and breakables, but nothing appears to be missing."

The knot of cold spread out. "Destroying furniture doesn't sound like burglary. It sounds like rage."

"I imagine they weren't happy when they had to leave empty-handed. Maybe they thought making a mess would slow us down or something." Again, her shoulders lifted and fell. "My insurance company is going to be *very* unhappy with me this week. First the hotel loses my laptop, then I total a rental car, and now this."

Alarms went off in his head. Vandalism like she described was usually done by kids, but kids weren't apt to break into a clothing designer's place of business.

"Are your offices on the ground floor?"

"No. We're on the tenth floor. There's even security in the building. Obviously, not very good security, but—"

"Any ex-husbands or jealous boyfriends in the wings?"

"You sound like Detective Huang. No ex-husbands. I broke things off with a man recently, and on the bright side, the police will probably give Ted a hard time."

"I gather you're no longer fond of Ted."

"Actually, I've hardly given him a thought since we broke up."

"Ted what?"

"Zillano, why?"

"Could he be angry enough over the breakup to destroy your office?"

"No way. Ted wouldn't bother to exert himself that far, Sheriff. Our breakup wasn't exactly amicable, but neither of us was devastated by it either."

"Why did you break up, if you don't mind my asking?"

She hesitated, looking embarrassed. "I found him in my bed with our twenty-three-year-old neighbor."

"Ouch."

"It was a shock, but other than that, neither of us was too broken up over the end of the relationship. I asked him to move out immediately and he did."

"Sounds like grounds for some bitterness there."

"My pride was dented, Sheriff. I would enjoy seeing Ted squirm a little, but we were together out of habit rather than undying passion. Ted is only passionate about the stock market."

"Maybe he was more upset than you realized."

"I don't think so. Ted's very good-looking and extremely successful. He'll have no problem finding another partner."

Dislike for the unseen Ted settled in his gut.

"Our parting was quite civilized, all things considered. I don't see him going to my office weeks later and destroying things. If he was going to do something that stupid, he would have torn up the apartment we shared."

"Do we know he didn't?" Noah asked thoughtfully.

"What?"

"Is someone looking after your apartment while you're gone?"

Her mouth opened soundlessly as the implication sank in.

"The man is obviously an idiot. Maybe he's an angry idiot."

Concern overshadowed her weak smile. "Thank you, but you don't know Ted."

"No, but whoever trashed your office might have gone to your apartment next if they were looking for something."

Her tongue flicked out to moisten dry lips.

"Does a friend or neighbor have a key?"

"No. My building has a security guard."

"So did your office."

"You're scaring me."

"Why don't we stop by my office and give Detective Huang a quick call?"

She crossed her arms over her chest and began to rub her

arms as though chilled. "He's probably gone home for the day."

"I think it's worth a try. Would you like me to talk to him?"

She only hesitated a second. "Yes. I think maybe I would like you to call him. If you wouldn't mind."

Detective Huang was still in his office and not at all thrilled by Noah's request.

"Sheriff, it's late and it's snowing again. Do you have any idea what a mess it is when it snows like this in New York City?" the detective asked, sounding aggrieved.

"I can imagine."

"The airports are so backed up they might as well have been shut down since yesterday. Vehicular traffic is at a standstill. Visibility is practically zero and every pregnant woman in town suddenly wants to give birth. And you want me to send a squad car to see if her apartment was vandalized?"

Noah didn't respond. He already knew the detective was going to do it. The man blew a gust of air into the telephone. "Hell. I have no idea when they'll be able to get there. Give me a number where we can reach you."

Noah gave him the office as well as his home number.

"This better not be a wild-goose chase," the detective muttered.

"Personally, I hope it is—for Ms. Diamond's sake."

"Yeah, there is that, isn't there? Okay. I'll get someone over there and let you know, but it may take a while. Could even be tomorrow."

"I'll suggest she stay here until we know something."

"Do that. I'll move my chat with the ex-boyfriend up a notch just to cover all bases."

Noah offered Sky what he hoped was a reassuring smile. "They'll let us know when they can. Let me call Lauren and tell her we're running late."

Lauren took the news in stride, promising to hold dinner

until they got there. Noah guided Sky back out to the police car. "You're taking all this very calmly," he told her.

"The body can only handle so many shocks in one day. I think I'm over my quota. After I first spoke with Detective Huang I ran the boardinghouse out of hot water. You'd be amazed at the calming effects of a steamy hot shower."

The image of her wet and naked, surrounded by steam, was not easy to put aside. "Nothing hurts from the crash?"

"My pride. I'm not really a bad driver, you know."

"Hey, I'd bet on you to win the Indy 500."

"Very funny."

"I saw your driving record, remember?"

"Then you know this was my first accident since I was seventeen."

"Your guardian angel must have been on break." His teasing was rewarded with a grin.

"But I still feel bad about the dog. I really did think he was a bear, you know."

"Understandable. He's big, black and shaggy looking, and visibility wasn't all that great."

"I'm not used to animals, living in the city like I do."

"Then you'd better brace yourself. My daughter has a habit of bringing home strays."

"Oh? Do I qualify?"

He angled another smile at her. "I'd say so, yes. Does that bother you?"

"Not at all."

He liked her ability to smile, despite the day she'd had. In fact, there were a lot of things he was coming to like about Skylar Diamond.

"Your daughter is very sweet," she told him. "But I was surprised that you allowed me to come tonight."

"Lauren didn't leave me much choice."

Her smile faded. "Look, if you're uncomfortable with me going to your home, turn this thing around and take me back to the boardinghouse."

Noah dropped his hand to cover her clenched fist where it rested on her thigh. She tensed and he wondered if she felt the same jolt of energy he did at the contact. He released her hand and gripped the steering wheel.

"Sorry. That didn't come out right. I'm glad you're joining us for dinner."

"I'm not hungry."

"If I don't bring you home with me, Lauren will want to stop by and check on you. My daughter worries about people. This way she can see for herself that you're fine."

And the truth was, he didn't want to take her back. There was something going on between them that had nothing to do with his daughter. Sky was an intriguing irritation, a puzzle he wanted to solve.

"I will ask that you promise not to say anything about modeling to her."

"You have my word. The subject won't even come up."

## CHAPTER SIX

LAUREN GREETED THEM at the door with an exuberant smile. "You're Skylar Diamond! I don't believe it. Dad, do you know who this is?"

"I—"

"Skylar's only the top designer of women's business attire in New York. I told Doug the name was familiar but I couldn't figure out why. Then it came to me, the Diamond Collection. I felt like an idiot. I even saw your picture in one of my style magazines. That outfit you have on is one of your originals, isn't it? What a great color. I love your bold use of color. Your stuff is fabulous."

Amusement warred with apology in her expression as Skylar met his gaze. Bemused, Noah listened as his daughter waxed on enthusiastically while Doug offered a limp shrug. "She's been like this since we got here."

The three dogs crowded around the newcomer in their midst. Skylar edged back against Noah as the largest of the trio tried to shove his muzzle in her hand for attention.

"Limpet, sit."

The big dog did, but Puddles and Leo rushed forward to sniff at her pant legs with interest. Sky held perfectly still against his side.

"Lauren, let's put the dogs outside. Ms. Diamond isn't used to animals."

"That's okay," Sky interjected. "You don't have to lock them up because of me. And Ms. Diamond sounds a bit pretentious, don't you think? The name is Sky." She jumped as Limpet leaned his considerable weight against her and tried once more to get her attention.

Lauren rushed forward contritely. "I'm sorry, Sky. I'm so used to these clowns, I didn't realize. Come on, guys. Dinnertime."

Three canine heads turned as one. The newcomer was forgotten as they hurried after their mistress. Fluffball, the orange tabby, leaped down from the couch, feigning disinterest, but followed the dogs to the kitchen.

"They're harmless," Noah told Sky.

She took a step away from his side, obviously embarrassed. "Do they know that?"

Noah smiled and the strained look began to fade around her mouth and eyes.

"I'm not afraid, exactly. I just don't know how to act around dogs. Especially when they travel in packs. Why is the big one called Limpet?"

"He clings to people like a limpet mine does to the metal hull of a ship," Noah explained. "He thinks he should be a lapdog."

"That would be some lap."

Doug laughed. "He watches Puddles and he's jealous. She curls up in Lauren's lap every chance she gets."

"Is that the little brown one?"

Noah nodded. "Lauren found her abandoned on the side of the road. We're guessing her original owners gave up when they couldn't housebreak her."

"She had a urinary problem requiring surgery," Doug interjected.

"I'm beginning to see a pattern here," Sky said. "That leaves…"

"Leo," Doug said. "You may have noticed he only has three legs. He had a nasty wound that had become gangrenous by the time he found Lauren. The vet had to amputate. She decided he had the heart of a lion so she called him Leo."

"Of course."

"If you'll excuse me," Noah said as Lauren returned sans dogs, "I'll go change before dinner."

"You've got about a fifteen-minute window before we're ready to eat, Dad."

Noah headed for his bedroom. His relief at learning Sky was who she claimed to be was tempered by the part of him that said there had to be more. His old fears skated around the surface of his mind. There wasn't much of a resemblance between the two women except for the eyes and the hair color, and more than likely, Sky's color owed at least a partial nod to someone other than Mother Nature.

If she *was* a relative, why not say so right off? He mulled over the implications while he showered and shaved. As he wiped the excess lather off his face he told himself he had not shaved because of Sky. It was simply that shaving went with showering. But he was attracted to her, he admitted. Any man would be. He tucked a clean shirt into a pair of good denims and headed for the dining room, feeling only slightly foolish. The tangy aroma of lasagna and garlic bread filled the house.

Doug was setting the casserole on the table as Noah entered. He looked up with an easy grin. "Brace yourself. You're about to learn more about women's fashion than mere men were ever meant to know."

"Many of the top designers are men," Noah corrected wryly.

"Uh-huh. Well, I'm warning you, unless you're interested in making a career change at this point in your life, they're talking terms like *selvage* and *cutting across the bias* and *drop waist* and *slash pockets* and all sorts of incomprehensible stuff."

Noah frowned. His daughter had always had an interest in fashion, poring over magazines with her friends as a girl. Yet her wardrobe was modest, and she wore jeans more often than not. Still, he should have warned Doug about

Skylar's intention to ask Lauren to model. He'd been so certain it was a ruse. And the truth was, he'd never considered that Lauren would be seriously interested if it wasn't. She wanted to be a vet. Didn't she? Had he underestimated the lure of high fashion?

Lauren was obviously enamored of Sky and her career. No matter how often Sky tried to change the conversation during dinner, his daughter brought it back around to the fashion industry. Doug didn't seem worried, so Noah worried for both of them.

"Lauren tells me you had another run-in with Franklin the other day," Doug said to him during a momentary lull. "Is that in your job description?"

Noah shrugged. "Living in a small town like this adds unofficial parameters to the job."

"Irascible neighbors included," Lauren said happily. "Talk about ornery. Dad tore his jeans and his shirt on a fence, trying to get out of his way."

Doug chuckled. "Poor old guy."

"Poor old guy my foot," Noah scowled. "He's mean and contrary even when he isn't lovesick."

Lauren giggled. "I'd have loved to see the whole thing. We could have sold tickets. Henry and Dad both got lines around him and Franklin still managed to drag them through a pit of mud."

Disgruntled, he frowned over the reminder that it had not been one of his better afternoons. Sky stared, looking appalled.

"Franklin is dangerous," Noah told them seriously. "He's more trouble than he's worth. And he's worth a great deal, as Henry explained when I offered to shoot him and put him out of all our misery."

"Oh, Dad. You know you'd never do that. Poor Franklin just thinks he's in love."

"Excuse me," Skylar interrupted, "I know this is Texas, and everyone likes the Wild West image and all, but I've got a real interesting picture going on in my head right now of a berserk sumo wrestler fighting to reach the woman of his dreams. Would someone mind explaining who Franklin is?''

Lauren and Doug erupted in laughter.

"Franklin is our neighbor's bull," Noah explained. "He keeps chasing another neighbor's cows."

"One cow in particular," Lauren added. "He thinks he's in love."

Sky frowned. "Why don't they just move the cow away from him?"

"They tried that," Lauren told her.

"He took down three fences and injured two hands when they put him in a remote pasture," Noah injected grimly.

"Jackson should just give in and pay Henry to let the bull service his cows," Doug suggested.

Noah shook his head. "Henry needs to sell him or shoot him before someone gets hurt. That animal is going to kill someone one of these days," he said seriously.

Everyone stared. Noah knew he sounded grumpy. Thinking about the bull, along with his daughter's fascination with Skylar, had left him feeling unaccountably irritable. He pushed back his chair and stood, dropping his napkin beside his plate.

"Lauren, the meal was terrific, but I need to go out to the barn before it gets too late. I hope you'll all excuse me."

"But we haven't had dessert yet."

"I'll get some later."

Lauren looked bewildered as her father walked away. Doug laid a hand on her arm and Sky bit down on her bottom lip.

"I'm sorry, Sky," Lauren said. "I don't know what got into Dad. He isn't usually like this."

"You don't have to apologize. It's been a trying day."

"But Dad's never moody. Something must be bothering

him. Well, whatever it is, he's never grumpy for long. He'll feel better after he comes back inside. You'll see.''

Doug studied Sky with a speculative gaze. She suspected he knew she was the source of the sheriff's grumpy demeanor. But it wasn't her fault Lauren had recognized her. And secretly, she was thrilled. She longed to tell Lauren who she really was. They could have so much fun together. Maybe after she got to know her a little better...

Only she wouldn't be sticking around to get to know her better.

The lasagna formed a lump in Sky's stomach. Lauren was happy with her life. It would be wrong to interfere. And given Sky's intense reaction to Noah, it was best to head back to New York before things got out of hand. She had wanted him to kiss her earlier.

She still did.

She helped clear the table, then excused herself to use the bathroom.

When she returned to the dining room, she found Lauren and Doug wrapped in a passionate embrace inside the kitchen doorway. They looked right together. Since neither of them saw or heard her, Sky backed out of the room quietly to give them some privacy. She had to swallow a twinge of ridiculous jealousy. Lauren was lucky.

The low murmur of voices in the kitchen told her when the couple came up for air, but Sky had no desire to walk in and see her daughter looking freshly kissed.

"Lauren, I'm going to walk over to the barn and talk to your dad for a few minutes," she called out, heading for the front door. She stepped onto the front porch. A swing sat crosswise on the porch at the far end, infinitely tempting. She resisted the impulse to sit there and absorb the scents and sounds of the evening. It was time to find Noah and go back to the boardinghouse. In the morning, once the rental company delivered another car, she'd make the long drive back to San Antonio and decide what to do with the rest of her life.

As she started across the grass, she quickly realized that high heels had been a poor choice tonight. They sank in the damp ground, making walking all but impossible. Hesitating only a minute, she pulled off her shoes. The grass was cold and wet, and she'd ruin her stockings, but Sky didn't care. The intense quiet of the land seemed almost eerie, yet it was also soothing. It had been too many years since she'd seen so many stars overhead.

Out of the darkness, something bounded in her direction. For a moment, fear held her motionless. Then she recognized the furry shape.

"Limpet."

He woofed a greeting and ran full tilt against her legs, pushing his muzzle in her hand demandingly. "Hey, take it easy," she said uneasily. Limpet was a large-size dog of questionable parentage, but his tail was wagging so hard she was pretty sure he didn't intend to sample her for his next meal.

"You're going to knock me over, dog." He gazed up at her adoringly, his large pink tongue hanging foolishly out of one side of his mouth. Tentatively, she stroked his head, amazed to find his fur was silky. His entire body quivered in pleasure.

"You're a fraud, you know that? You look big and dangerous with that row of teeth, but you're just a big baby, aren't you?"

"I think she has your number, Limpet."

The quiet words came out of the darkness and caused a surge of adrenaline to shoot right through her. Sky peered around and Noah detached himself from the fence where he'd been leaning, invisible in the shadow of a large pecan tree. The other two dogs bounded toward him from the field beyond the fence. A group of horses were grazing there, unperturbed by the canine visitors.

"You startled me," she told Noah.

"Sorry."

He didn't sound sorry. He sounded remote and still angry. At her? Probably. He didn't like her.

But he wanted her, just as she wanted him.

She pushed aside her lingering fantasies about the man and drew on her professional persona as she stepped over to where he stood. "You don't have to apologize, Sheriff. I was wondering if I could bother you for a ride back to Bitterwater."

"No need to eat and run."

"It's getting late. I want to start for San Antonio as soon as they deliver the new car in the morning."

He pushed back the brim of his hat. "Why?"

"Why what?"

"You weren't in any hurry to leave before."

"No one had broken into my office before. I need to get back and be sure everything gets straightened out."

"You said your staff could handle the office."

"They can, but there isn't much point to my staying here any longer. I can work on my designs more easily at home."

"We don't know that your home is secure yet" he said mildly. "Detective Huang hasn't called back."

"I'm sure everything is fine. Someone just wanted my designs."

"Maybe. But it would be safer if you stay here until they arrest whoever broke into your office."

Ha. She definitely wasn't safer staying here. She could smell his aftershave on the breeze. A subtly masculine, tantalizing scent. His nearness started a whole new longing inside her for things that could never be.

"Tell me something."

Her body tensed, fearing what he might ask.

"Is this reaction we're having to one another something you've ever experienced before?"

She released her breath on a wave of tingling excitement. "No."

He took a step closer.

"That's what I thought."

She held up a hand. "But this isn't smart. You and me. You don't even like me."

"Oh, I like you all right. I just don't trust your motives," he told her softly.

On the other side of the fence a horse snorted and went racing down the field. The other animals immediately took flight as well.

"You're hiding something."

She shivered.

"But that's something apart from this," he said. "Isn't it?"

"Yes."

The chemistry swirling between them had nothing to do with Lauren and everything to do with the incredible excitement building inside her.

"Who are you really, Skylar Diamond?"

The softly voiced question was compelling. She shook her head, wanting to confess and afraid of what he would say when she did.

His curse was as soft as the night. "Come here."

Her feet moved her forward while her brain urged her to run in the opposite direction. She couldn't take her eyes from his shadowy shape. Her lungs had forgotten how to breathe. He lifted her chin and her entire body began to tremble.

"I need to kiss you."

"Yes."

Noah cupped her face, knowing he was going to regret this, but unable to stop himself. He lowered his head and took possession of her mouth. His hands threaded the silk of her hair, drawing her up against his body, rigid with need. Her shoes fell from her fingers with an audible thunk. Then the world ceased to exist as her lips softened under his and parted, allowing him to explore.

Noah knew he was in serious trouble at the first intoxicating taste. It wasn't enough. Not nearly enough.

She moaned as her hands came up to circle his neck, pulling him closer. He bit at the fullness of her lower lip and she arched against him, her body ripe and full and vital. This time it was he who groaned as desire swept aside rational thought. He clenched the soft curves of her buttocks, drawing her against the straining hardness seeking release. She whimpered softly as she pressed against him, trying to get closer still. Her teeth suddenly nipped at his jaw, then soothed the bite with licks of her tongue.

His hand shaped her, sliding upward to explore the curve of her hip, the line of her waist, rising to trace the fullness of her perfectly shaped breast. He could feel the nipple pressing against his palm through the flimsy material covering it.

"Noah!"

"Yes. Say my name again," he whispered fiercely.

She smiled. A woman's smile of power. "Noah."

His mouth swallowed her cries of pleasure as he gently pinched and rubbed that pointed nub. Her questing hand slid down over his thigh, seeking to trace his outline with her fingers. And the dogs suddenly sprang to life, haring off across the open expanse of grass toward the house.

Noah stilled. She made a sound of protest, but his fingers released her as the porch light came on. His daughter and Doug were silhouetted against its glow. They walked over and took a seat on the porch swing.

Noah pulled Sky against his body, feeling the shudders of unfilled desire rack her. He was confident they were deep enough in the shadow of the tree that the kids couldn't see them. Finally she drew in a deep trembling breath and stepped back.

"We shouldn't have done that."

She was right, but it angered him just the same. "If you're waiting for an apology—"

"I'm not."

"Good, because I've been wanting to do that since I first saw you outside the café."

She bent and retrieved her shoes. "I'm leaving tomorrow."

His gut tightened. "Stay. At least until we hear back from Detective Huang."

She hesitated. "I can't."

"Why not?"

This time the hesitation was longer.

"You could come with me tomorrow," she said so quietly he barely heard the words. "We could spend the night in San Antonio."

Noah drew in a breath while his body and mind ignited at the unexpected invitation. The hunger inside him swelled. He controlled it with effort. "One night?"

Her eyes glittered, mysteriously silver in the moonlight. "What do you want from me, Noah?"

And that, of course, was the crux.

"I wish I knew."

DETECTIVE HUANG didn't call until nearly eleven the next morning. His mood sounded even more sour than it had the night before.

"What do you know about the Diamond woman, Sheriff?"

"Only what she's told me. She arrived a few days ago, why?"

"She planning to stick around?"

"No, as a matter of fact she intends to go back to New York tomorrow. Why?"

"Someone used her apartment to vent a lot of rage. She doesn't have much of a place to come back to anymore."

Noah's fingers tightened around the telephone. "She believes a business rival was responsible for her office."

The detective snorted. "The kind you wouldn't want to meet in a dark alley, maybe. Hard to tell if they were searching for something or simply bent on destruction. Looking at the mess, you come away with the impression that someone doesn't like your Ms. Diamond very much either way."

Noah stopped himself before he pointed out that she was hardly his.

"We'll be taking a close look at the ex-lover. According to people who live in her building, the two of them just called it quits after five years together. Whoever got inside both places either had a key, or he was very, very good with locks."

"Anything taken?"

"Hard to say. I looked around this morning. Looked to me like Ms. Diamond planned to be gone for an extended period of time."

"How extended?"

"Most of her clothing, jewelry and personal effects are gone. Frankly, it looks like she skipped town. Her assistant says she's been acting remote since the breakup. I think *brooding* was her actual term. The assistant figured it had to do with the breakup. Zillano called the office several times at first but Ms. Diamond refused to talk to him."

"She didn't change her locks after he left?"

"Apparently not. The assistant says she got a call out of the blue one evening at home telling her to cancel everything on Ms. Diamond's schedule until further notice."

The ominous feeling that had settled inside him began to expand. "She told me she came here for inspiration for next winter's line of clothing."

"She seem nervous?"

Only of him. "Not really, no."

"Mr. Zillano isn't answering his phone and he didn't

make it into work today, but then half the city is still snowed in. You plan to see her again today?"

"Actually, she was driving into San Antonio today, why?"

"If Zillano—or whoever—found out where she went, he could be on a flight heading in your direction right now."

Worry sunk its sharp teeth into him.

"You might want to have someone keep an eye on her while she remains in your vicinity. At least warn her to stay alert."

"I'll see what I can do."

All morning he'd been looking for a reason to drive over to Bitterwater before she left, while telling himself not to be a fool. Lauren and Doug had driven her back to the boardinghouse last night on their way to meet some friends for the rest of the evening. He'd told himself it was better that way. He wasn't looking for a one-night stand and that's all he could have with a woman who was going back to New York. Besides, "the fashion designer and the sheriff" had a ridiculous ring to it.

So why was he so pleased to have a reason to go and see her again?

## CHAPTER SEVEN

"I'M SORRY, SHERIFF," Daisy Merrill told him. "Ms. Diamond rode into town with my husband. The car rental place told her they can't get a car out here until tomorrow for some reason, so she decided to spend the afternoon in town. Such a nice, polite woman. Very neat, you know. Picks up after herself. Not a bit of trouble. I hope everything's all right."

Noah shook his head noncommittally. She hadn't left! "Thanks, Daisy."

"My pleasure. Will I see you at the barn dance tonight?"

"I'll be there." Keeping the peace at the monthly barn dance outside Darwin Crossing was part of his job. It generally drew quite a crowd and every so often things got unruly.

"I'll see you there, then," Daisy said.

Bitterwater was three times the size of Darwin Crossing, which admittedly wasn't saying much, but it boasted a downtown shopping district as well as a small shopping center outside of town. The possibilities where Skylar could be were fairly limited. Noah found her sipping a soda in a corner booth at the restaurant.

She was not alone.

Lauren sat across from her, talking animatedly. Magazines were spread all over the table. Skylar listened intently, nodded, and pointed to a picture. The two of them bent over it while Sky began sketching something in the border of the magazine.

His chest tightened with conflicting emotions. Relief that she was there and unharmed, but anger that his daughter was sitting with her. It was ridiculous to feel threatened, but he wished he'd remembered to tell Detective Huang about Finders Keepers.

Sky's eyes widened in welcoming pleasure when she glanced up and saw him approaching. The pleasure quickly faded.

"Dad! Hi!" Lauren said, looking up. "What are you doing here?"

"I was about to ask you the same question."

His tone came out curt. Lauren blinked in surprise.

"Doug and I came into town to pick up a couple of things and have lunch. We're going riding this afternoon with some friends. We ran into Sky in the bookstore and invited her to have lunch with us."

"Where's Doug?"

"He ran over to the post office for a minute. Is something wrong, Dad?"

"I need to speak to Sky for a few minutes."

"Funny, I was beginning to feel invisible," Sky said with a hint of dark humor.

Lauren was obviously puzzled by the undercurrent.

"Hardly invisible in that outfit," he told Sky.

She raised her eyebrows coolly. "You don't like it?"

Oh, he liked it, okay. A little too well. Today's suit was a vivid royal-blue that brought her eyes sharply to life. She'd removed her jacket, setting it over the back of her chair. The unusual V cut of her silky blue-green blouse drew his gaze more powerfully than any magnet. A large blue-green opal rested against her pale skin, and matching earrings dangled from each lobe. Even her ring and bracelet matched. She looked every inch the wealthy designer, haughty, professional, in complete control.

He longed to see her as she'd been last night, breathless from his mouth and hands.

"Nice shade of blue," he said, managing to sound neutral.

"Dad has no sense of style," Lauren said quickly in an obvious attempt to diffuse some of the tension. "I was showing Sky some wedding gowns and bridesmaid dresses. I'm trying to decide what style I want and I thought she could advise me."

A mother's duty. But Beth wasn't here to help her. Noah knew it only made sense for her to turn to Sky. There was no reason for him to be feeling defensive.

A glance down showed that Skylar had made several drawings in the borders and white areas on the magazines. In a few simple strokes, she'd captured the essence of several of the gowns, altering them slightly by changing small things that added up to a completely different look.

"Sky said as long as she's stuck here in town for another day, she'd be willing to come up with a couple of design ideas just for me."

His daughter's eyes glowed, bright blue with excitement.

Noah didn't want to dim that glow, yet he couldn't stem his misgivings. "That's real friendly of her."

"Oh, Daddy, you have no idea what an opportunity this is! It's unbelievably fantastic! Sky commands extraordinary prices for original designs. She's offering to do this for me for free!"

Why? He knew Sky recognized the question hovering on the tip of his tongue. Only Lauren's sparkle kept him from voicing it out loud.

"Lauren, I need to speak to Ms. Diamond in private for a few minutes."

"Is something wrong, Dad?"

"Nothing you need to worry about."

She looked far from convinced, but she didn't argue. "Do you want to join us for lunch then? I can have the waiter set another place."

"Thanks, but no. I have to get back to Darwin Crossing. Ms. Diamond?"

Sky inclined her head and started to rise, but Lauren slid out of the booth. "You can talk here. I'll go and see what's taking Doug so long."

Her eyes turned gray with worry as she all but fled toward the front door. Noah scowled. He settled in the seat his daughter had vacated across from Sky and tried not to stare at the delicate sweep of her throat or the way her hair tempted his fingers. Sky looked cool, calm and haughtily unapproachable. Now that he knew about the heat simmering beneath that cool facade he wasn't about to be fooled by her demeanor.

"Want to explain what's going on here?" he asked quietly.

"Your daughter just did that."

"I thought we agreed that you wouldn't pursue her."

"I'm not."

Noah indicated the table, the magazines and their surroundings with a sweep of his hand. "You said you were leaving."

"They can't deliver—"

"The car until tomorrow, I know. But if you're leaving in the morning, when are you going to have time to do up some designs for her?"

"This afternoon. I have an entire day to kill."

He knew exactly how he'd like to help her kill the day. His hunger for her was more frightening than her presence here with his daughter. He'd never felt this need for a woman before. She haunted him, awake or asleep.

"I can't afford to pay your price."

Puzzled, she cocked her head to one side. "There is no price."

"Isn't there?" he asked softly.

Her lips parted in sudden understanding while her fingers gripped the edge of the table. He watched understanding yield to anger, sending a flush of color to her cheeks. Abruptly, she took a deep breath and leaned back, her implacable mask once more in place. Noah was impressed by her control. His wasn't nearly that good.

"I happen to like your daughter and her fiancé. Designing a gown for her would be a pleasure. Normally I design business clothing. This would let me do something different. A challenge." Her eyes were glittery green shards of anger. "And it has nothing to do with you and me." Her tight expression dared him to contradict her.

"All right."

"Whatever you think, I didn't arrange this meeting. I fully expected to be on my way out of town by now. Is there some other reason for the unexpected pleasure of your company?"

"I heard from Detective Huang this morning."

Her eyes clouded, but she waited in silence.

"Your apartment was more thoroughly destroyed than your office."

For a moment, she stared at him blankly. Then her face lost all color. "What?"

"I'm sorry," he said more kindly. "They believe the person either had a key or knew how to manipulate your locks."

She shook her head in denial. "Destroyed how?"

"Furniture broken or slashed open. Trinkets, mirrors, basically anything breakable was broken. Anything that could be cut with a knife was slit open. Any idea who did this?"

She shook her head.

"What about Zillano?"

"Of course not."

"Why 'of course not'? You just broke off a five-year relationship. You told me yourself it wasn't a happy parting."

"No, but it wasn't spiteful, either. If anyone had a right

to be angry it was me, not Ted. And if you knew Ted, you'd know how ridiculous it is to suggest he would do something like this. He doesn't have a vicious bone in his body. Believe me, I wouldn't have stayed with him all this time if he did. He's a stockbroker, witty, urbane, intelligent. Not at all the sort to wantonly destroy my apartment.''

"What about someone new?"

"I haven't dated anyone since Ted left."

He didn't like the primitive sense of satisfaction he felt at her words. "Your assistant told Detective Huang that you left New York in a hurry."

The green of her eyes darkened. "I'll have to have a few words with my assistant. My coming here *was* an impulse. The weather was rotten, my mood was rotten and I decided to chuck it all. I wasn't getting any work done in New York. I picked a spot, booked a ticket and here I am."

"Most people would book a spot in the Bahamas or Florida," he offered mildly.

"I'm not most people."

"I'll grant you that one, but why here? Why Bitterwater and Darwin Crossing?"

"Why not? It's a totally different environment from New York."

He wished he could believe her, but it didn't add up. Without thinking, he leaned forward and covered her hand with his own. The arousing impact from merely touching her was as sharp as before. Noah had to work to ignore her sensual pull as their gazes locked.

"Skylar, if you're in some sort of trouble, I can help."

Her hair swung, shimmering slightly as she shook her head. "I'm not." She looked down at his hand resting over hers.

He let her go and sat back. "Yes, you are, whether you choose to admit it or not. This wasn't some random prank. Someone deliberately chose you to victimize."

"It doesn't make any sense. If it wasn't someone trying to steal my designs, I haven't got a clue."

Her bewildered expression looked so genuine, he found himself wanting to protect her and offer comfort. It was much harder than it should have been to distance himself emotionally and get on with his job.

"Do you always pack everything you own when you go on a trip?"

"I do when I'm not sure where I'm going or how long I'll be gone. Look, Sheriff—"

"Noah."

"What?"

"Last night you called me Noah."

Pink tinged her cheeks. The pulse in her neck began to throb. She was remembering, the same as he was.

"Last night you weren't acting like a sheriff. And I think it would be best if we both forget about last night."

"I agree, but I don't think that's going to be possible, do you?"

She wouldn't meet his eyes. When she lifted her head, her expression changed and she gazed past him. He could tell Lauren and Doug must be returning. He slid out of the booth.

"According to Detective Huang, they haven't been able to locate Ted Zillano."

"What do you mean?"

"He's not at his apartment or at work."

"There was a snowstorm. He's probably bundled up with his latest…companion."

"Do you have a name?"

"I think they've been changing on a weekly basis."

"Okay. The airport resumed regularly scheduled flights this morning."

"And you want me on the next plane out of town?"

"No, I want you to be careful. Whoever tore your place apart may be on his way here to Texas."

THE MUSIC WAS LOUD. Probably so it could be heard over the crowd, Sky decided. People must have come from miles around to jam themselves into this huge old place out in the middle of nowhere. Despite her mood, the lively music called to her. She'd never been to a barn dance held in a genuine converted barn before. She watched the dancers and tried to remember if she'd ever known how to do a Texas two-step.

She hadn't wanted to come. When Lauren had invited her, she'd pointed out that she had nothing appropriate to wear, but her daughter had spiked that argument.

"Wear anything. Jeans to skirts and dresses. Nobody cares."

But Sky did. Foolish or not, she wanted Noah to see her looking good. And when the nice couple who ran the boardinghouse offered to let her ride with them to attend the dance, Sky went through her wardrobe and came up with her calf-length brown skirt, leather boots and her high-necked ivory lace blouse. In the general store in town, she found a wide belt with a Western buckle and a pair of crystal-and-gold earrings in the shape of horseshoes.

Now, standing amid the revelers and tapping her toes in time to the music, she didn't feel the least bit out of place. Several men had invited her to dance, but she'd refused all offers. As a teen, she'd never been to a dance in her life.

"Sky, you came! You look fantastic! Wow. Great earrings."

"Thank you. You look pretty terrific yourself, Lauren. And your date's not so bad, either."

Doug grinned. "How come you aren't dancing?"

"I'll let you in on a little secret. The Texas two-step isn't real big in my part of New York."

"Ah."

"We'll have to educate you," Lauren said. "New York doesn't know what it's missing. Come on."

"No, really, Lauren, that's okay."

But her daughter and Doug were undeterred. Soon the three of them were laughing. Two other young couples joined them, obviously close friends. So did several hopeful, single men of varying ages. Everyone was more than happy to teach the newcomer how to dance Texas style. After a bit Sky began to relax and really enjoy herself.

And if her eyes continued to sweep the crowd, she told herself she wasn't actually looking for Noah, just keeping her eyes open like he'd told her to. Twice she spotted a sheriff's uniform, but both times it turned out to be a young deputy.

The line dance ended and she came off the floor winded and thirsty. Instantly, two hopeful suitors sped off for refreshment.

"You know something, Lauren, a person could get used to all this attention. Maybe I should spread the word in New York. Come to Texas for a great time."

Lauren laughed and sobered quickly, looking over Sky's shoulder.

"May I have the next dance?"

Sky's heart skidded against the back of her throat. She turned, looking up into Noah's face. "You'd be taking a big risk. I haven't mastered the Texas two-step quite yet," she told him, forcing the words past her dry mouth.

"It's a slow song."

He was right. The band had changed the tempo to a slow ballad. Before she could object, Noah took her hand and led her firmly onto the floor.

"I'm not much of a dancer," she told him nervously.

"That's okay, neither am I."

He gathered her into his arms and her heart began to thud wildly.

"Relax."

"Easy for you to say."

He grinned. "This will work better if you let *me* lead."

Embarrassed, she met his gaze and saw he was teasing. "I'm used to being in charge."

"I've noticed." He nodded toward where her two hopeful companions waited with drinks in their hands. "But let's give it a try—my way."

He held her firmly against his chest as he began to lead them in and around the other dancers. Sky wondered if he could feel the pounding of her heart through his uniform. Gradually, she relaxed, forgetting about her feet and letting her senses enjoy the scent and feel of being held by him.

"You look very pretty tonight," he said quietly. "I like that blouse. It has an old-fashioned sort of look that suits you."

The compliment surprised her. "Thank you. Do you always come to dances dressed in your uniform?"

"When I'm on duty."

"Oh. Should you be dancing?"

His eyes met hers. "Definitely."

Desire, thick and heady, stirred in his hungry gaze. Her body responded instantly. Beneath her white lace bra, her nipples tightened. Electricity hummed between them so strongly she was surprised they weren't lit like a Christmas tree.

"You want me." She hadn't meant to whisper the words out loud.

"With every breath," he agreed.

His honesty zapped her mind of coherent thought, even as her body reacted with matching need. The music stopped. Noah didn't let her go. He led her across the floor, through the crowd. She followed blindly until he reached a door marked Private. He ignored the sign and twisted the handle.

She wanted to ask where they were going, then decided she didn't give a darn. Anywhere away from prying eyes was fine with her. She wanted his mouth and his hands and—

He twisted the lock then spun her around. She was flattened against the hard, cold wall. His mouth sought hers in the darkness of the room. The kiss was hot and wet and wild—exactly what his eyes had promised. She clung to him, fiercely demanding as well as receiving.

His teeth grazed her lip, fueling the fire they were stoking ever higher with each caress, each touch of lips against skin. She kissed his face, his neck, his ear, pleased when he groaned in pleasure.

"I told myself I wouldn't come near you tonight," he whispered against the curve of her jaw.

"Am I so scary?"

His hand brushed her breast, stirring her nipples to aching awareness.

"Extremely. You've got every man in the place panting after you, yet you stand there looking prim and untouchable."

She arched enough to force his hand to cup the breast it hovered over. The glint of his teeth reflected what little light filtered in the room from the window across the way, and she knew that he smiled.

"Know what's driving me crazy?"

"What?" His mouth sought the pulse point in her neck and she shifted to allow him better access. He gave a throaty laugh, a deep rumble of masculine satisfaction. His hand skimmed down her body, leaving tendrils of excitement in its wake. He found the side slit in her skirt. She tensed as his hand paused there.

"This is driving me crazy."

The warmth of his callused hand against the sheer nylon of her hose added another layer to the seduction as his palm slid slowly up her leg.

"All night, I've been watching this slit and the glimpse of leg you've been showing."

His hand skated up the slit with indecent laziness, bunching the material of her skirt higher and higher. His fingers feathered between her nylon-encased thigh. Sky shivered.

"I've been wanting to touch you here, like this."

She bit down on her bottom lip to keep from crying out

as his fingers stroked higher, lightly touching the sensitive apex. His masculine smile was nothing short of predatory as he felt the proof of her arousal.

"You've been wanting this as well."

"Yes."

She drew his mouth down to hers for a drugging kiss. Her senses were vividly alive. Pulsing with a craving she couldn't articulate.

"I've never wanted a woman the way I want you," he said against her mouth.

"Good."

He chuckled again, then used his lips and tongue to further arouse her, inserting his leg between hers so she was practically riding his thigh.

The sound of raised voices had him lifting his head away. She uttered a mew of protest. He pressed a finger to her lips and listened hard. His curse was low and inventive.

"I have to go."

She shook from head to toe. "I know."

"I won't be able to come back," he warned, releasing her and stepping away.

"I know."

He straightened his shirt, doing up buttons she didn't even remember undoing. She adjusted her skirt and blouse without looking at him.

"You could come with me tomorrow," she said tremulously.

There was a beat of stillness before he answered. "Or you could stay."

"Isn't Lauren living at home? I doubt it would do your reputation any good to spend the night with me at the boardinghouse, even if those nice people would allow such a thing."

He ran reckless fingers through his hair. The voices were louder now. Male voices, sounding happy—sounding drunk.

"Give me five minutes before you leave here. The rest

rooms are to your right. If anyone says anything, tell them I let you in here to make a phone call." He paused as he reached for the door. "I'll see what I can do."

She stood in the darkness, listening without hearing the words as he braced the three young men beyond the door. Her fingers touched lips that still throbbed with the taste of him. Her body ached with unfulfilled longing.

It was a lot longer than five minutes before she had herself under enough control to open the door. She stepped out directly into the path of a large, greasy-looking man.

"Excuse me."

"My fault," he said with a leer.

He smelled of beer and sweat and other things better not identified. His dark eyes were glassy as he looked her up and down. His smile of approval knotted her stomach.

"My fault and my pleasure," he told her.

She gave him a withering glare. "Forget it." Tussling with a drunk this size was not something she wanted to do. Relief surged through her as he gave a careless shrug.

"Another time. Have you seen Sheriff Beaufort?"

"Not for a while."

But she'd kissed him and touched him and let him touch her. And her skin still felt branded by the feel of his hand.

"I'll find him."

His gap-toothed smile had a feral quality that made her shiver. To her profound relief, he strode away, trying not to stagger.

As she reached the main barn, Lauren and Doug hurried over to her. "There you are! We've been looking everywhere for you."

And she was very conscious of the fact that her lipstick was gone and her lips had a puffy, well-kissed feel to them. If the kids noticed, they were too polite to say anything. But Lauren seemed to be trying hard not to stare at her neck. Had he left a mark? They'd probably seen Noah lead her off the dance floor like some stallion with an eager mare.

"The Merrills went home a while ago. I promised we'd give you a ride back to the boardinghouse."

"I'm sorry. I didn't realize—"

"No problem," Doug assured her. "We'll be happy to run you over there."

"Dad said to tell you he would have done it if he could, but he had to take a couple of kids to his office to wait for their parents. They got into the punch someone spiked and they're snockered good."

"Snockered?" Sky found herself smiling. "Where'd you ever hear that term?"

"Beats me."

"Are you ready to leave?" Doug asked.

More than ready. "Yes, thank you."

"Are you really driving back to San Antonio tomorrow?"

"I'm afraid so, Lauren, but I finished a couple of designs for you to take a look at. I'll run in and grab the sketches so you can take them home. I incorporated the beading you liked from—"

"Here we go again," Doug said good-naturedly.

Lauren elbowed him into silence, then came to an abrupt halt, her excitement fading. Doug's car was parked at the far end of the dark lot. Only one other car was still parked near it. Two figures were hunched beside the rear of the second car, shadowy shapes in the dark. Even as they watched, one figure straightened.

Doug came alert, but Lauren abruptly relaxed. "It's Mr. and Mrs. Jenkins."

As they drew closer, the problem was quickly apparent. The older couple had a flat tire. The once-robust elderly man had fingers that were gnarled by arthritis. Doug quickly offered to change the tire for them.

"Look, why don't you run Skylar back to the boarding-house while I change the tire. I'll wait for you at the main entrance when I finish. You can swing by and pick me up."

"Good idea. Sky and I can discuss fashion without boring you to tears."

"That was the general idea," he agreed with a grin. He kissed her forehead and handed her his keys. "Drive carefully."

"I will." She turned to Sky. "I was thinking about what you said about the bridesmaid dresses."

They talked all the way back to the boardinghouse. Listening to her daughter plan her wedding was one of the hardest things she'd ever done. Sky was horribly tempted to tell Lauren the truth, but she resisted the impulse.

"It will only take me a minute to get the drawings," she promised her daughter. The porch light was off when they pulled up. Sky hoped the Merrills hadn't locked her out. It was after midnight and she'd hate to have to wake them.

"I'll come in with you. Do you really have to leave tomorrow? Couldn't you stay another day or two?"

Sky thought about how badly she'd like to do exactly that and shook her head. "No. I have to get back. I'm sorry."

"Me, too. I think my dad likes you."

Her heart skipped a beat. "What makes you say that?"

"I think it was the way he was practically eating you alive out there on the dance floor tonight."

"Lauren!" Heat stormed her cheeks as they stepped up onto the dark front porch.

"I got the impression you liked—"

Lauren's indrawn breath was the only warning Sky had. The shape rose out of the deep shadows of the porch and lunged toward them.

# CHAPTER EIGHT

THE MOON reflected the glint of silver in his upraised hand. Sky thrust Lauren aside so hard the girl tripped and fell down the wooden steps to the sidewalk. Sky felt the slashing cold bite of steel against her shoulder. There was no time to think. She brought her booted foot up, kicking out with all her might.

The kick connected. He grunted in pain. Lauren screamed. The sound startled Sky as well as their attacker. He twisted toward her daughter and she ran for the car. Sky launched herself at the knife arm, kicking, pummeling, gouging at his ski-masked face with her fingernails. He shook her off, backhanding her with enough force to knock her into the porch railing. Her head connected with a thunk.

"I've got a gun," Lauren yelled from behind the open car door.

Sky wanted to tell her to run, to get away, but she needed her breath to scramble to her feet and charge at him again. He hit her once more, this time with a fist. Air sailed from her lungs on a whoosh of sound. She sank down on her butt, desperately trying to fill her emptied lungs. He didn't turn away from her this time. Sky saw him raise the knife, felt the raw fury of his anger, and knew he was going to kill her. Yet she couldn't move.

A gunshot exploded. Something thudded into the porch beside him. With a portion of her brain, Sky acknowledged her surprise. Lauren really did have a gun. The attacker jumped over Sky and raced across the porch. He disappeared over the railing into the darkness on the other side.

"Sky! Sky! Are you all right?"

She tried to tell Lauren she was fine, but she couldn't summon enough oxygen to form the words. Her ribs burned like fire as she tried to draw in more air. She wondered if he'd broken her rib, and if he had, if it had punctured her lung.

"Oh, God, you're bleeding!"

She was? Well, darn. Her arm hadn't even hurt until Lauren pointed that out. Her blouse was darkly soaked in warm blood. She'd never get it clean. And this was her favorite blouse!

"Police emergency," Lauren said breathlessly into a small cell phone.

Still in a daze, Sky saw that Lauren continued holding the gun in her other hand. She was impressed and slightly stunned by her daughter's familiarity with the weapon. Obviously, Noah had trained her well. Lauren was prepared for all emergencies.

Good thing somebody was. Sky closed her eyes and concentrated on filling her lungs some more.

NOAH LEFT the inebriated young teens in the custody of his deputy, who would wait for their annoyed parents to arrive. He returned to the barn to make another sweep of the grounds, checking for anyone else who had imbibed too heavily, was up to some mischief or was feeling too amorous for his date.

At least that's what he told himself he was doing. The truth was, he'd hoped to catch Sky before she left. No matter that it was insane, he was still perched on the keen edge of arousal. That mind-boggling session in the back room had only made things worse. He'd nearly taken her right there against what had once been the tack room wall.

And she would have let him.

The knowledge was heady stuff. It didn't seem to matter that he didn't trust her. The chemistry between them was overriding his common sense. He hadn't behaved like this since he was a randy teenager. Hell, he'd never behaved like this. Sky had his head spinning. And his only consolation was that she seemed to be every bit as affected as he was.

Even as he thought about that, his headlights picked up Doug crossing the mostly empty parking lot. Instantly, he marshaled his thoughts and pulled over to find out what was wrong. Doug was explaining about the flat tire when Noah heard a call come in over his radio. The second he heard the address, his body turned to ice.

"Get in!" he ordered.

"What is it?"

"Lauren and Sky."

Noah barely waited for Doug to scramble inside and close the door before he hit the siren and the lights and tore out of the parking lot. The hollow taste of fear filled him. He called in a response, silently offering up a prayer.

Doug sat in puzzled silence while the dispatcher relayed a lookout for a male attacker, six-two, 175 pounds, dark clothing and a ski mask—armed with a knife.

Noah told himself Lauren and Sky were okay, but he couldn't make himself believe it. He kept remembering Detective Huang's description of Sky's apartment. "Sure looks like somebody has a powerful dislike for this lady," the detective had said.

Noah's heart threatened to stop altogether when the dispatcher added that shots had been fired.

"Someone got shot?" Doug exhaled sharply.

"Someone was attacked at the boardinghouse in Bitterwater," Noah said tersely.

"My God! I told Lauren to take Sky home while I changed the tire." Stricken, the younger man stared at him. "I should have made them wait until I finished."

Privately, Noah agreed, but nothing would be gained by saying so. "Lauren was armed," Noah told him. "She knows how to use a gun."

"If the attacker didn't take it away and use it on her."

Noah forced that horrific image from his mind and shook his head. "If that had happened the dispatcher would have said the suspect was armed with a gun instead of a knife. Lauren was the one who fired."

He stated it with far more confidence than he was feeling. His daughter didn't like guns, but she had a great deal of respect for them. If she'd fired her weapon it was because she'd seen no other choice.

An ambulance was being dispatched.

"Someone was hurt," Doug said, his eyes as wild as Noah felt. They both knew the possibilities were limited. He prayed the ambulance wasn't for his daughter or Sky.

"Someone must have followed them home from the dance," Doug continued, his voice filled with fear and shock.

"Or they walked in on a situation," Noah suggested.

Like the person who ripped up Sky's place in New York? Noah gripped the steering wheel even tighter as they flew over the mostly empty roads. He'd been a cop a long time. Long enough to know what they could be heading toward.

"What about that convict you told Lauren to watch out for?"

"Francis Hartman wants a piece of me, not my daughter."

"But isn't that why you told Lauren to be careful? Because he might try to use her in retribution?"

Noah swore softly. He hadn't even considered that possibility. Recklessly, he pushed the speedometer up another notch. "Hang on. We'll have our answers in a few minutes."

Official vehicles plugged the driveway as Noah rolled up behind the ambulance and cut the lights and siren. The first thing he saw was his daughter standing on the front porch talking to the police. His incredible relief was short-lived when he spotted Sky sitting down, leaning against the porch railing and surrounded by people.

Doug didn't wait for the car to rock to a complete stop before he was out the door, flying across the lawn. He reached Lauren well ahead of Noah. Lauren flung herself into the young man's arms. For just a moment, Noah felt his chest constrict, seeing his daughter reach for Doug instead of him. But that unsettling instant of disorientation faded the moment he turned his attention to Sky and saw the darkly spreading stain on her blouse in the beam of a powerful flashlight someone held.

He felt as though he'd been punched in the stomach. Sky had been hurt. Two paramedics bent to examine her.

"Did you have to cut it? It was my favorite blouse."

"Sorry, ma'am," the woman said kindly. "I'm afraid it was already ruined. Where else are you hurt?"

"It's just a scratch."

"One that needs a couple of stitches."

Sky muttered something pithy. "Can't you just stick a bandage on it?"

Noah's relief was almost painful. If she could give them a hard time, she couldn't be hurt too badly. He wanted to pick her up and hug her the same way Doug was doing with Lauren. "Stop giving the paramedics a hard time," he scolded softly.

Her face lit when she saw him and his heart gave a funny lurch.

"Noah." She managed a wobbly smile. "I'd stand up, but they won't let me. I'm fine."

"If you were fine, you wouldn't be sitting there bleeding all over what's left of that blouse."

Fear ghosted over her face. "It's only a cut, thanks to Lauren's fast thinking. She saved both our lives tonight."

Noah had to swallow before he could summon any words. "Is she okay?" he asked the paramedics.

"The wound isn't deep, but we should take her over to the clinic and let the doctor check her out."

"I don't need a doctor," she protested.

"You heard the paramedic. Let the doctor check you over. I'll come get you after I'm done here. Promise."

She blinked back sudden tears and nodded. Noah turned away reluctantly as Lieutenant Devlin Bateman tapped him on the shoulder.

"What happened here, Dev?"

"According to your daughter, they were attacked as soon as they stepped on the porch," he said without preamble. "Apparently the guy was inside the house when the Merrills came home. Back door's unlocked. Mr. Merrill claims it wasn't when they left, but there's no sign of a forced entry. The suspect was completely dressed in black including a black ski mask that covered his face and hair. We don't have any kind of a description beyond height and weight. He forced the Merrills down in the basement at knifepoint. Mr. Merrill was cut when he tried to resist. The suspect threatened to slit their throats if they didn't cooperate. Mr. Merrill believes he would have done it."

Noah glanced back at Sky, who was being transferred to a gurney. Devlin watched him sympathetically.

"My guess is he'd have done exactly that," Devlin told him. "The Merrills are going through the house with one of my people to see what's missing. He wore gloves so no prints. We already know Ms. Diamond had some opal jewelry sitting on a dresser. It appears to be gone. Looks like a burglary at this point. We think he was leaving the house when your daughter pulled up, trapping him on the front porch."

"Why didn't he simply take off? Why jump them?"

Devlin shook his head. "Good question. Your daughter

gave us a clear account. It's a good thing she kept her head. She scared him off with a shot.''

Noah surveyed the porch. The dim light beside the front door did little to illuminate the shadowy recesses. A burglar could have waited there undetected, or jumped over the railing and been away before they even caught a glimpse of him. "He jumped them deliberately.''

Dev didn't seem surprised. "Possibly.''

"He was lying in wait for them.''

"Someone they know?''

"Skylar's New York office and apartment were trashed the other night.''

"Does she know who did it?''

"She says not. A Detective Huang is handling the case.''

"Puts a different slant on this. You want to have a look around?''

"If you don't mind. Okay to send Doug home with Lauren?''

"Sure. I've got her preliminary statement. I can talk to her tomorrow.''

"Thanks.'' He walked over to where Doug continued holding Lauren as if he'd never let her go.

"You okay, honey?''

"I'm fine, Daddy.''

Her lips trembled, but she was dry-eyed. "Sky saved my life. He came out of nowhere with that knife. She pushed me out of the way and he cut her instead. We were coming inside to get the wedding dress designs she did for me. I should have known something was wrong. There were no lights on inside or out, but I wasn't paying attention. We were talking.''

His hands fisted helplessly at his side. He forced them to relax. "Sky says your quick thinking saved both your lives. I'm proud of you, honey. You kept your head and chased him off.''

"But I rushed my shot. I missed him.''

He wanted to hug her the way he had when she was little and scared. But that was Doug's job right now. He offered her a smile instead. "Don't worry about it. We'll get him. Doug, would you mind driving Lauren back to the house?"

"No, Daddy, we're going to the clinic. I have to be sure Sky's okay."

He understood. He wanted to go as well. Realistically, he knew his place was here right now.

"I won't let her out of my sight, Sheriff," Doug promised.

Doug was obviously feeling a full measure of guilt. "All right. I'll catch up with you there or at home."

The boardinghouse offered up nothing particularly useful. The couple was badly shaken, but the older man's wound was superficial. He refused treatment beyond a bandage. Sky was their only guest at the moment and nothing appeared to be missing except the jewelry that had been sitting out. They found the rest of an impressive collection inside a large jewelry box in one of Sky's suitcases.

"The lady has good taste," Dev muttered. "This either wasn't a robbery or the guy was too inept for words. This pendant alone would fence for a pretty penny."

Noah ignored the jumbled contents. His gaze landed on the drawings she'd been coming inside to get. The detailed sketches were sitting on the small desk, neatly marked with Lauren's name. She'd even sketched a fair likeness of Lauren wearing the dresses.

"Mind if I take these?" he asked Dev. "Sky was coming inside to get them for Lauren."

"Go ahead. Ms. Diamond sure doesn't believe in traveling light, does she? Look at this mound of luggage."

Noah eyed the stack of suitcases. No wonder Detective Huang thought she was skipping town. She couldn't have left much behind.

"She's a fashion designer."

"Yeah? I wonder how many closets she has."

Noah narrowed his eyes and scanned the room again. "Where's her briefcase?"

"I didn't see one."

"There should be one. She carries it almost everywhere."

After a brief search they found it lying open, partially hidden under the bed.

"Looks like it fell after he ransacked it, and got kicked under here. Let's have a look," Dev said, placing it carefully on the bed.

As far as Noah could see, everything inside, and the items that had spilled on the carpeting, related to her job. The file with Finders Keepers on it and the one Alma claimed to have seen at the café with his daughter's name on it were no longer there.

Noah brooded about that all the way to the clinic. Maybe she'd put them in her car. He made a mental note to stop by the garage and check. First thing tomorrow morning he was going to try calling Dylan Garrett again.

Doug was pacing the waiting room when Noah reached the tiny clinic that served the area. He was alone. "Lauren's in back trying to convince Sky to spend the night at your place. They took seven stitches in her arm. She's got a couple of bruises, but otherwise the doctor says she's okay."

"How are you holding up?"

Doug smiled without humor. "My nerves are shot. I'm not sure how I'm going to leave here tomorrow morning. I'll be a wreck worrying about her being here while I'm at school. If I didn't have a major paper due—"

The door swung open.

"—isn't necessary," Sky was saying to Lauren. His daughter brightened, spotting him.

"Dad! Maybe you can talk some sense into her. I told Sky she should come back to the house with us and spend the night."

Sky's eyes locked with his. Several emotions flickered over her features, but she stared at him mutely. Her blouse had been replaced by a sweater he recognized as one of Doug's. The younger man must have had it in his rental car. The sleeves had been rolled up and pushed back and the material draped in sloppy folds over her curves. She should have looked ridiculous with her hair all tangled and her eyes smudged and shadowed. But she didn't. She looked like an endearing waif. Noah resisted an impulse to walk over and put his arms around her.

"You and Doug head home," he told his daughter gruffly. "I'll take care of Skylar."

"All right, Dad," Lauren agreed, sounding oddly subdued.

"Oh. Here. I think these are the papers you wanted her to have?"

Sky glanced from the drawings he thrust toward her to his face. "Yes. Thank you." She handed them to Lauren, who hugged her tightly. Noah saw Sky wince, though she didn't protest.

"Come on, Lauren, it's late," Doug urged.

"And you have to get up early," she agreed. "I'm sorry, Doug. Sky, thank you."

"Thank you."

The women shared a look of understanding. "You won't leave without saying goodbye?" Lauren demanded.

"I promise."

Doug slid his arm around Lauren and led her outside.

"You raised a terrific young woman, Sheriff," Sky said. "Are you going to start grilling me now?"

Fatigue stamped her features. She gathered her haughty demeanor around her like a shield.

"That's Dev's job. I'm here to provide taxi service."

Her lips parted, her confusion evident.

"Come on," he said kindly. "Let's get out of here."

"You don't have to say it twice," she said in relief.

"How's the arm?" he asked as they headed for his cruiser.

"Right now I don't feel a thing. They numbed it so they could stitch it up. I suspect it will hurt later on. The doctor gave me something to help me sleep."

"But you aren't going to take it, right?"

"Taking up mind reading?"

"Sometimes it's not hard. You're a stubborn, independent woman. You don't want to take something that might leave you groggy and vulnerable."

"Something like that, yes."

"In your shoes, I wouldn't take it, either," he confided. Before she knew what he intended to do, he lifted her carefully and set her inside the front seat of the high vehicle and closed the door.

He went around and got in on his side with a lopsided grin. "And yes, I know you could have gotten in without my help."

"Actually," she said softly, "with this arm I'm not so sure I could have. Thank you."

The woman was full of surprises. "You're welcome. Doug said it took seven stitches to close your arm."

"So they tell me. I wasn't keeping count."

He started the engine and put the car in reverse. "It's my turn to thank you."

"For what?"

"For keeping my daughter safe."

"You've got it the wrong way round. She saved me. He was about to stab me again when she fired that gun and scared him off."

Noah took a deep, steadying breath. "You were both lucky."

"I know."

Sky sat in the safety of Noah's police car and tried to keep the shaking inside where it didn't show. She thought she'd done a pretty credible job holding it together until now, but she was starting to feel the aftermath of everything she'd been through. The doctor had explained this was likely to happen. She just hadn't realized how jangled and raw her nerve endings would feel. Fear was suddenly welling up inside her again.

"You may have been right, Sheriff."

She felt him glance her way but kept her gaze firmly on her clasped hands. She'd broken several nails, she saw. Her manicurist would scold her.

"Right about what?"

"That man tonight…it probably sounds paranoid, but I had the impression…he seemed so angry. The attack felt almost personal. As if it were me he wanted to hurt."

"Maybe it was," he said quietly.

She shook her head, unwilling to believe that, because if it was true, she'd put her daughter in harm's way. And that made the shaking so much worse. She couldn't endanger Lauren. The thought was unbearable. It was going to be difficult enough to go back to her hectic, empty New York life knowing she'd left her daughter behind, but if something happened to Lauren because of her…

"You think tonight was connected to what happened in New York."

"Don't you?" he asked.

"How could it be?"

"Did you leave anything in your apartment that would have told someone where you'd gone?"

She started to say no, then thought about the pad next to the phone. Had she thrown away the sheet she'd made notes on? She couldn't remember.

"It's possible."

"You must have some idea what he wants from you."

"None. I mean it."

"Originally you said a competitor?"

"When it was my office, that was my first thought. I had some drawings stolen a few months ago. The fashion industry is big business, Noah. Theft isn't all that uncommon. But I've never heard of anyone carrying it this far."

He was silent for several minutes. Sky tried to relax, but her body still hummed with tension. Her mind kept replaying those terrifying minutes on the porch.

"According to Detective Huang, the damage appeared maliciously directed."

"That just doesn't make sense. No one has any reason to hate me personally."

"Except Ted Zillano."

"No. I can't believe that. I *don't* believe that. I told you, we were together out of habit. There was no great passion in our relationship."

"For five years?"

"Is that so hard to understand? We live busy lives. It was nice to come home to someone at the end of the day."

"You could have gotten a cat."

She managed a weak grin. "Except a cat can't escort you to business functions or social gatherings."

"Did you do a lot of that? Go out socially?"

"Yes and no. We went out a lot because of our jobs. Socializing was an extension of our professional world."

"So what did you do for fun?"

"Fun?" A novel concept. Had she ever done anything just for fun? Looking into his features she realized the only fun she could remember having since her mother died was at the barn dance that night. "We went to parties and plays and concerts, but always because it involved another couple one or the other of us knew through work."

"You and Zillano never did things together just as a couple?"

"No." And until this moment that hadn't really seemed strange. "I told you, we just sort of fell into a relationship."

"Are you sure Zillano viewed your *association* the same way? I sure wouldn't."

The atmosphere altered in the beat of her heart. Noah watched the road, but she could practically feel the tension in his taut frame. No. He wouldn't feel the same way. She couldn't imagine a relationship with Noah that would be lacking in passion the way hers and Ted's had been. Somehow she knew this all-consuming awareness would always be there between them, lurking in the background of their relationship.

"You're nothing like Ted."

"I'm glad you realize that."

A shiver went down her spine.

"You threw him out for sleeping with another woman."

"No, I threw him out for bringing a young girl into *my* bed in *my* apartment." Remembered anger filled her voice. "He could have taken her to her place or his own apartment."

"Wait a minute. I thought you lived together."

"We did, but Ted still maintained an apartment close to his office. Apartments are hard to come by in New York. You don't let go of a decent one unless you're certain you're never going to need it again. Ted wasn't real big on commitment."

"And you wanted him to make a commitment?"

"No! Well, maybe at first I thought things would take a different path for us. I would have liked someone special in my life, a family, the usual things. But I was busy trying to create an identity in the fashion world and that consumed most of my energy and spare time. When I met Ted at a party, he was comfortable. We seemed to be on the same page with things. I did think maybe something more would happen at first, but it didn't take long to realize we were never going to have more than what we already shared."

"Yet you stayed together for five years."

"Yes. I don't think I can explain it to someone like you."

"What's wrong with me?"

"Nothing." And that was part of the problem. Everything seemed unbelievably right about Noah. Except that he lived here in Texas and was her daughter's father.

Noah accepted that, though something changed briefly in

his expression. "So did Ted play around a lot while you two were together?"

"No. Not at all. He didn't have any more time in his life than I did. I would have known if there was someone else."

"But there was."

Sky shook her head. "Ted brought that girl to my place deliberately. I'd recently started one of those discussions men hate about commitment and goals. I was feeling restless. I don't know. I'm about to turn forty. I suddenly realized I probably would never have a family of my own. Ted couldn't imagine having a family with his busy lifestyle—and he wasn't about to alter that for any reason. I think he was concerned I was hinting about marriage to him. I wasn't, but I suspect the girl in my bed was his way of ending things."

"Why not simply say goodbye?"

"You'd have to know Ted to understand."

"I don't think I'd like to know Ted," he growled.

Sky blinked. "Yes, well, I don't think he'd take too kindly to you, either. Anyhow, he never liked what he called 'messy emotions.'" She glimpsed a signpost as it rushed by. "Where are you going? Wasn't that the turnoff for Bitterwater?"

"We aren't going to Bitterwater. We're going to my place."

"But—"

"Do you really want to spend the rest of the night in that house by yourself? The Merrills went to a neighbor's."

"But…I can't go home with you."

"Why not?"

Sleep in the same house with him? When despite everything she still wanted him and knew he felt the same way? She straightened up in her seat. "Because I don't have anything to wear," she said primly.

A chuckle escaped his throat. "Yes, you do. Your suitcases are in the back."

She twisted around to look. "All of them?"

"Even your briefcase."

She gave a guilty start, and hoped he didn't notice. Had he looked inside? Had he seen the file with the map and the notes from Finders Keepers? Did he know who she was?

"Do you always keep your briefcase under the bed?" he asked mildly.

"Of course not."

"Then you'd better check the contents as soon as we get to the house."

"My designs are in there! My disks… My God, Noah, maybe it was about my job, after all."

He shook his head. "There are disks and work files inside. You'll have to see if any of them are missing, of course. The case had been opened and gone through."

Why didn't he mention the file on Lauren? He must have seen it. Lauren's baby pictures, the notes his wife had sent every year, all of that was in the file plainly marked with Lauren's name. Yet he didn't say a word. Why not?

"Doug is sleeping in the spare room so you'll have to take my bed."

For a split instant she froze. The file, the attack, everything faded as his words penetrated. The memory of his kiss inside that darkened office became so vivid she could feel her body starting to respond. She stared at him.

"I'll take the couch," he continued, unperturbed.

Sleep in his bed, where he slept night after night? Who was he kidding? She wouldn't sleep a wink.

"I'll take the couch!"

He spared her a glance. "With Lauren and Doug in the house, your virtue is perfectly safe."

"My virtue isn't interested in safety," she said in exasperation as he returned his attention to the road. "And that's exactly the problem. I want you, too."

He drew in a sharp breath. His head swiveled to stare at her. "Are you always this candid?"

"Too much so at times, or so I've been told." Feeling like a fool, she shrugged. "It saves misunderstandings."

"We can't sleep together with my daughter in the house."

"On that, we are agreed. But do you really think either of us is going to sleep knowing I'm lying on your sheets, in your bed, in your room."

Noah cursed.

"Exactly what we *can't* do."

He strangled on a chuckle.

"And I'm still going to leave in the morning," she warned him.

He didn't respond.

Her broken nails dug into her palms until she nearly drew blood. "You could still come with me."

The whispered words exploded in the silent confines of the car. A muscle twitched in his hard-set jaw. Sky leaned her head back and closed her eyes. It was going to be a long night.

# CHAPTER NINE

SHE WAS STILL thinking that same thing three hours later. Only now her arm throbbed, she had a headache, and muscles she hadn't even known existed ached from the attack. But those weren't the reasons she was still awake. It wasn't even Noah's presence in the room down the hall, though she couldn't stop thinking about him. What really worried her was the fact that Lauren's file and the directions to Finders Keepers were the only things missing from her briefcase. Only one person would have any interest in that file.

Noah.

But if he'd seen it, why hadn't he said something? The troubling question had no answer. If she weren't so tired, maybe she could think. Nothing made sense anymore.

Sky drew on her robe after pacing the den floor for several minutes. Doug had insisted she take the spare bedroom, but Noah finally agreed to let her use the couch when she pointed out that she might need to sit up if her arm bothered her too much.

Her arm was the least of her worries. She made her way as silently as possible through the dark house to the front door. Limpet startled her by appearing from somewhere to join her, his tail swishing happily. She touched his head hesitantly, not sure if she should let him outside at this hour or not. His presence was sort of reassuring, however, so she decided to take a chance.

The front door made little noise when she opened it. Leaving it ajar, she closed the screen silently. Belatedly, she realized she should have put on slippers. The boards under her feet were cold as she made her way across the porch to the swing. Limpet jumped up beside her when she sat down and the swing squeaked loudly in protest.

"Shh, Limpet. Get down." He looked at her with what she fervently hoped was a wide doggy grin and thumped his tail. "Missed out on obedience training, huh?" Well, who was she to tell this massive beast where he could sit?

"All right, but you are not a lapdog no matter what you may think. Next to me, dog. Not on top of me," she whispered. "My arm hurts and my lap's too small."

As if he understood perfectly, he curled beside her and settled his large heavy head in her lap with a sigh.

"Thanks. Are you trying to be sympathetic?"

She stroked his head and he sighed again, this time in obvious contentment. The night air had a decided nip to it, but that was okay. She was oddly unafraid sitting out here in the dark despite what had happened. Probably because she knew Noah was only a yell away. His presence was definitely reassuring. She breathed in the scents of the night and closed her eyes, rocking gently back and forth and scratching behind the large dog's ear.

What would her life have been like if she'd chosen another path? Would she be struggling to make a living so her daughter could go to college as her mother had done for her, or would she be some rancher's wife by now? If she could go back in time, would she change the choices that she'd made?

What she had told Noah about her life tonight was nothing short of the truth. When her mother was alive, she'd been Sky's best friend and confidante. Sky was willing to do anything to see her mother smile. But after she passed on, there wasn't anyone but single-minded career types coming her way. Everyone was climbing ladders, including her. It had been enough.

No. She was lying. If it had been enough she never would

have come looking for her daughter. Hadn't she secretly hoped to become part of her child's world—to make some sort of connection in her life—and to absolve herself from guilt?

"You two make quite a picture."

Startled, she gasped at Noah's softly voiced words. He opened the screen and stepped outside. Limpet wagged his tail in welcome as Puddles and Leo joined the party.

"Are you trying to give me a heart attack?"

"Sorry."

"Some watchdog you turned out to be."

Limpet jumped down and trotted over to Noah to have his head rubbed, then sniffed at the other two dogs.

"I heard you come outside," Noah told her.

"I didn't think I made much noise."

"You didn't. I was awake."

"Shall I mention that I told you so?"

She couldn't draw her gaze from him. He'd obviously just come from bed. His hair was mussed and tangled as if he'd been running his fingers through the strands. He'd put on a shirt, but only fastened the middle button. Not that it was any big deal, she told herself. Pick up any magazine and you could see a man's bare chest.

Only the men in those pictures weren't standing two feet away from her and wearing a pair of snug-fitting jeans with the button undone. She couldn't stop wondering if Noah wore anything under those jeans. Did he sleep in the nude? Probably. Lots of people did.

Like hers, his feet were bare. Her imagination shouldn't be jumping in excitement this way, but like the rest of his rumpled appearance, there was something very sexy about those bare feet.

Because they belonged to Noah.

"Arm's hurting, huh?"

She jerked her head up to meet his eyes. "A little."

"Want some company?"

Too much for comfort. The smart thing to do would be to send him away or go back inside herself. She wasn't feeling particularly smart tonight, or maybe she was just a glutton for punishment.

"Sure."

"Scoot over."

"You're going to sit here?"

He tipped his head to one side. "It's a big swing. I don't take up as much room as Limpet."

"You aren't as soft and furry as he is, either."

His teeth flashed in the darkness as he smiled. "How can you tell?"

She was searching for a comeback when his next words altered everything.

"If I lay my head in your lap, will you pet me, too?"

A disturbing sensual energy hovered in the air between them. Like a charge waiting for the fuse to be lit, it sat there, needing only a match to set it off.

"What are you doing?" she asked hoarsely.

"Making a fool of myself, I suspect. Come here."

"I don't think this is smart."

"Hell, I *know* it isn't smart, but I want to hold you all the same. Just hold you."

Her heart thundered in her chest. She could almost hear the strike of the match as she warily shifted position to lean her head against his chest. He gently repositioned her so her head fit comfortably into the curve of his shoulder. With a sigh, she snuggled right in. It was if she'd been designed to fit there.

Mindful of her injury, Noah slid his arm around her and felt her tremble.

"Cold?"

"Not really."

He smiled against her hair. The scent of her shampoo filled his nostrils. He stroked her arm through the sleeve of her silky robe and was rewarded with another slight shiver.

"This material is almost as soft as your skin. No, don't pull away. All we're going to do is talk."

She stayed where she was, but he could feel the tension humming through her. It was only fair. His own body felt as if it were plugged into an electrical current.

"Just talk, huh?"

"Unless you want to try making love on a porch swing."

She sucked in a breath while his body tightened hungrily at the image of her naked and vulnerable, sitting astride him here on the swing.

"Sounds interesting. Is this some fetish I should know about?" she asked. He noticed she didn't sound too upset at the idea.

"More like a recent fantasy."

"How recent?"

"Since I stepped out the door and found you sitting here in the moonlight looking as tempting as sin in this sexy scrap of nylon."

"It's silk."

"Pardon me." He continued to stroke her arm through the material.

"I thought we were just going to talk."

"We are talking." His fingers touched the start of the bandage beneath her thin robe and he felt her tense.

"Hurting bad, huh?"

"Some."

"On a scale of one to ten, how much is some?"

"Don't worry about it."

"Ah. A twelve. You didn't take that pain pill, I gather."

"I told you I wasn't going to. It's very peaceful here."

He almost smiled at her quick change of topic. "Yes, it is. Darwin Crossing is quite a change from Dallas." After a moment, he felt her relax against him again.

"Is that where you used to live?"

"Uh-huh. I used to work for the Dallas Police Department."

"Why did you leave?"

"My wife died."

She tensed.

"Tell me about her," she said softly.

"Why?"

She gave a tiny shrug. "I was making conversation. If it bothers you to talk about her—"

"It doesn't."

The three dogs wandered down the steps out into the yard to investigate something. They were quickly swallowed by the velvet darkness of the yard.

"Beth was a quiet person. Almost shy. All she ever wanted was to marry and have children. Only she couldn't conceive so we adopted Lauren."

Sky didn't comment on the adoption, she simply waited. She felt oddly right nestled against him like this, he decided.

"Beth was the perfect cop's wife. I worked undercover for the Dallas Police Department in those days, putting in long hours to build a name for myself inside the department. She never complained about the hazards or the hours. She was always there, cheerfully waiting when I'd come home. I didn't notice when she started not feeling well and she never said a word—until it was too late. She died of ovarian cancer when Lauren was five."

Sky covered his hand with her own. "I've read that ovarian cancer is like that. Usually by the time there are symptoms, not much can be done."

Her matter-of-fact tone and the warmth of her hand were more soothing than words of sympathy would have been. Noah leaned his chin against the top of her head.

"It must have been hard, raising Lauren by yourself," Sky said quietly.

"At first it was. Lauren didn't really know me. I hadn't been home much." And he knew Sky could hear the guilt he would always live with for his neglect of his wife and child. "I stopped doing undercover work immediately, but

I soon realized I wanted to make a complete change. The county was looking for deputies, so I applied. They hired me on. Then when the sheriff's position came open, I ran for that without really expecting to get the job."

For several long seconds, she didn't reply.

"And now you're the father of the bride."

"Yeah."

"You don't sound happy."

"Oh, I am. Lauren's young, but she's mature for her age and I really like Doug. The two of them are a good match."

"But…?"

"Now who's reading minds?"

"You're right. Sometimes it isn't hard."

"I guess there's a part of me that selfishly doesn't want to let go of my little girl. We had some rough moments, but the two of us became pretty close."

Her fingers stroked the back of his hand. "I think that's nice. Lauren's a very lucky woman to have two men in her life who love her so much."

He remembered Sky had said she never knew her father.

"How come you never married?" he asked.

She dropped her hand back to her lap. Immediately, he missed the warmth of her fingers.

"No one ever asked me."

"I find that hard to believe."

She spread her hands. "I spent years establishing a career in a cutthroat industry. The men I tend to meet are either married, gay, or like Ted, not particularly interested in commitment."

The back of her hand accidentally brushed his bare abdomen. She drew in an uneven breath as his muscles contracted at the unexpected touch. Awareness closed them in a tight cocoon, making him totally cognizant of every inch of her slight body where it brushed against his own.

"It's getting cooler. You should button your shirt."

"Does the sight of my bare chest bother you?"

She lifted her face, putting her mouth within inches of his own. "What happens if I say yes?"

He'd planned to keep everything platonic, but the remembered taste of her was like a fever in his blood. Awareness sizzled between them. He wanted more. Lots more.

"I guess it would depend on *how* it bothered you," he said huskily.

The tip of her tongue moistened her lips. "And if I said I found it...sexy?"

"Ah. Then this happens."

He fit his lips over hers, savoring the texture and the taste of her mouth. She shivered delicately once more, sending uncontrollable currents of hunger skating through him. He wanted her with shocking desperation. It made no sense; it simply was.

The slow, hot glide of her tongue over his teeth set his body on fire. Their tongues and lips mated freely. She leaned into his body, molding herself against the hard wall of his chest. They fit together as though they had been fashioned as one unit.

She pulled back, her eyes glittering in the moonlight, her body quivering. "You said just talk."

He stroked her face, running his thumb over her well-kissed lips. "We did." Even in the darkness, he knew her eyes changed color again. It was a little disturbing to realize how well he was coming to know her.

She relaxed, melting against him. "So we did."

That was all the invitation he needed. He lifted her onto his lap while the swing groaned in protest.

"The kids," she whispered.

"Their rooms are in the back of the house."

"Good."

His chuckle was as ragged as his breathing. Her lips parted and his tongue took full advantage to duel with her own. His fingers sought and found the knotted belt of her robe. The heady fragrance of her body was like a drug to his system. He had to have her or die of frustration.

He eased the robe open and she helped him lower it down and off her arms. A blouselike top with narrow spaghetti straps covered the gentle swell of her breasts. The hard, pointed nipples tented the silky material. Noah cupped the sides of each breast through the fabric, shaping them. She stared, open-eyed, like a doe caught in headlights.

"Do you like this?" Lightly, he ran his thumbs over her nipples and watched as her lips parted on a soft sound he took as assent.

He leaned over and closed his mouth over one full breast, right through the material. She shuddered, uttering a soft, keening cry. His fingers closed over the other nipple, tugging it, even as his teeth raked its mate.

"Noah!"

Her broken plea nearly unleashed the raging passion inside him. He wanted her, but he wanted her as mindless with need as he was himself.

"Stand up for a minute."

He set her on her feet in front of him, steadying her when her knees threatened to buckle.

"What are you doing?" she asked.

"What are you wearing?"

"You want a fashion lesson now?" she asked incredulously. "It's a camisole and tap pants."

"Take them off."

"What?"

Surprised by the boldness of his own words, he nevertheless watched the slow heat build in her expression. Another woman might have died of embarrassment, but he knew that wouldn't be Sky's reaction. He sensed a restless hunger in her that matched his own.

She tilted back her head as if she'd heard that thought and smiled a slow, sensuous smile that teased at the hunger in his gut. "So you want a striptease?"

Noah nearly groaned out loud. "What I want is to rip those bits of silk from your body and plunge inside you until we can't tell where one of us leaves off and the other begins," he told her honestly.

"Oh."

"I was trying not to be quite so primitive."

She stared at him intently. He wondered if he'd pushed the limits of this intangible connection he'd sensed between the two of them.

"If the answer is no, now would be a real good time to go back inside," he said. He was fully, heavily aroused, and the words cost him, but he knew it was true. He wanted Sky in the most basic way, but only if she wanted the same thing.

Still without saying a word, she clasped the hem's edge of her top and began to inch the fabric up. He thought his recklessly racing heart would tear right through his chest at the sultry expression on her face.

"Primitive sounds...exciting."

His blood heated to just below boiling. "Keep teasing me like that, and we're going to find out how exciting. What is that?"

She stopped moving, the undersides of her breasts barely exposed. "What is what?"

But he was already leaning forward to lightly touch the ugly dark bruise in the center of her chest.

"Oh. That's where the attacker hit me tonight."

Rage washed over him. "He hit you?"

Lightly, she touched his jaw. "Does it turn you off?"

Her concern tempered his fury. "Of course not. But it almost makes me wish Lauren's shot hadn't missed."

"You don't mean that," she said with certainty.

"You're right. I don't. Not really." He tugged her forward, between his legs, and placed a gentle kiss in the center of the bruise. "On the other hand, I would take great personal pleasure in giving that bastard a few reciprocal bruises.''

"Later." Her lips curved slightly as she reached for the buttons on his shirt. "Let's get back to this primitive stuff."

He was still furious with the bastard who had hurt her, but it was hard to stay focused on anything as she pulled her top over her head, leaving her bare breasts within inches of his mouth.

Skylar was like no woman he'd ever known. Boldly sensual with an underlying vulnerability that appealed to every part of him. Moonlight bathed the tops of her breasts, highlighting the puckered nipples while throwing the rest of her body into the deeper shadows cast by the porch railing. Noah leaned forward and ran his tongue over the soft contours of her stomach. She inhaled sharply, her stomach muscles rippling.

"I don't understand what it is about you that makes me feel so unbearably wanton and naughty," she whispered.

The husky thread of her voice was fuel for the growing fire inside him. "That's just how I want you. Naughty." He laved the underside of each breast. "And wanton."

He drew a nipple into his mouth and sucked strongly, drawing a helpless cry from her throat. The sound was incredibly intoxicating. He let his teeth just graze the tip before moving to suckle her other breast.

She thrust her hands through her hair and arched her back, allowing him better access. He took full advantage, pulling her down to ride one denim-clad knee as he sampled her breasts.

"Noah! I want to touch you, too."

Oh, yeah. He wanted that as well. He licked the exposed length of her throat, kissing the sensitive skin of her neck. "Where do you want to touch me?"

"Everywhere," she said breathlessly, kneading his shoulders.

He grinned wickedly. "Soon."

His fingers crept under the waistband of her silken shorts and her stomach contracted. She trembled helplessly as he helped her to stand again, sliding the shorts over her hips until they slithered down her slender legs, exposing the light-colored triangle of hair to the moon's view.

"I want to be inside you. Right now." It was all he could do not to follow through when his body was urging him toward completion.

Her breathing hitched, becoming audible as her tongue glided across her lips. Her eyes were half-closed in arousal. The womanly scent of her was a heady aphrodisiac. Using one finger, he traced the path his tongue had taken earlier down her body until he reached the line of curling hair. With his fingers, he threaded a path to the secret moist place those curls covered.

"I see you want that, too. Don't you?"

"Yes."

He probed gently. She made a small arousing sound, her fingers tangling desperately in his hair. He shuddered, inflamed with his own need. Only the desire to bring her as much pleasure as he could kept him from drawing her down then and there.

Sky took the initiative away from him, sliding her hands over his shoulders, inside his shirt and down his chest until she found the nubs of his nipples with her fingers. She scraped a nail across them gently, sparking an electric current of white-hot desire. He had to close his eyes against the force of his need.

"You're killing me."

She smiled. "Not yet."

Her hands glided over the planes of his stomach, caressing his skin with piercing sweetness until she came to the band of his jeans. Her smile widened. She looked right at him as she ran her fingers over the zipper of his jeans, bringing him to pulsating life. Deliberately, she traced his outline, taking his measure, then stroking him through the material lightly. But when she started easing beneath his waistband, he stayed her questing fingers.

"Sorry, but you're testing my control to the maximum. If you touch me there, I won't be able to wait, and I want to take this slow."

Her gaze deliberately stayed on the hard bulge his pants concealed. Her fingers reached for the zipper. A touch of moisture marred the dark material of his jeans and she knew he was perilously close to losing control.

"Slow is for beginners," she said huskily.

The sound of the zipper was loud in the silence of the night.

"I don't think either of us qualifies, do you?"

"No."

The time for teasing was over. Noah helped to free himself, positioning her across his lap. The swing squawked in protest when he probed carefully at her soft, wet passage. Her eyes widened and then dilated to mere slits. It took all his remaining control not to greedily thrust into that enticing warmth. He let her set the pace, but her left nipple was only inches from his mouth. He bathed its nub with his tongue and lips as she settled herself to accommodate his length.

Her muscles began to contract around him at once, deliciously hot and moist. The swing rocked. He gripped the supple skin of her buttocks and entered her fully, his deep strokes setting the rhythm for their bodies.

Her mouth settled over his in an open kiss of blatant carnality. Her tongue thrust inside his mouth—just as he was thrusting inside her. He stirred helplessly, knowing he couldn't hold on much longer. The heat rose in him, demanding release. He reached between their bodies, finding and rubbing the slick wet nub.

"Noah! Oh, my—"

She convulsed around him in a climax that sent him flying over the precipice as well. With his release came a sense of contentment unlike any he could remember.

Sky collapsed against his damp chest and he held her tightly, rubbing her back and rocking them both in silence while their sweat-slicked skin cooled in the night air.

"That was—"

"Incredible?" he volunteered.

Sky opened her eyes and lifted her face to smile at him. "Yes."

Noah kissed her lips with a tenderness that brought a lump to her throat. Oh, lord, what had she done?

Making love with him had been inevitable. On some level she had known that from their first meeting. She'd told herself she could indulge in one uninhibited night of passion without consequence, but she'd *lied*. How was she going to walk away from Noah now? Falling in love with him was just plain stupid. He would never forgive her if he learned who she really was.

"Are you all right?"

His concern was nearly her undoing.

"I didn't hurt you, did I?"

She stroked his jaw and tried not to cry. Why couldn't they have met under different circumstances? She tried to control the trembling of her fingers without success as she explored the stubble along his jaw. Her foolish heart was his for the taking and she couldn't say a word. She drew on her professional armor, projecting a confidence she was far from feeling.

"Of course you didn't hurt me. I was the one on top, remember?" She managed a smile that felt much too bright and forced. "Did I hurt you?"

His chuckle was mellow. But he sobered quickly and swore.

"What's wrong?"

"I didn't use protection. I can't believe I forgot—"

"Shh. It's okay. The timing is safe."

"Only virgins or fools believe in that method of birth control."

"Yes, well, it isn't something we can undo, is it? So unless you have some disease I should know about—"

"No, of course not."

"Me, either. There, you see? Nothing to worry about." She slid off him quickly, reaching for her scattered night-clothes. Not bothering with the tap pants or camisole, she donned the robe, knotting it quickly.

"Are you sorry we made love?"

His soft-voiced question knifed right through her. She turned around to face him. "No. I'm not sorry we made love, Noah." Because that was what it had felt like. Not a mindless coupling, but a loving. "I've never known a man like you. I only wish we'd met twenty years ago."

"What's wrong with right now?"

The compulsion to tell him was strong. She swallowed and shook her head. He came off the swing and bridged the gap between them.

"Why do I feel like something is wrong here?"

"Because you're too perceptive by half?"

"What's that supposed to mean?"

She met his gaze. "It means you live in Darwin Crossing, Texas, and I live in New York City. I'm leaving in the morning, Noah."

He gripped her arms, careful of her injury. "We'll talk about that in the morning."

"We can talk, but it won't change a thing."

He wove his hands through her hair and kissed her with aching tenderness. Her body still tingled from his lovemak-ing, yet she suddenly wanted him all over again.

"Get some sleep."

And they both knew neither one of them was apt to get much sleep tonight. But at least he'd given her something to dream about besides faceless men coming at her from the darkness.

She heard Noah whistling for the dogs as she made her way down the hall to the bathroom.

Twenty years ago she'd left behind her daughter here in Texas. This time she was going to leave behind her daughter and the one man she could have loved.

NORMAN SMITH let himself into the darkened motel room, frustrated and furious. He slapped the file folder he'd taken down on the dresser in muted fury. The client wanted the job done this weekend. Once again he'd planned everything carefully, only to watch things disintegrate before his eyes. His professional reputation was at stake—and all because of that woman. She must have hidden the computer case somewhere. He'd gone through her room quickly tonight, but there had been no case, no money, no C4.

He didn't care about the case, and he'd get the money back one way or another, but he hated having to change his plans at the last minute like this. That's how bad mistakes got made. Yet he had no choice. He'd have to find a new source of explosive quickly, or make his own. Neither option pleased him. His risks increased either way.

His shin throbbed where she'd kicked him. A knot had already formed over a huge bruise. She'd even managed to claw his face right through the ski mask. He touched the angry red scratches, barely restraining his anger.

Getting away and out of the area tonight had been dicey. The cops had been better prepared than he'd expected. If he hadn't parked his car so far from the isolated house... But no, that would have presented other problems. He'd done the best he could. It was all the woman's fault. At least he'd had the satisfaction of knowing that she hadn't walked away totally unscathed. And the other one. Who would have figured the younger one would really be armed?

It was actually a good thing, he reminded himself. Otherwise he would have killed Skylar Diamond right there on the porch and he might never have recovered his money. She was going to pay for all the inconvenience she'd caused him. He fingered the opal necklace he'd taken from her room at that boardinghouse.

He had to do the job on Monday without the C4. But once he finished, he'd find Skylar Diamond again. Then he'd claim his property and he'd teach her a lesson she'd take to her grave.

# CHAPTER TEN

SKY COULDN'T BELIEVE she'd not only slept soundly, but overslept. Both Noah and Doug were gone when she awoke the next morning, aching in places that had nothing to do with cuts or bruises.

She heard Lauren outside, calling to the dogs. She reached for the telephone before she could change her mind. Maybe the rental company could still divert the driver out to Noah's ranch instead of Bitterwater.

"But, Ms. Diamond, we had a call this morning canceling the second car." And she didn't have to ask who had placed that call.

"I'm afraid there has been some confusion, but I desperately need transportation immediately. I'll be happy to pay an additional premium if you can send me out another car right away."

The dangled promise of more money did the trick. They did have another car available. "But it's not a luxury sedan like you requested. All we have available right now is a small white coupe."

She spared only a moment to consider her stack of luggage. "Fine. Whatever you can do, as soon as you can do it. Just bill it to the same credit card."

"Yes, ma'am. I assume you'll also want full coverage on this vehicle?"

"Definitely. I'll endeavor to avoid police cars." And sexy sheriffs as well.

With time to kill, she set about packing just one bag,

selecting only what she might absolutely need to take back with her. She would send for the rest later. The jewelry box was the first discard item. She could wrap a few individual pieces in a scarf or something. Which reminded her that she needed to notify her insurance company about the stolen opals.

She was about to close the case and set it aside when she remembered the letter. Lifting the loose lining, she withdrew the soiled white envelope she'd hidden underneath years ago. The penciled words, *To My Daughter,* were still clearly legible. Hard to believe this had been written so long ago. She could close her eyes and it was yesterday—only hours after signing the papers forever giving up all rights to her baby.

Sky had intended to give the letter to the social worker to put in her daughter's file—in the event her child ever asked about her birth mother. But somehow, she never had. Instead she'd taken the letter home with her and hidden it away, unable to throw it out, unwilling to mail it to the agency.

For years, her infant had been someone she could only imagine. Now that she knew her adult daughter, she wondered what Lauren would think of her letter? Sky still remembered every word, every thought and emotion that she'd tried to convey. They were etched on her soul forever. Somehow, she thought the Lauren of today would understand.

Once more, temptation reared its ugly head. All she had to do was walk outside and hand this envelope to her daughter. Both of their lives would forever change. But for good or bad?

Sky knew her mother had been right all those years ago when she'd urged Sky to give the baby up without holding her or seeing her. Knowing her child made it that much harder to walk away a second time. Quickly, she stuffed the envelope back inside the jewelry box and finished packing.

She would look forward, not back—even if it was tearing her apart.

Lauren looked depressingly perky, obviously none the worse for what had happened last night. By contrast, Sky knew there were shadows in her eyes and bags underneath. She felt every one of her thirty-nine years and then some.

"You are so incredible," Lauren greeted her. "I can't believe these sketches! Any one of those dresses would be the stuff of fairy tales, but I really liked the one you marked *A* the best. It's so fantastic. Are you sure you wouldn't mind if I used the design? I mean, you could make this up and sell it yourself. It's so gorgeous."

Her heart lightened at her daughter's effusive praise. She had to swallow past a lump in her throat before she could talk. She covered the moment by pouring another cup of coffee and petting Limpet on the head as the other two dogs sniffed at her feet, searching for crumbs they might have overlooked earlier.

"Thank you. I wouldn't have created them for you if I didn't want you to have one. I did have a thought, however. Would you mind if I had the dress made up for you?"

Her daughter's lips parted. Her eyes sparkled blue with excitement, but they quickly faded back to gray as she shook her head. "I couldn't let you do that. You have no idea how much I'd like to, but—"

"Hear me out." Sky thought quickly, the idea sketching itself in her mind even as she spoke. "That dress was designed for you. *A* was my favorite pick as well. What if I make it up in your size and give it to you with a stipulation? You let my photographer take your picture in the gown. I'll have you sign the usual release form. That way I'll be able to use the picture to pitch a line of bridal gowns and bridesmaid dresses for the professional woman."

Lauren's jaw dropped. "You're kidding, right? You want me to model for you?"

Noah was going to kill her. Sky knew she would never

be able to redeem herself in his eyes for this, but what did it matter? She would never see him again anyhow and it was suddenly vital that she be part of her daughter's wedding in some way. If she couldn't fulfill her role as mother of the bride, at least she could know that her daughter was getting married in the wedding gown she herself had never had, but had dreamed of all her life.

"I only want you to model this wedding gown, nothing else, Lauren. We have to be clear on that. You'd be doing me an enormous favor, though. If, after you get the gown, you don't like it, you don't have to wear it for your wedding."

"Are you kidding? I'd kill to wear this gown."

Her features froze. Sky knew Lauren was remembering the night before when she'd fired into the darkness at their attacker. She met her daughter's stricken expression and summoned up a smile. "Fortunately, murder isn't required. All you have to do is let me take your measurements. Do we have a deal?"

Lauren's tension eased. "Deal."

"There's just one more thing." Sky took a deep breath. "Your father is going to be very unhappy over this."

Lauren's eyes sparked with sudden mischief. "Somehow, I don't think so."

"No, listen, Lauren. We had a misunderstanding when I first came to town. I told him I wanted you to do some modeling for me and he was very upset."

"You did?"

"I had to promise him that I wouldn't offer you a modeling contract. When he finds out about this, he's going to think I broke my promise."

"I don't understand. Why would Dad be upset over you asking me to model?"

"I think he's worried that it will alter the course of your life—and not for the better." Her crooked smile lacked any trace of humor. Despite the incredible moments out of time last night, Noah didn't really like who Sky was. And he definitely didn't want his daughter following in her footsteps in any way. "You already have goals and plans in place. He didn't want my offer messing any of that up."

"That's crazy. I would have been flattered—I am flattered—but there's no way I'd put off my marriage or my schooling to go to New York and be a model."

"I thought as much."

Her gaze clouded. "Are you asking me not to tell him? Because I don't keep secrets from my dad."

"And I wouldn't want you to. I just want you to understand the situation, Lauren. I'd rather give you the dress without strings, but I know you wouldn't be comfortable with it as an outright gift. This way we both get something we want in an even exchange. If you'd rather say no, I'll understand. You can still feel free to make up the design yourself."

"You really wanted me to model for you?"

Sky shrugged, guilt riding her for the lie. "It was a passing idea that I had."

"I don't know what to say."

"How about if we go ahead and take your measurements now? You can think this over, talk to your dad and Doug about the dress, and let me know after I get back to New York."

"Sure. Okay."

The morning flew past. Sky savored every minute of their time together, trying to lock away her daughter's smile and the sound of her laughter for future moments. She threw herself into a discussion of Lauren's plans for the wedding, offering occasional suggestions, but mostly just listening and trying not to play what-if. They were having lunch when the telephone rang. Sky knew it was Noah even before Lauren answered. She wasn't a bit surprised when Lauren handed her the telephone a few minutes later.

"Dad wants to talk with you."

It was silly to feel all fluttery at the sound of his voice, but she couldn't seem to still the butterflies that had launched themselves in her stomach. Her mind insisted on fast-forwarding through every second of the night before.

"How are you feeling this morning?" he asked.

"It's afternoon, in case you hadn't noticed," she pointed out with false cheer. "And I'm feeling pretty good, all things considered. What about you?"

"I'd be feeling a whole lot better if I was there with you instead of here at work. Sorry I couldn't phone sooner. I got called in on a high-speed chase that ended in a multicar pileup out on the highway first thing this morning."

"Ouch."

"Yeah. That was followed by a fugitive arrest warrant that didn't get served according to plan, either. I think I'm getting too old to chase down a twenty-year-old on foot."

"Oh? Last night I had the impression you could hold your own with anyone."

"Yeah?" If he'd been a cat, he would've been purring. Sky smiled. "Yeah."

"This is the first five minutes I've had." His voice lowered. "But I've been thinking about you. How's the arm?"

"As sore as I expected. I'm glad you called. I wanted to thank you."

"For what?"

Aware that Lauren was listening unabashedly, she hesitated. "Everything."

"Oh. That." His voice lowered to an unbearably sexy octave. "Believe me, it was my pleasure. I'll never look at that swing the same way again."

Sky felt the color stealing up her neck. "You Texas men and your sweet talk."

His low, throaty chuckle warmed her all over. She found herself grinning, wishing he was there in front of her. Suddenly, Noah swore. "I don't believe this. I've gotta go. I'll talk with you when I get home."

"But, I won't be…here," she said softly to an empty line. Two cars were coming up the long driveway even as she hung up.

"Someone's coming up the driveway," Lauren said in alarm.

"It's okay. It's just my rental car."

"What do you mean?" Lauren demanded. "Dad said he canceled it."

"I reinstated it." She faced her daughter, a longing ache blooming inside her.

"But you can't go!"

"I told you I had to leave today."

"Why?"

"I have a meeting tomorrow, Lauren."

"Cancel it."

Sky shook her head, trying to keep her emotions at bay. "I have to go. I hope it's okay if I leave some of my things here. They could only rent me a small car this time."

"Does Dad know you're leaving?" Lauren demanded.

"You heard me try to tell him."

"You have to at least stay until he comes home."

"Lauren, I can't."

"I don't understand."

Her daughter's eyes, so like her own, mirrored the hurt inside her. "I know you don't, and I can't explain."

"I thought you and Dad… I mean…he's been so different since you came to town. I think he likes you."

"I like him, too. Believe me, I wish things could be different, but my life is in New York."

"Only if you want it to be."

The dogs scrambled for the front door, barking for all they were worth. Sky turned away and started after them before she lost her tenuous control and released the tears burning her eyes.

"Sky, wait!"

She turned at her daughter's imperious command and

time came to a complete halt. Lauren held a revolver in her hand, steely determination replacing her anger and pain.

"What are you doing, Lauren?"

"You don't know who's out there. After last night, Dad said we weren't to take any chances."

Sky tried to calm her racing pulse. She spoke softly, but firmly. "It's okay, Lauren. You can put the gun away. The rental company told me it would be a white coupe. The second car is the driver's ride back. You can see they're wearing the right uniforms. I promise you, it's my rental car."

"But…"

Sky tugged the dogs away from the door to let the man with the papers inside. Lauren disappeared. Sky guessed she was trying to call Noah. She signed for the car, tipped the man handsomely, and went to the den to collect her briefcase and the one suitcase. Looking around at the very masculine room, she hesitated. She couldn't leave him without an explanation. She wrote Noah a quick note, propping it conspicuously in the middle of his desk.

Lauren met her in the living room. She looked close to tears. "I couldn't reach Dad. He's out on a call."

"I know."

"I wish you wouldn't go."

Sky set down the bag and opened her arms, hugging her daughter for the very first time. She had to blink back her own tears when she let her go.

"Will you come back?"

"I'd like that very much, Lauren. Especially since I'm leaving more than half my wardrobe here."

"Good. You'll have to come back because I won't mail it to you. And for sure you'll come to the wedding."

"If you invite me, I'll come. Take care of yourself. And give your Dad and Doug a hug from me."

"I wish you wouldn't go."

"I wish I didn't have to go."

She put on her sunglasses and headed outside with a heavy heart. Chances were good she'd never see Lauren or Noah again. She wasn't sure which thought brought more pain.

"WHAT DO YOU MEAN, she's gone?" Noah clenched the telephone receiver so tightly he was surprised it didn't crack. "When? Did she say where? Did she mention a hotel? Okay, listen to me, Lauren. I want you to pack a bag. See if you can stay with your friend Carmella for a couple of days.... Yes, I'm going after her.... Yes, I'm stopping at home first. I can't leave unless I know you have a place to stay.... All right. I'll see you shortly."

Skylar had run. He hadn't expected it, but he guessed he should have. She'd told him all along what she planned to do. Canceling the car hadn't worked. He should have known better, but the whole day had been crazy from the moment he got dressed. He hadn't had lunch, let alone dinner, yet, and he had a dozen messages sitting on his desk waiting to be returned. Two of them were from Zach Logan. One was from Detective Lee Huang in New York.

He tried that number first. The detective was out of the office. The woman who answered didn't think he was coming back until morning.

"Noah?"

He looked up to find his deputy standing beside his desk.

"We just got a call. Henry's bull got loose again."

"Of course it did."

The deputy blinked. "Uh, what do you want me to do?"

"Shoot it."

The young man's mouth fell open. Noah sighed.

"Never mind, Terry. I'll take care of Franklin. I was on my way home anyhow. And just so you know, I won't be in tomorrow."

"Uh, are you okay, Sheriff?"

He rubbed his jaw ruefully and reached for his hat. "I'm

not sure. I'm starting to feel sympathy for the damn bull. What does that tell you?''

He left his deputy standing there speechless. But it was true. The poor lovesick bull only wanted to get to his favorite cow. While Sky was anything but a cow, Noah knew exactly how the poor old boy felt.

*Why had she run?*

She had to know he was going to follow her after last night. He was too old for games. So was she. He wanted answers and he wanted her. He intended to get both.

THE KNOCK on the door of her San Antonio hotel room brought Sky bolt upright in bed, heart pounding. She hit the light switch and reached for her robe as the commanding sound came again.

Before she made it to the door, Noah's voice carried clearly past the flimsy barrier. ''Open the door, Sky.''

She took off the dead bolt and flung it open in shocked surprise.

''Noah! What are you doing here?''

''I was invited, remember?''

His tone was hard, his expression coldly forbidding. In his hand he held a small duffel bag. He was still in his uniform, right down to the gun belt, but his outfit no longer had that crisp, neatly pressed look. In fact, it looked like he'd been rolling around in the dirt and mud. There were grass stains and a small tear at the shoulder. Mud had splattered his legs and hat. She'd never seen Noah look so tired or irritable.

''Are you going to let me inside?'' he demanded.

''Yes, of course.'' Thoroughly rattled, she stepped back.

''Thanks again,'' he said briefly to someone in the hallway.

''No problem, Sheriff. Ma'am.''

Only then did she realize he wasn't alone. A security man

stood behind him holding a passkey. He tipped his head in her direction, then Noah was inside and closing the door.

"How did you find me?"

"It wasn't hard. One phone call, in fact." He dropped the bag on the end of the bed and removed his hat.

Her heart stuttered, then began racing hell bent for leather. His dark eyes swept her, taking in her robe and tousled hair. She knew exactly what he was thinking. This was what she'd worn last night. His hands went to the tie at his neck.

"What are you doing?"

"Getting undressed, what's it look like I'm doing?"

Her mouth went bone dry under the intensity of his stare.

"Don't look so shocked. You must have expected me."

She shook her head mutely. With deft, economical movements, he removed his gun belt and set it on the bed. Then his fingers skimmed down the buttons on his shirt.

"You should have. You invited me." He shrugged out of the shirt, dropping it on top of the gun.

"I left you a note.... Oh, God, what happened?"

She reached out to touch the large bruise that started below his last rib and disappeared beneath the waistband of his pants. His indrawn breath made her hesitate, her fingers barely touching the warmth of his skin.

"Does it hurt?" she asked into the hushed silence that filled the room with waiting expectancy.

"About the same as yours did last night," he said quietly.

His fingers touched the robe covering her chest, just below her breasts. They responded to his touch, swelling with desire to have those fingers move up the few inches necessary.

She dropped her hand to her side as if burned. His lips twisted wryly and he lowered his hand as well.

"H-how did it happen?"

"Henry's bull," he said succinctly. His hands went to his belt and began to undo it, but his eyes never left her face.

She moistened her lips. He watched her with a banked hunger she could all but feel. Yet there was still anger coiled in the depths of his expression. It was the anger that left her feeling unnerved and uncertain.

"What...did he do to you?"

"Nothing I shouldn't have expected. He chased me over a fence. Unfortunately, there was a large rock where I landed. Can't blame the bull for that. He was simply giving vent to his frustrations. Males are like that, you know. They don't like being deprived of what they consider theirs."

His words reinforced her guilt. She shook it off, knowing she couldn't afford to show any weakness or she'd be lost in the maelstrom of longing that was pulling at her emotions.

"I don't belong to anyone but myself."

His lips curled without mirth. "I thought we were talking about the bull."

The sound of his zipper was loud in the silence of the room. Sky realized she'd forgotten to breathe. His thumbs hooked in his waistband. She waited for the slow slide of his pants, but he surprised her by suddenly sitting down. With a deliberate smile, he began tugging off his boots.

"I'm not sure there's any difference," she told him.

The smile widened. "Now that you mention it, me either."

The second boot dropped to the floor and the sock followed.

"Like I told my deputy tonight, I'm starting to have a lot of sympathy for that poor old bull. He knows what he wants and he's going after it the only way he knows how."

She swallowed hard at the passion she could sense in him. Her own body clamored with excitement. The rush of heat was heady, but she tried to maintain control.

"Are you by any chance comparing me to a cow?"

"Not by a country mile. But you have to admit, the situation is similar. You left. I followed."

"I told you I was going!"

"And you invited me to come along."

She bit her lip, knowing there was no answer she could make. She had invited him. And she did want him, with every beat of her heart.

He stood up and dropped his pants in a single smooth motion. He was heavily, incredibly aroused. "I'm going to take a shower. You can scrub my back."

Unconcerned by his nudity, he strode into the bathroom. The sound of water cascading into the tub brought her out of her daze. She found him adjusting the water temperature.

"We can't make love in there."

His eyes glittered, darkly promising. "Want to bet?"

He pulled the lever, stood, and stepped into the tub.

"Coming?"

The heat pooling low in her abdomen sent her trembling fingers to the belt of her robe. This was completely insane. She should not be doing this.

But he was right, she discovered. They could make love in the shower.

FOR THE FIRST TIME in what had proved to be an extremely long day, Noah allowed himself to relax. Nestled beside him, her arm spread across his naked chest, Skylar slept deeply. Despite the exhaustion tugging at his mind, he stared up at the ceiling and listened to the muted sounds of the hotel around them.

He'd planned to question her as soon as she came out of the bathroom, while her defenses were down—when the intimacy they'd just shared might keep her from lying to him. Only she'd slipped into bed beside him, her eyes more closed than awake, her mouth swollen from his kisses, and curled into his arms, more trusting than a kitten.

And he hadn't asked her a single question.

Silently, he called himself a fool even as he unconsciously pulled her more closely against his side. He hadn't been a monk since Beth died, but there hadn't been all that many women, either. Not for lack of interest. But he'd had a daughter to raise. Indiscriminate couplings had never appealed to him. He'd thought he wanted what he'd had with Beth, yet none of the very nice women he'd met over the years had stirred more than mild interest in him. Until Skylar Diamond waltzed into town and blew away all his preconceived ideas.

She was nothing at all like his gentle wife. Skylar was fiercely independent, filled with coldly polished sophistication that melted into incredible passion whenever they touched. The attraction between them was nothing short of incendiary and he couldn't understand why it should be this way. He told himself it was lust. She was a burr beneath his saddle, so to speak. This hunger for her would burn itself out quickly if he gave it half a chance. They weren't just opposites, they were practically antagonists.

So why did he feel this possessive hunger for her?

He'd found her note right before he left the house. Anger had sent him reaching for the telephone. Thinking about the note, he knew he was worse than a fool.

*Noah, There's a part of me that would give anything to stay, but we both know I have to go. Staying here would put us all at risk, from more than just a faceless man with a knife. I know you'll be angry over the dress, but I swear to you that I didn't break my word. Not really. Please let me do this for your daughter. I will never forget you. Sky.*

Instead of taking time to change, he had called his daughter as soon as he read those words. His anger had cooled considerably on the drive into San Antonio, especially after he started putting some of the pieces together. He might be wrong, but he didn't think so.

Only a total idiot would fall in love with a woman who had the power to destroy his entire world.

# CHAPTER ELEVEN

THE TOWN OF Trueblood, Texas, sat right outside the city of San Antonio. She had never been there before, but it appeared to be a nice, lazy little town, about the size of Bitterwater. At the gas station, they gave her directions to the Garrett ranch.

Noah was going to be furious, of course. Enraged was probably more like it. But on waking, she knew if she was going to make her morning meeting with Lily Garrett Bishop, she would have to leave before he awoke.

Finding herself nestled against the man she loved had required all the discipline she possessed not to roll over and begin again the slow, sweet prelude to loving him. His features were relaxed in sleep, making him look younger, almost boyish.

That would change the moment his eyes opened. She knew Noah would demand answers. And he was going to be even angrier than the bull at the ones she had to give.

Leaving him a note on her pillow, she'd slipped away like a thief.

Now, as she drove down the long narrow driveway of the Double G Ranch, she reached a massive two-story house in brilliant white stucco with a red tile roof. Inside, heavy exposed beams and an imposing stone fireplace dominated the great room, but the doghouse peaks flooded the insides with natural light. The effect was quietly elegant.

She was directed up the flight of oak stairs to the second floor that overlooked the great room. Obviously intended as a waiting area for clients, the room housed comfortable chairs while one entire wall was filled with books and periodicals. A stone half wall separated the working office of a dynamic, red-haired woman dressed in a colorful skirt and blouse ensemble.

Sky would never have thought to put quite those shades of rust, lime, deep purple and blue together, but she had to admit that on this woman, the combination, while eclectic, was not garish.

"Welcome. You must be Skylar Diamond. I'm Carolyn Mulholland. May I get you some coffee?"

"No. Thank you."

Carolyn's smile was open and friendly. "Are you sure? I'm hopelessly addicted so I always have a fresh pot brewing."

"No, thank you." Despite the woman's outgoing manner, Sky could barely contain her impatience. She wanted to have this meeting with Lily over and done so she could catch the afternoon flight back to New York. Keeping her professional expression in place was an effort.

A petite young woman with blond hair appeared around the half wall holding an envelope and a file in her hands. "Carolyn, I set two more files over there. Once we're finished going through these old files, I'm heading back to Pinto. Hello. You must be Skylar Diamond."

"Ms. Garrett Bishop?"

This blonde wasn't what she'd been expecting, either.

The young woman smiled and shook her head. "I'm Calley Graham, an associate. Lily asked me to apologize profusely. She and her husband are moving into their new house today. They were supposed to be in last week but there was an unexpected glitch and they had to move today."

"So she isn't here?"

"No, but she's expecting you. She wondered if you'd mind meeting her at her house instead of here. I know it's a bit of an imposition, but she insists on supervising the men.''

"The doctor should never have lifted her restriction," Carolyn said.

"She's only supposed to be doing light duty," Calley agreed. "But I guess technically, supervising falls into that category."

Carolyn gave a ladylike snort. "If that's all she does. Want to place any bets?"

"Ashley's with her. She promised Cole to keep Lily out of trouble."

Sky took a chokehold on her frustration. She had no idea who all these people were and she didn't care. "Is it far?"

"Oh, sorry. No," Calley said. "Their new house is at the back end of the ranch. It's not quite completed, but they're moving in just the same. I'm going there now to take this file to Lily. I can take you there."

"I'd prefer to follow you."

"Sure. Suit yourself."

Carolyn handed Calley another folder. "Don't forget this. Dylan needs to look it over."

"Right. Back in a minute."

"Take your time."

The house Lily Garrett Bishop and her husband had built was so new there weren't any shrubs, plants or even grass out front yet. What there was, was a truck with two good-size men unloading furniture.

Calley greeted the two men with a wide smile. "Hey, Dylan! Hi, Max. This is Skylar Diamond."

The two men paused on either end of a long couch to say hello.

"Thanks for coming out here like this, Ms. Diamond," the man with the sun-streaked brown hair offered. "I'm Dylan Garrett, Lily's brother and partner."

Sky studied the man curiously. Laugh lines framed his eyes and mouth and a dimple flashed when he smiled. "We don't generally meet clients this way, but my sister didn't think we could do this job without her personal supervision.''

''Ma'am.'' The quiet, dark-haired man called Max nodded politely toward her and then grunted at Dylan, shifting his weight under the load. ''If you want to talk we need to set this couch down.''

''Sorry, Max.''

''Please, don't let me interrupt,'' Sky insisted.

Calley followed the two men inside, leaving Sky to trail behind.

''Any idea where Lily is?'' Calley asked the men.

A tall, tousle-haired man in well-worn jeans and Western shirt entered the mostly empty great room. ''My wife and her sister are in the nursery. Hi, there. I'm Cole Bishop. You must be Skylar Diamond.''

Lily's husband held out a hand to Sky. Despite his gruff exterior, he had a firm, friendly grip and warm eyes.

''Go on up. She's expecting you.''

''Thank you.''

Uncomfortable surrounded by all these people who were so easy with one another, Sky started for the staircase. She hesitated when Calley remained behind talking with Dylan, but he waved her up the stairs as Cole and Max went back out to the truck.

The sound of women's voices led her down the hall to a bedroom that was being decorated in a cheery cowboy plaid by a gamin-faced young woman with short-cropped black hair.

''You know I'm happy for you, Sis, but this whole motherhood thing isn't for me. I'm young. I can't see myself getting married and raising kids. At least not for years and years.''

''You'll change your mind. I did.''

''Maybe fifteen years from now or something, but there's

so much I want first. I want to establish a successful career. Meet people. See the world.''

The stylishly dressed young woman glanced toward the door and Sky knew by the widening of her eyes she'd been seen.

"Actually," Sky said, walking forward, "having a career is nice, but as you get older you realize it's no replacement for having people you love in your life."

"That's exactly what I've been trying to tell her." The tall, slender woman with long, wavy black hair came forward, hand outstretched. "You must be Skylar Diamond. Hi. I'm Lily Garrett Bishop. This is my sister Ashley."

Now this was more like what she'd been expecting. Except for the rounded stomach of course. Lily Garrett Bishop was pregnant. "Hello."

"Oh, wow. Skylar Diamond," Ashley said, her brilliant green eyes growing wide with approval, "of the Diamond Collection?"

Sky nodded, feeling unaccountably pleased.

"Your styles are awesome. Really. I have several of your business outfits. I absolutely love your designs. Skylar's so great, Lily. You know that red pantsuit you like of mine? That's one of her designs. Wow. Meeting you is incredible. I hope you won't mind my saying that the newspaper pictures of you don't begin to do you justice."

"Thank you." Sky took the comment as it was intended. She'd capitalized on her Grace Kelly looks ever since she realized what an asset they were in her business.

Ashley Garrett was exactly the sort of woman Sky had in mind for many of her designs. Ashley would definitely show a Diamond suit to advantage. However, Sky would dress the young woman in greens and blues with those eyes.

"My sister is what's known in our family as a clothes horse," Lily confided, smoothing her hands over the rounded dome of her stomach and the baggy maternity shirt that covered it.

Sky allowed her lips to curve. "I'm glad to hear it. Without people like Ashley, I'd be out of business."

"So there," Ashley said, sticking her tongue out. Her sister laughed good-naturedly.

"I'm afraid I'm more out of clothes than into them at the moment," Lily said.

Sky hoped her smile wasn't as bittersweet as it felt. "When is your baby due?"

"In two months."

"But only if you stay off your feet and follow the doctor's orders," Calley said, entering the room. "Cole's going to tie you to a chair if you don't start behaving. Here's the file you need. I have to go back and help Carolyn. We're nearly finished sorting through the last of the old case files."

"Great. I really appreciate it, Calley. And thank you for escorting Ms. Diamond out here for me."

"No problem. Nice to meet you, Ms. Diamond."

"Thank you."

"I'm going to go down and see if the men need anything before I leave. What about you ladies? There isn't any coffee, but I think we have some cold drinks in the fridge. Can I bring you something?"

Sky shook her head, wondering impatiently when her meeting with Lily would begin. "No. Thank you."

"I'll go with you, Calley," Ashley said. "I need to ask Cole something."

Lily watched the women disappear then turned to Sky with a warm smile. "I'm sorry for all the confusion. It's nice of you to come out here like this. When I made our appointment I thought we'd already be moved in by now. Please, have a seat, Ms. Diamond."

A lovely carved wooden rocking chair and two folding chairs sat beside a small card table that held an array of appliques. The room was empty of other furniture at the moment. Lily cleared a space on the card table and set the file down, taking one of the folding chairs.

"As we discussed, your daughter is living in a small town called Darwin Crossing, which is about ninety miles from here. She's been attending Texas A and M in College Station."

Sky kept her face impassive. "That's a fairly prestigious school, isn't it?"

Lily smiled. "Yes. Lauren is enrolled in their veterinary program, although she's taking courses online this semester to allow her time to prepare for her wedding. Lauren is engaged to marry a young man who will graduate this spring. I believe that's how the two of them met."

Lily continued talking, but Sky wasn't registering much of what she was saying. She was picturing her daughter as she'd seen her yesterday and wishing she could change her own life somehow.

"We could contact them for you. Pave the way, as it were," Lily was saying when Sky's brain reengaged.

"No. Thank you, but no. That won't be necessary."

Lily watched her intently. "Why do I get the feeling I'm telling you things you already know?"

"I already went to see her," Sky confessed. "It's okay, she doesn't know who I am. I have no plans to interfere in her life. I just…I never had any other children."

Lily's expression softened. Sky didn't want to see pity there, so she found herself talking quickly. "I was busy building a career—like your sister wants to do. Only I was so busy I never took the time to do anything else with my life. Now that it's too late, I just wanted to assure myself that I didn't make a mistake all those years ago."

"I think I understand. But I'd hardly say it's too late. You're still young."

"I'm turning forty."

"Many women are having babies in their forties."

"True. But those women are fortunate enough to have husbands and fathers for those babies. You're very lucky, you know." She gazed at the woman's rounded stomach.

"I had nothing to offer my child twenty years ago. I'm afraid I really don't have anything to offer her now, either." And that thought lay bitter in her mind.

"I'm sure that's not true. I think she'd like to know who you are. I would, if I were her," Lily said gently.

Sky couldn't manage a smile, but she nodded her thanks even as she reached into her handbag for the check she'd prepared in the coffee shop this morning.

"Why didn't you tell her who you were?" Lily asked.

"There were…complications." She could hardly reveal to the investigator that she'd fallen in love with her daughter's adoptive father. "It's better this way."

"And if she decides to come looking for her birth mother one day?"

"She won't. She's a very well-adjusted young woman, happy with her life. It's what I needed to know to move on with my own life." Sky blinked back sudden tears. "Thank you for finding her for me." The thanks came from her heart.

"You're welcome. Reuniting families is the best part of my job. Are you sure you don't want to tell her the truth?"

"I'm sure."

"All right. I think I can understand, even if I'm not sure I agree."

Sky lifted the folder and rose to leave as Cole Bishop entered the room. Lily's eyes lightened in welcome and love. Sky felt an intense stab of jealousy. She hurried from the room before the growing surge of emotion could rinse away her calm resolve. She clutched the folder like a shield all the way to her car. Inside was everything the agency had been able to compile on her daughter, including a recent photograph. She touched Lauren's features lightly, before putting the folder inside her briefcase. She was glad she had given Lily a nice bonus. The detective had earned it. She headed back into Trueblood and the pharmacy she had seen there.

There was an empty parking space next to a beautiful green Jaguar. A man squatted on the far side of the car, doing something inside. She didn't even glance his way as she hurried toward the pharmacy. There was a dull throbbing ache in her shoulder that the aspirin she'd swallowed with her coffee this morning wasn't helping. She still didn't want to take one of the pain pills the clinic doctor had given her. With any luck, the pharmacist could recommend something over the counter that would be a little bit stronger than aspirin, but less dramatic than the prescription stuff.

Fifteen minutes later, she headed back to her car, stuffing the plastic bag and its contents inside her bulging briefcase. She was startled to see the man who'd introduced himself as Dylan Garrett standing on the sidewalk next door. He didn't see her because he was deep in conversation with a large, muscular man with jet-black hair and a strong jawline. The man's tailored clothing gave him a sleek, expensive look that she might have once found attractive. She'd take bets he went with the Jaguar parked next to her.

As she reached for the car door, she heard someone call her name. She looked up, expecting it to be Dylan. Shock held her motionless long enough for Noah to shut the door on his truck across the street. Excitement warred with trepidation.

Crunch time.

Pulse racing, she hurried across the empty street to meet him. And the world exploded at her back.

HE WATCHED as the force of the explosion sent the woman tumbling forward. Shards of metal catapulted through the streets, raining down in all directions. The man sometimes known as Norman Smith smiled in satisfaction. Crude, but effective. He hadn't lost his touch. The man talking with Cooper sprinted toward a bleeding woman. He punched in the final digit on his cell phone and hit Send. Then he waited while the connection was made and the phone began to ring.

"Hello."

He smiled. Sebastian Cooper sounded dazed. The man was the only one on the street not moving in one direction or another. He remained perfectly still, staring at the remains of his car in total shock. The client would be pleased.

"Call it a friendly warning, Cooper," the man calling himself Norman Smith told him. "There are people who don't like the way you've been overstepping your authority. They think maybe you don't want to take orders anymore. That isn't smart, Cooper. Not smart at all."

"Who is this?"

Cooper's head swiveled in all directions as if he sensed his adversary's presence nearby.

"You need to get back on the team," Smith told him, unperturbed. "Think about this—you could have been inside that Jaguar."

He pressed the End button and hit Power to turn off the phone. Then he sat back in the stolen truck to study the scene. The man who had called to Skylar Diamond was now at her side, tenderly cradling her body.

Interesting. The daughter's father, if he wasn't mistaken. Maybe the biological father? Either way, a terrific break for him. This opened up all sorts of possibilities.

The Diamond woman stirred. That was good. She wasn't dead. He hadn't really wanted to kill her. Not like that. Doing her wasn't business. He planned to make it pleasure.

She'd given him a real bad moment when she pulled up on the scene while he was placing the second explosive inside the car. He was afraid she'd notice him and call attention to what he was doing before he set the second timer, but he doubted she'd even noticed him as she hurried inside the store. That she had parked next to the Jaguar was actually fate.

The temptation to hurt her a little had been irresistible. Too bad he didn't have a cell phone number for her. It might have been fun to string things out with her. But the important thing was to get his money back and eliminate the only person on the face of the earth who knew, or could guess, who and what he was. As a pro, he couldn't afford to leave her alive. And thanks to that file in her briefcase, he had all sorts of leverage to use against Ms. Skylar Diamond should it prove necessary.

Careful planning, that was the key to everything. He fingered the worst of the scratches she'd inflicted. It ran down his cheek to his lip. He owed her. He continued to watch the scene unfold from inside the stolen truck. Parked in the shadows on the facing side street, he had a perfect view of the action.

NOAH SAW Sky stumble, then fall to the ground as the concussion propelled her forward. He was running toward her before the debris stopped falling.

"Sky!"

Flames shot upward. Noah realized the gas tanks on the two mangled vehicles could go at any minute, causing further explosions. He turned Sky over gently. Her eyes were open, but unfocused.

"What...happened?"

"I'm guessing a pipe bomb or something similar."

He lifted her carefully, grabbing her briefcase at the last second. There was a hair salon directly in front of him across the street from the burning cars. He carried her inside and set her on the first chair he saw.

"Where are you hurt?"

"I'm okay."

Her eyes were clearing, the dazed expression fading somewhat.

He handed her the briefcase. "Wait right here."

At least one of the gas tanks blew before he could stand up. The plate glass window of the salon cracked in half. He threw himself over her body as the top pane collapsed, falling inward. Screams, shouts and sirens filled the air. A car alarm shrilled uselessly. He stood, crunching glass beneath his boots.

"Are you hurt?"

She looked stunned, her pupils huge and midnight black. Even as he asked the question, he could see her pulling herself together.

"I'm all right. You've got glass stuck in your hat."

He pulled off his Stetson and found a large shard embedded in the dirty hat. Three women milled about unhurt, but much too close to what was left of the window.

"Get back," he told them. "The other gas tank may go as well. If it does, so will the rest of that window."

His plan to leave Sky here and go and help the people who were injured dissolved with the second explosion. There was no doubt in his mind this was somehow connected to Sky. He couldn't risk leaving her alone for even a minute.

"Can you walk?" he demanded.

"I think so."

"Let's go. My truck's over this way."

"But I have a rental car."

He looked across the street at the flames. The two former cars were now nothing more than so much worthless scrap metal. "Not anymore."

"Oh, my God. They're going to cancel my insurance for sure."

Another time, her woebegone expression might have been funny. As it was, he saw nothing humorous in the moment. The two empty vehicles were completely destroyed, but they could just as easily have contained people.

"Come on."

Police cars were arriving. Dylan Garrett was issuing instructions even as he tended to a bleeding woman. The part of Noah that wanted to rush over and help the stunned people milling about was overruled by the instincts screaming inside him to get Sky away from the scene. He scanned faces and doorways and parked cars as he led her to his truck and helped her inside.

"Your windshield is cracked," Sky pointed out.

"Yeah. So's the driver's window." And that crack ran the entire length of the window. Fortunately, he could see around the cracked windshield well enough to drive.

He had to skirt the hood of the Jaguar, which had blown into the middle of the road, but he got them away from the scene before it was cordoned off. He drove carefully, hoping his tires wouldn't pick up something that could puncture them.

"We can't just leave, Noah. My suitcase is in that car."

"I don't think you're going to want to wear anything that survived," he said grimly. He drove with an eye on the rearview mirror.

"What are you watching for?"

"Anyone who might be following us."

"Why would anyone follow us?"

"That's what you're going to tell me as soon as I'm sure we aren't being followed."

"You aren't making any sense."

She was serious. Noah shook his head without responding. Not a single vehicle followed them out of town. He bypassed the highway and turned down the second road he came to, pulling off in a church parking lot.

"What are you doing?"

"We're going to talk. You're going to tell me why someone just blew up your car."

Her face paled. Her mouth opened and closed twice before she got any words out. Dirt ran from her chin to her eyebrow. He resisted an urge to wipe at the smear.

"You think someone blew up my car? On purpose?"

"Yours or the one parked beside it. What do you think just happened back there?"

Her bottom lip began to tremble. She shook her head

helplessly. He reached out to remove something trapped in her hair and she flinched.

"Hey. Take it easy. I was just reaching for this," he said softly.

She didn't even look at the twig in his hand. She shuddered, her face devoid of all color. "I don't understand."

No one could fake that sort of reaction. Noah knew in her present state she was incapable of lying to him.

"Does your ex-boyfriend know anything about explosives?"

He hadn't known her eyes could go that wide. "I don't know."

"Well, we're going to find out." He pulled out his cell phone and pressed a button. "This is Beaufort. I need the number off my desk for Detective Lee Huang in New York. He did? How long ago? Okay, thanks."

"Why would someone blow up my car, Noah? It isn't even mine. I only rented it. My insurance company is going to drop me like a stone. First the computer is stolen, then the office and apartment are destroyed, then I run one rental car into a police car and have the second one blown up. I don't think I'm even going to be allowed catastrophic coverage after this. And, Noah, I think I'm going to be sick."

Her face was drained of all color. He tucked the phone under his chin, firmly pushing her head down. "No you aren't. Put your head between your knees. That's it. Take deep breaths. Good. Nice and easy." He rubbed her back while she shuddered.

"Detective Huang," a voice crackled in his ear.

"Beaufort, here."

"I can barely hear you, Sheriff."

"I'm on a cell phone."

Sky raised her head. Some color had returned to her cheeks and her eyes didn't look as glazed as they had a minute ago.

"What do you have on Zillano?"

"Say again?"

"Zillano," he repeated.

"We questioned him yesterday." The voice faded and static crackled in Noah's ear, making him wince.

"Yesterday? So he's there in New York? You're sure?"

"—here, Sheriff…go…see…an hour."

Noah cursed as the voice broke up. "Look, I'm going to have to find a real phone and call you back. But you're sure Zillano is in New York right now?"

The static mercifully cleared for a moment. "Definitely. Is there a problem?"

"Someone just blew up Skylar Diamond's rental car." He waited out another moment of static. "Look, I'll call you back."

"Do that. I'd like some—"

Dead air replaced the rest of his words. Noah disconnected, trying to think.

"I told you it wasn't Ted," Sky said quietly.

"So you did. But you said something else a minute ago." He played back the words she'd spoken right before she'd started feeling sick. "You said something about a computer being stolen. What computer?"

"My laptop. I don't know that it was stolen exactly, but it disappeared when I first arrived. There was a huge convention checking into the Grand and they delivered someone else's laptop bag by mistake. So far, no one has turned my case in."

The hairs at the back of his neck rose. "You have someone else's computer?"

"No. I did have someone else's computer bag, but to tell you the truth, it was awfully light to have a laptop inside. The bag had some weird lock on it, so I don't really know what was inside."

"What did you do with this bag?"

"Turned it over to hotel security."

"Does anyone know about this?"

Her laugh had an edge. "Most of the hotel staff. I've been calling there every day since it happened. What does this have to do with someone blowing up my car?"

"I don't know, but we're going to find out."

## CHAPTER TWELVE

NOAH USED the cell phone on the way back to San Antonio while Skylar sat huddled quietly beside him, her arms crossed over her chest as if she were cold, despite the unseasonably warm day. It took him a while to reach Devlin Bateman's brother Liam. At first the judge was reluctant to issue a court order to open the mysterious computer case.

"Liam, someone could have been killed."

Sky suddenly stiffened. "Someone was."

"What? Hold on a second, Liam."

Animation lightened the tension in her features. "The morning I checked out, security discovered someone had been murdered in the hotel. It may not be connected—in fact, it probably isn't connected—but—"

His voice roughened. "Liam, we've got a murder at the hotel the night of the mix-up. Now, given the fact no one came forward to claim this computer case and Ms. Diamond's computer was never returned— What? No. I don't know who's in charge of the investigation. Uh-huh. So is it enough? Yeah. That's what I thought. Yes, I'd appreciate it. No, I'm en route to the hotel now. Thanks, Liam." He broke the connection and nodded at Sky. "Liam's going to get us the court order."

He made two more quick calls arranging to meet the detective in charge of the murder investigation. "If there is a link it will be the first lead we've had," the man said.

"We're almost in San Antonio now," Noah told him. "We'll check in with hotel security and wait for you."

He ended the call and frowned at Sky. "Why didn't you tell me about the murder and the missing case before?"

"I never thought about it until you started talking to that judge. Is he related to the lieutenant I met in Bitterwater?"

"His brother," Noah said tersely. "Didn't it occur to you to wonder about the coincidence here?"

"No. Okay? It didn't. I'm sorry, but my mind just doesn't work that way. I wasn't seeing conspiracy connections all over the place."

Noah reined in his frustration. She'd been through a lot in the past few days. So had he. Watching her nearly blown to bits had rattled him in a way little else could have. He realized he wanted to do whatever it took to keep her safe.

"We'll be there in a few minutes," he said more kindly as she pinched the bridge of her nose. "Got a headache?"

"A big one," she agreed, looking pointedly at him before shutting her eyes.

He ignored the jab. She was entitled to a show of temper. He knew she wasn't really angry with him, but at the situation.

"Maybe we should head for the hospital and have you checked out."

Her eyes flashed open. "It's a tension headache. I get them frequently. Especially when someone blows up my car. I've got some pain reliever in my briefcase."

Abruptly she sat up straighter in alarm. "My briefcase! Did you get my—"

"Your briefcase is right here."

He plucked it from beside the seat and instantly she relaxed. "Thank you."

She reached inside and pulled out a small shopping bag that contained a bottle of water and an over-the-counter headache remedy.

"If you pull lunch out of there I'm going to start to worry."

"Will a candy bar do?"

He grinned, but her pinched features worried him. "You sure you don't want to have a doctor check you over?"

"I'm fine."

"I don't think I'd be feeling fine if someone had just blown up my car."

She blinked in surprise at the curtness of his words.

"Look," Noah said evenly, "our tempers are both a little frayed right now. I'm sure there are a lot of things you haven't told me because I didn't ask the right questions. Tell me about checking into the hotel."

She seemed to marshal her thoughts for a moment, then concisely explained about the convention checking in at the same time, the toilet problem and subsequent change in rooms. He resisted an urge to prod her with questions, letting her tell the story in her own way first.

"So there was plenty of time for the switch to have been made either on purpose or by accident."

"Why would someone switch the cases on purpose?"

"Depends on what's in the case. Where did security find the body?"

"They said it was in one of the rooms."

He saw her shiver. "What?"

"The man's throat was slit."

Noah tried to ignore the chill that slithered down his spine. Sky and Lauren had been attacked by a man with a knife. Before he could point that out, her eyes widened in horror.

"Oh, God, Noah, now that I think back on it, the woman said it was one of their maintenance people. I'm almost sure that's what she said. What if…you don't think…?" She trembled visibly.

Yeah, he did think, because he was pretty sure his mind had jumped to the same conclusion as hers. He laid his hand against her arm. "Take it easy."

"But what if someone killed that poor man who came to

fix my toilet because I had the wrong computer case? That's what this is all about, isn't it? It has to be!''

''We don't know that.''

''Of course we do! It's the only thing that makes any sense! I told you all along no one had a reason to be doing these things to me. All this time I worried it had to do with my designs, but it was never about them. Someone wants that computer case!''

''Hold it. Before you start jumping to conclusions here, let's analyze this.'' A tractor trailer suddenly switched lanes to avoid a merging car. He heard Sky's sharp intake of air as he steered around them.

''Good job,'' she told him. ''What is there to analyze, Noah?''

''How did anyone know what room you were in?''

''Like a fool I announced my name and room number to the desk clerk and—''

A dawning comprehension slackened her lips.

''You thought of something.''

She nodded mutely, her eyes wide open. ''I think I know who's doing this. I mean, I don't know him personally, but—Oh, God—it feels right. I even wondered at the time if he was stalking me.''

''For crying out loud! You've got a stalker? I asked you who—''

''I don't have a stalker. At least not in the normal sense of the word. There was a man on my flight who acted interested in me at the airport. I had absolutely no interest in him, so I cut him with a look. I didn't think anything of it at first.'' Quickly she described what had happened.

''He could have switched the cases right there at the airport,'' she continued. ''I'd given them to the skycap and I wasn't paying as close attention as I should have been.''

A hint of color tinged her cheeks. Before he could wonder about that, she shook her head.

"He wasn't carrying anything when I first saw him in the baggage area, I'm sure of it. Yet later, he was."

"He could have checked the case."

"A computer case that fits easily under the seat? I don't think so."

"Okay." He had to control his own rising excitement. "But we still have a problem, Skylar. Your office and your apartment were destroyed in New York. That would have happened after you got the wrong case."

"Exactly."

"But assuming it was the same man, why would he go back to New York when you were here in Texas?"

"Because he didn't know I was still here." Her eyes glittered as she considered the possibilities. "Think about it, Noah. If I'm right about the who, he hears me give my room number. He calls to make sure he heard the right room. I answer, but by the time he gets there, they've moved me to another room. Only, he doesn't know that. All he knows is I'm gone and the room is empty. How is he going to find me? The hotel wouldn't tell him anything even if he asked. The only identification inside my laptop case has my name and my business address."

"I see where you're going, but we still have a problem. All he had to do was go to the desk and tell them the wrong case had been delivered to him, same as you did."

"What if he couldn't? He might not have been registered at the Grand if he switched our cases at the airport. Even if he was, say the switch was made at the hotel by accident, security wouldn't turn it over without proof that the case was his."

"You did say it had a distinctive lock. If he had the key or combination or whatever…"

"Sure, if. But maybe he didn't. Maybe the case doesn't belong to him. Maybe he stole it from someone else. Or maybe he couldn't risk anyone finding out what he has inside. There are lots of reasons he might not want to come forward and claim the case. I mean, how would he even know I'd discovered the switch? And even if I had, he'd have no way of knowing what I did with the case. I could have opened it and kept the contents. I could have thrown it away. I could have done all sorts of things. And even if he figured I turned it in, wouldn't hotel security at least ask him to identify the contents?''

Noah frowned. ''Possibly. But I still don't buy that he'd go back to New York.''

''What else could he do to find me? At my office, he would discover where I live. Once he got inside my apartment, there's a pad next to the telephone where I make notes when I'm talking. I'm sure I wrote down my reservations.''

''Including the boardinghouse?''

''I'm afraid so.''

''So he comes back to Texas, drives to Bitterwater, and breaks into the boardinghouse looking for the case.''

''Only we come home as he's leaving.''

Noah rubbed his jaw thoughtfully. ''How is attacking you going to help him find the case? You can't answer questions if you're dead.''

''But he didn't kill me. Lauren was the one he struck out at initially. I just got in the way. And everything happened pretty fast.''

Noah thought of several more holes he could poke in her theory, but he could see she was really warming to this idea. Unfortunately, so was he.

''It all comes down to the contents of that computer case. What would be worth killing someone over?''

THE DETECTIVE in charge of the murder investigation at the Grand Hotel whistled tunelessly. His tall, scrawny partner swore under his breath. All five of the people inside the security office stared at the stacks of unmarked bills sitting beside the now unlocked computer case.

''There's one heck of a lot of money in here.''

"Certainly enough to be worth killing someone," Noah agreed.

The detective unzipped another section and reached inside. Noah sucked in a breath when he saw the lump of claylike material.

The detective's partner swore steadily, without once repeating himself. Sky looked from one face to the next. "I don't understand. What is that?"

"C4," the detective said softly.

"Enough to blow a sizable hole in this building," his partner agreed.

Ray Ellenshaw, the Grand's security man, uttered his own expletive.

"C4 is an explosive," Noah explained for Sky's benefit. "And I think we can safely say this explains why someone is very angry with you right now."

"Hey, I didn't do anything—"

"But why kill our maintenance man?" Ray Ellenshaw interrupted.

"At a guess, I'd say wrong place at the wrong time," Noah told him. "Whoever wants this back probably walked in on him while he was fixing the toilet."

"But why kill him?"

It was the police detective who answered, his jaw tight. "Because the maintenance man could identify him."

Every gaze in the room turned to Sky.

"Thanks. You gentlemen are making me feel so much better."

She ignored the hand Noah laid on her arm. She was cold right down to her toenails.

Eventually, the afternoon turned into evening. They ate cold pizza and subs at the police station. The police had been wanting to question Sky ever since they learned she had briefly been assigned to that room. Sky answered repeated questions until she was hoarse. She helped an officer work up a composite sketch of the man from the airport.

She looked at mug shots until she was bleary eyed. Then the detectives insisted on putting her in protective custody. Sky refused, feeling close to panic.

The police were checking airport security cameras and the passenger list from her flight with airport officials. Sky felt overwhelmed.

Noah had disappeared right after she finished working with the computer sketch artist. Now she sat in the crowded, busy detectives' office, where telephones rang and people with guns moved around her with purpose, and she fervently wished Noah was still at her side. She hadn't realized how much she'd come to depend on his presence, even though he couldn't help her now. No one could. She wondered what would happen if she just got up and slipped out the door. The thought was inviting. But where would she go?

"Ready to leave?"

Noah had come up behind her without a sound. He looked as tired as she felt.

"Go?"

"Come on. Grab your briefcase and let's get out of here."

"But they said—"

"You could leave with me."

Her heart pounded even as she jumped to her feet. It was full dark outside and she inhaled the cool air deeply.

"Where are we going?"

"How would you feel about sharing a cheap motel room for the night?"

Her heart stuttered. "With you?"

"I thought you might prefer it to a couple of strangers in a safe house somewhere here in San Antonio."

She willed herself to stay calm. "At least I know you don't snore."

Noah offered her a tired smile as he started the truck. "There is that."

Sky leaned back and closed her eyes. They drove in companionable silence. Next thing she knew he was shaking her awake. The motel was small, in the middle of nowhere, and the unit he ushered her inside housed a giant double bed. Sleep drained from her the moment she saw the bed. She looked from it to Noah.

"We're just going to sleep. Okay?"

Staring into his tired eyes, she nodded gratefully. "Okay."

They fell into bed fully dressed except for her shoes and his boots. She tried to slow the erratic bump of her heart as they lay in the dark intimacy of the room, listening to the quiet that encased them. Despite her heightened awareness, there was something soothing about being here with him like this.

Noah, with his easy laid-back air was nothing at all like Ted or any other man she had ever known. Maybe that wasn't so surprising. The only men she'd met in New York were intensely focused businessmen, as engrossed in their careers as she'd been in her own. There had never been any room for a deep, meaningful relationship. What she'd hoped she'd found with Ted had soon proved as shallow as her previous relationships. Only Ted had been more comfortable than the other men, so it had been easy to remain with him all that time.

But what if she had stayed here in Texas twenty years ago? Would she have met someone like Noah? A man who might have been willing to share more than surface emotions with her? A man who obviously accepted her daughter as his own. Could she have kept her child, or would she have ended up like her mother, aged before her time, as she tried to support the three of them?

For months now, the knowledge had been chipping away at her mind that she was nearly forty and would likely never have another child, never be part of a tightly knit family unit. She had needed to know about her baby. If nothing else, all these years of feeling guilty, of wondering if she'd made a terrible mistake, needed to be put to rest. She couldn't undo what she'd done, but maybe she could buy her conscience a pardon with the knowledge that her daughter had grown up happy and loved.

"Sky?"

The deep rumble of Noah's voice tugged her from her thoughts.

"I don't want to wake up again and find you gone. No more pithy little notes on my pillow."

For some reason, that made her smile. "Got it. No more notes on your pillow." She hesitated. "I'll pin the next one to your shirt instead."

There was a moment of complete silence before she heard his choked chuckle.

"I'm not going anywhere, Noah," she promised him. "It's a scary thought, but I realized sitting in that police station that I don't have anywhere to go."

"C'mere."

She hesitated, then scooted to the center of the bed until they touched. He slipped a comforting arm around her, and for several long seconds she lay there, curled up against his warmth.

"Pithy?" she asked quietly.

His laughter rumbled in her ear. "Go to sleep. We'll discuss it in the morning. Along with a few other things," he added pointedly.

Yes. She would savor tonight. In the morning, she would tell him the truth. "Good night, Noah."

Only for some reason, all thought of telling him anything disappeared when she woke to find him standing in the bathroom door wearing nothing but his jeans. He must have taken a quick shower because his hair was damp and there were still tiny beads of water on his chest. Her reaction was as elemental and basic as it got. She was pretty sure she saw a spark of answering desire as he crossed the room and reached for his shirt.

"I'll pick up a fast-food breakfast while you get ready," he said quickly.

"It'll only take me a minute," she promised.

"Not if I stay here," he told her gruffly.

Sky inhaled sharply, but he was out the door before she could find anything to say. The things he made her feel went beyond the hot craving that lingered so explosively between them, and she didn't know how to handle those emotions.

She was still thinking about that when he returned, acting calm and unruffled, as though nothing simmered between them. Sky was more than willing to follow his lead. This was all becoming too difficult. Her brain was on overload. Only her treacherous body seemed to know what it wanted.

Noah.

The hot, dark coffee hit her system with a needed caffeine jolt. When they stopped for gas, Noah excused himself to use a phone. He was gone long enough that Sky started to worry.

"Everything okay?" she asked when he got back in the car.

"Everything's fine. Lauren is spending the night with a friend, but she's going to run over to the house and feed the menagerie after work."

"Oh."

"She told me about the dress," he said out of the blue.

Sky tried to gauge his mood. "Are you angry?"

"I was."

"I wasn't trying to break my promise or go behind your back to recruit her, honest. I just wanted her to have the dress and I knew it was the only way she would accept it. She's got a stubborn streak."

"I know." His lips curved. "I figured that was what you were doing."

His cell phone rang, startling both of them. She gathered from Noah's terse conversation that he was talking with his office. Sky did her best not to eavesdrop. She stared out over the landscape, trying to assimilate the fact that he wasn't angry over the dress. She didn't know if she'd ever understand this man. But she knew she wanted to.

"We need to stop by my office," he told her when he disconnected. "There are some people meeting there I need to talk with. Zach Logan is chief of detectives for the Dallas Police Department. I used to work for him. He's got a man undercover who might know something about that computer case."

"Oh."

Fear was a great motivator, she discovered. Her hormones retreated. By returning to Darwin Crossing, she might be inviting a cold-blooded murderer to follow. Noah, Lauren and anyone else who got between her and the man who wanted the case would be in potential danger.

Marissa Hurtado was on the telephone when they stepped inside Noah's office. She waved a greeting, while speaking to the person on the other end of the line.

Two men sat at Noah's desk. Sky got a shock when she realized Dylan Garrett was one of them. Comfortably ensconced in a chair, he was talking with a distinguished-looking man with dark hair and a mustache.

Noah smiled and waved the other man back down in his seat when he made to rise. "Stay put, Zach."

"Noah. Glad you could make it." Dark eyes took her measure as the Dallas detective surveyed Sky, making her all too aware of her soiled clothing.

"This is Skylar Diamond," Noah said.

"Ms. Diamond." He nodded in greeting. "This is Dylan Garrett."

Dylan had risen. "We've met," Dylan said. "Good to see you again. And in one piece. You weren't hurt in the explosion?"

"No." She was aware of Noah's sudden tension. The man called Zach Logan leaned back in Noah's chair, stroking his mustache thoughtfully.

"Dylan," Noah greeted a tad less warmly. "So you two know each other?" His voice was low and soft with no inflection. A sure sign that he was upset.

"We met yesterday," Dylan said calmly.

This wasn't the way Sky wanted Noah to learn of her relationship with Lauren. She should have told him when she had the chance. "I hired Finders Keepers, but I was working with Dylan's sister," she explained without explaining.

Obviously aware of the tension, Dylan jumped in before Noah could ask the logical next question. "Zach was filling me in on the mob investigation," he said.

Zach had been watching the byplay intently, and now he nodded. "We're waiting for Jesse Brock. He's our man inside right now. Apparently, J. B. Crowe is still calling the shots from his prison cell. However, there are rumors of dissention in the ranks. I've got a picture I want to show you, Dylan, but before we get started, you can tell your people to stand down, Noah. Francis Hartman won't be coming after you or anyone else. He was positively identified in a liquor store holdup not far from here. The clerk's brother-in-law was an off-duty officer who happened to be in the store at the time. They had a shoot-out and Hartman lost."

Noah grimaced. "He always did have rotten timing."

"Yeah, well, at least the state won't have to pay for his upkeep any longer." Zach tapped a paper sitting on the desk. Sky glanced down at the man's face.

"I saw this man."

Something crawled in Noah's belly. "Where?"

"At the barn dance the other night. He was…he was looking for you."

Zach raised bushy eyebrows.

"You actually talked to him?" Noah demanded.

She nodded, and moistened her lips. "Right after you took those boys outside. He was in the hall when I left the office. He asked me if I'd seen you. He was dirty and un-shaven and he smelled bad. I told him I didn't know where you were. I was pretty sure he'd been drinking.''

"When was the barn dance?" Zach asked.

Noah answered absently. The thought that Francis Hart-man had actually been at the barn dance was unsettling.

"That was a near thing," Zach remarked.

"Yeah." He looked at Skylar, then quickly away. "Too near. You're sure he's dead?"

"We've got a positive identification."

"Good." Marissa gestured to Noah from the doorway. "Excuse me a minute," Noah apologized. "I'll be right back."

"I didn't want to interrupt," she said, "but I thought you might want to know that Henry's bull is missing."

"What do you mean, missing?"

"Henry says the animal went berserk. The bull went through another fence and took off before anybody knew he was loose again. Henry says they can't find him. Jackson moved his herd near your west pasture. The two of them had just come to terms over the cow this bull has his heart set on."

"I don't think it's his heart," Noah said bluntly. "But either way, I don't have time for this right now. Where's Terry?"

"Dealing with an accident over near Willow Tree."

"Let him know not to take any more chances with this bull. I don't want any of our people getting hurt. Make it clear. He's to use whatever force is necessary to protect lives."

"Yes, sir."

The front door opened and a dark-haired man strode in-side. He had the sort of dangerous appearance that would make any law enforcement official take a second look. Hollywood would have typecast him as the villain even without the scar over his left eye.

"Jesse Brock?" Noah asked.

The man inclined his head, his dark eyes assessing Noah with sharp intelligence.

"Noah Beaufort. Zach and Dylan are already here. This way."

"Yes," Dylan Garrett was saying reluctantly as they approached the group. He handed a photograph back to Zach Logan. "That's Sebastian Cooper. Damn it. I still can't believe he's connected to someone like Crowe."

"Unfortunately… Ah, here he is. Come on back, Jesse. I see you already met Noah, you know Dylan and this is Skylar Diamond. I'm not sure how Ms. Diamond fits into this meeting, but Noah assured me she has something to contribute."

"I do?" Skylar turned a puzzled expression on him.

"The man at the airport," Noah told her. He swung around another chair for the newcomer, but remained standing, half leaning against his desk.

Zach frowned as he handed the newcomer a photograph. "Have a look at this, Jesse."

"I've seen this guy around the Crowe estate a number of times, but I don't know his name."

"Sebastian Cooper," Dylan supplied grimly.

Noah peered at the picture and turned it so Sky could see as well.

"Oh. Him."

"You know him?" Zach Logan demanded of her while Noah's gut tightened another notch.

"No, but he was with Dylan yesterday right before someone blew up my car."

Dylan jumped on her words. "Your car?" he demanded. "Wait a minute. You've got things backward here. The pipe bombs weren't in your car, they were in the Jaguar."

# CHAPTER THIRTEEN

NOAH TOWERED over Dylan's chair. "What are you talking about? I was there. Her car blew up."

"Because of its proximity to the Jag. With the amount of explosives he used in those pipe bombs, I'm surprised he didn't take out the whole city block."

Noah swore. "Pipe bombs? Not C4?"

Zach Logan held up a hand. "Okay, let's take this from the top and give Jesse and me a chance to play catch-up. Someone blew up Sebastian Cooper's car yesterday?"

Dylan nodded.

"Then we were wrong," Sky said in relief.

Noah shook his head. Tersely, he explained the recent events to the others. Zach questioned Sky on several points. He had her go over the description of the man she'd seen in as much detail as she could remember, but both Dylan and Jesse shook their heads.

"Doesn't ring any bells," Jesse said.

"Now I see why you thought her car was the target," Dylan said with a considering frown, "but according to Devlin Bateman's people, there were three pipe bombs in the Jag."

"Bit of overkill, wasn't it?" Jesse Brock asked laconically.

"It made a substantial mess, yes," Dylan agreed.

"Were the bombs on timers?" Noah asked.

"Dev didn't think so," Dylan replied. "He's pretty sure someone manually detonated them."

Noah frowned. "That means the bomber was there. He knew the car was empty."

"Not necessarily. He could have seen Sebastian and me heading toward the car and not realized we'd stopped to talk for a minute."

Zach Logan toyed with his mustache, scowling.

"What did Cooper have to say about what happened?"

Dylan's expression darkened. Sorrow flitted past his eyes, hardening to resolve. "He lied to me. To tell you the truth, when it blew, both cars were so badly destroyed we couldn't tell what had actually happened. At first I thought a gas line had exploded. Then I saw it was just the two vehicles, so I figured the explosion was aimed at Sebastian. I lost track of him for a few minutes after it happened, but he was as badly shaken as a man could be. I couldn't get him to admit a thing. He kept saying he didn't know what had happened, he didn't understand. But I knew he was lying."

At his grim expression, Sky shuddered. Whatever the men's relationship had been before the car bombing, it had undergone a terrible transition since. She did not envy the man called Sebastian Cooper.

"Excuse me," she said, looking from one face to another, "but I'm confused. Is the car bombing connected to the computer case or not?"

"Bottom line? We don't know," Zach Logan told her. "Any idiot can figure out how to make a pipe bomb these days."

He straightened decisively, laying his broad hands flat on the surface of the desk. He inclined his head at Noah, then offered Sky a professional smile. "Ms. Diamond, thank you for the information. I may need to get in touch with you after I've talked with some people. Rest assured, you're in safe hands with Sheriff Beaufort. He's one of the best officers I've ever worked with."

It was a clear dismissal. Sky stood quickly. Noah stepped

beside her. He seemed embarrassed by the unexpectedly effusive praise from Logan.

"I'm going to run Sky out to my place."

"All right. I'll be in touch, Noah."

Sky remained mute until they were outside, moving down the road in Noah's truck.

"Interesting, but more confusing than helpful," she said. "Zach Logan thinks pretty highly of you."

Noah felt his neck redden. "He's been trying to get me to come back to work for him."

"Going to do it?"

"Nope. I like my current job."

"Well I'm feeling a trifle dense this morning. What just got decided in there?"

"You weren't the intended target yesterday." He returned Alma's wave as he drove past her café.

"So no one is trying to kill me?"

"I didn't say that. You're still the only link to a computer case full of money and explosives."

"Thanks for reminding me. Couldn't you have lied to make me feel better?"

Noah's lips curved involuntarily. "I think you can handle the truth."

Guilt flooded her face, turning her eyes a deep gray. He saw her fingers flex nervously. A cold lump of unease settled at the base of his gut.

"Something you want to tell me?"

"No, but I guess I have to."

Before he could respond, his radio demanded attention. Marissa patched him through to a deputy in the next county who had a situation and wanted Noah's advice. Since Noah had handled this particular domestic situation more than once, he knew the family involved and was able to suggest a temporary resolution. "Not that they won't go back to feuding over something else tomorrow."

"Yeah. Thanks, Noah."

With an apologetic glance at Sky, he used the radio on his shoulder to call Terry. His deputy had just finished up the accident scene and agreed to meet him at the house. Noah didn't want to leave Sky there with someone potentially coming after her.

"I'm going to have to go back to work," he told Sky as he disconnected and signaled to turn into his driveway. "But I'll make us some lunch first so we can talk."

"You don't have to do that. I know my way around a kitchen, and to tell you the truth, I'm not very hungry."

"We should—" Noah stopped the truck short of the house.

"What's wrong?"

"I'm not sure."

He couldn't define the prickle of unease, but looking at the house sent all his senses on alert. Everything looked exactly as it should. And yet...

"Wait here while I check out the house," he told her.

Anxiety pinched her expression. A protest hovered unspoken on her lips.

"I'm fairly sure everything is okay, but if something happens, take the wheel and head back to town. Understand?"

"You're scaring me."

He knew the feeling. "Just sit tight, keep the doors locked and stay alert. I want to make sure everything is okay before we go inside."

He slipped from the truck, tugging his gun from its holster. There was absolutely no sign that anything was amiss, but he couldn't stop the nagging feeling that something about the silent picture was wrong. It felt strange to be checking his own house this way, he decided as he crept from window to door, looking for signs of intrusion. Nothing appeared to have been tampered with. Yet his unease persisted.

He glanced back at the truck. Sky had moved behind the steering wheel and was watching him intently.

He checked the barn inside and out. The horses were peacefully grazing in the pasture. Nothing looked odd.

He lowered his gun, but didn't resheathe it as he headed back to the house. Mindful of the bombing, he checked the front door carefully before inserting his key. The dead bolt clicked open like always.

Noah went through the silent rooms one by one, but there was nothing out of place and no sign of anything wrong. He was letting nerves get to him, he decided.

Satisfied, he motioned to Sky. She drove up and parked directly in front of the house, her relief evident.

"Everything looks fine," he said as they started onto the porch.

"Where are the dogs?" Sky asked.

"Hell!" He grabbed her arm. "Back to the truck!"

His subconscious had been trying to tell him all along it was too quiet. Sky complied with his order instantly. Noah blocked her body with his own, even as he reached inside the truck for his cell phone.

"This is Sheriff Beaufort," he said when the vet's receptionist answered. "I need to talk to Lauren."

"You just missed her, sheriff. I think she was on her way home for the afternoon."

"Did she have the dogs with her by any chance?"

"Yes. She brought all three of them in with her this morning. I think one of them was due for a checkup or something."

Noah relaxed. "Okay. Thanks.... No. No message." He disconnected. "The dogs are with Lauren," he told Sky.

"Then everything's okay?"

The surge of adrenaline had left him even more edgy. "As far as I can tell. Good observation on your part," he told her. "I'm so used to the dogs running all over this place, I didn't even think to wonder where they were."

"I don't see the cat, either," she pointed out.

"Fluffball's idea of expending energy is getting up to

investigate the food dish. She's probably curled up in a closet or something.''

"Just thought I'd mention it.'' She headed for his study and stopped dead. "Noah!"

His hand automatically reached for his weapon at her tone.

"My suitcases aren't in the den anymore!"

"I moved them into the spare bedroom,'' he said, trying to relax again. "Don't worry. They're all there. I saw them a minute ago.''

"Sorry.''

"It's been a long couple of days. I want you alert, not worried. The man who's looking for the computer case has no way of tracking you here.''

Guilt twisted her expression again.

"What's wrong?''

"Maybe he does know how to find me. Did you remove a file from my briefcase?''

The warning prickle was back. "No. What file?''

Bleakly, she met his stare. "The one I had on Lauren.''

Noah forgot to breathe. Her eyes burned green with trepidation. Her fingers curled, the nails biting into the palms of her hands. He found himself oddly reluctant to ask the next question.

"A file on her wedding dress?'' But he knew that wasn't what she was talking about. She'd had a file with Lauren's name on it before she'd offered to design a wedding dress for his daughter.

Sky drew in a shaky breath. Now that the moment had come, she wasn't sure how to tell him. Everything would change after this. She didn't want to see the anger and rejection in his expression when she told him the truth. His opinion mattered, far more than it should have.

"No. I lied to you.''

His body went still. He watched her with a quiet that went soul deep. Sky wanted to lie again and keep on lying. She wanted to cling to the man who had held her so compassionately last night, but he was gone in the blink of an eye. This was a police officer, bracing for the worst.

"The file contained her baby pictures and the notes that Beth sent the adoption agency every year until she died."

Iciness pervaded his body, mercifully numbing his mind. He stared at the woman he had started to let past his defenses. All he could think was that he didn't want to hear this.

"You hired Finders Keepers to locate my daughter."

"Yes."

He fought the rising panic. "Why?"

She didn't flinch at his tone and she didn't look away, but he saw the anguish in her expressive eyes.

"Lauren is my biological daughter."

The words exploded like an expected thunderclap in the room.

"No!"

Startled, Noah and Sky spun as one toward the shouted protest at their back. Lauren stood in the kitchen doorway, her expression stricken. He'd been so focused on Skylar he hadn't heard Lauren drive up or enter the house. Now that other sights and sounds penetrated, he heard the dogs barking outside.

"You aren't my mother! You can't be!" Car keys slipped from her fingers and clattered to the floor unnoticed.

Tentatively, Sky reached out a hand. "Lauren, I'm sorry. I didn't want you to—"

"You're lying! Dad, why is she lying?"

"No. Lauren, listen to me—"

"I won't listen! I won't! You're not my mother. You'll never be my mother! My mother died of cancer when I was five."

Stunned, Noah stared at his daughter. "Lauren. You've always known you were adopted."

"I was adopted because the woman who gave birth to

me didn't want me." Her rising voice broke on a sob. "She gave me away like an unwanted puppy."

Pain filled Sky's expression. "Lauren, that isn't true. Please. You don't understand."

"Of course I do. I *liked* you. I *really* liked you. And all this time you were playing some sort of sick game with me." Tears choked her voice. She pivoted and fled down the hall toward her room.

Sky stood there, her hand outstretched in supplication, tears welling in her eyes. Eyes that were just like Lauren's.

"I never wanted this to happen. I didn't mean for her to know," she said brokenly.

Noah hardened his heart. His own sense of betrayal ran so deep he could barely think. "When did you plan to tell me?"

Sky shook her head from side to side. "I wasn't ever going to tell either of you. I only wanted to see her, to know she was happy and loved. I never meant to hurt either of you."

Noah swallowed the bile that rose to the back of his throat. She'd lied to him all along. And he'd known. On some level he'd known. The resemblance wasn't strong but it had been there in her eyes, in the way she held her head, in many small, subtle ways.

Face it, he hadn't pushed Skylar for answers because he hadn't wanted to know the truth. His nightmare had finally made its way out of the shadows, and the result was more devastating than he'd anticipated.

"Why didn't you tell me the truth from the start? Why lie about wanting her to model for you?"

Eyes of liquid gray stared at him beseechingly. "Because I didn't want you to think what you're thinking right now."

"Lady, you have no idea what I'm thinking right now." There was a roaring in his head making thought all but impossible. He choked down the angry bile. "You used me to get to my daughter."

"No! You can't believe that!"

"Can't I?" He wasn't sure he could ever forgive her. "Terry will be here in a few minutes," he said coldly, trying not to feel, trying not to think. "I'll arrange to move you to a safe house. In the meantime, stay away from Lauren."

She nodded and shut her eyes against the tears that slipped down her pale cheeks unchecked. He refused to let her pain touch his own. She'd lied to him.

Without a word, she followed her daughter down the hall, entering the spare bedroom and closing the door. Noah found himself standing in the kitchen, badly shaken.

He needed to talk to Lauren. Only he wasn't sure what to say to her. Beth had always felt his fear that one day Lauren's birth mother would want to claim her was foolish. The adoption was perfectly legal. The birth mother had no rights.

Yes, well, tell that to Lauren right now. Tell that to a daughter whose world had just been turned upside down by the woman's arrival. Hadn't he known that no one could give away a child as perfect as Lauren without wanting her back one day?

Noah drove his fist into his hand over and over again. Skylar had suckered him good. Anger and pain were all tied up with his guilt over Beth's death and the feelings he'd begun to have for Skylar Diamond. How could he have ignored his original instincts like that?

He picked up Lauren's car keys and set them on the table. With a heavy heart, he walked down the hall and paused at his daughter's door. He heard her weeping and hesitated, hand raised to knock, but he was unable to complete the action. Instead, he went into his room and began taking off his clothing, reaching for the only clean uniform he had left.

He was pulling on his pants when he heard his daughter's bedroom door open. Almost simultaneously, Sky's door opened as well. He stumbled over a pant leg in his hurry to avert a further catastrophe.

Sky froze when she saw Lauren standing there. Her daughter's blotchy red face was a match for her own. "Here," Sky said, thrusting the envelope at her daughter.

"I don't want anything from you," Lauren said thickly.

"I wrote that letter to you a few hours after you were born."

"I don't care."

A noise came from the master bedroom across from them, but neither of them glanced in that direction. Lauren didn't drop the letter. And she didn't retreat back into her room but remained standing in the hall. Sky forced the words past her clogged throat.

"I was only nineteen years old. My mother was ill and I was about to make her dream come true by getting a full scholarship to become a designer."

"How nice for you."

"No. It wasn't nice at all. I was scared to my soul that I'd just made the worst mistake of my life and I didn't know how to fix it. So I wrote my child a letter. I intended to give it to the adoption counselor. I wanted it placed in your file in case you ever wanted to know about me."

"Why would I want to know anything about a person who could give away their own baby?"

"I didn't have a name to call you, and I didn't know how old you'd be if you ever read the letter, so I skipped a salutation and just started writing from my heart. 'I'm lying here in this cold sterile bed and my heart is breaking,'" she quoted from memory. "'For nine months you've been a living part of me and now you're gone. I'll never get to see you, or hold you, or nurse you, or watch you grow up to be a woman in your own right.'"

"Stop it. I don't want to hear this."

"'I'm only nineteen years old and I don't know what else to do. It's just your grandmother and me. We've been living hand-to-mouth all our lives, but your grandma has been getting sick a lot lately. She thinks I don't know how sick, but I do. She's spent her whole life raising me, doing her best, trying to keep us out of poverty. All she ever wanted was for me to go to college and make something of myself. And I was trying so hard. But I did something really stupid one night. My actions were stupid, not the result. You were a miracle.'"

Her voice broke, but she refused to stop. "'I want so much to keep you, but I can't and it's tearing me apart. We've had days when all we had to eat was soup and crackers. I don't want that for you. I can't bear to think of that for you. And I know your grandma can't, either. The doctor says she needs an operation, only we don't have the money and I'm so darn scared. The lady from the adoption agency told me they only adopt babies to couples who can afford to see you won't want for anything at all.'"

Lauren began to cry silent tears. Sky swallowed her own sorrow and finished the recital.

"'I'll pray every single day that you are happy. I love you so much, even though I never got to see you or hold you in my arms. Please don't hate me. Please forgive me. I have to do what I think is best for all of us even if it's killing me inside. Have a happy life. I will miss you always. Skylar Diamond.'"

Lauren sobbed once. She crumpled the envelope in her fist and ran down the hall. A moment later, Sky heard the front door slam closed. Defeated, she went back inside the spare room, her eyes blinded by tears as she closed the door.

An arm snaked out of nowhere. A gloved hand clamped itself over her mouth. She couldn't breathe as she was pulled back against a hard masculine body. The blade of a knife was shoved against her throat hard enough to cut the skin. She could feel the warm trickle of blood as it ran down her neck.

"Very touching," a voice whispered. "If you make a

single sound I will kill you. Then I will kill your daughter and her father. Nod if you understand me.''

Frantically, Sky nodded. The knife bit a little deeper. Oddly there was no pain, only an all-consuming terror that made it hard to stand still. The fingers slipped a little. Desperately, she inhaled through her nose, trying to fill her empty lungs.

A hand rapped against her door. The sudden sound would have made her scream if the hand hadn't still been covering her mouth.

"Open the door, Sky."

"Tell him to go away," the voice whispered so softly in her ear she could barely hear his words over the hammering of her heart. "If he opens that door you will both die."

Her mouth was suddenly free, but the knife never wavered, nor did those hard arms relax their fierce grip.

"G-go away!" she choked out. "Please!"

The doorknob twisted. Sky stopped breathing.

Slowly, it twisted back. The door didn't open. After a second, she heard Noah's booted footsteps walking away, down the hall.

"A wise decision," the voice whispered. "We're going to be leaving here in a few minutes. Just the two of us. You aren't going to give me any more trouble, are you?"

Deliberately, a gloved hand squeezed her injured shoulder. She gasped at the unexpected pain and shook her head.

"I didn't think so. I want my computer case back."

Blood trickled down her chest from the cut, pooling stickily between her breasts. She couldn't stop shivering. "I—I don't have it."

He squeezed her shoulder again, much harder. She bit back the cry of pain as he sent her stumbling facedown on the bed. He followed her down, his voice in her ear.

"Where is it?"

"At the hotel," she cried into the bedspread. "The Grand Hotel. I turned the case over to security."

"You're lying. You'd better be lying or I'm going to carve you into little pieces right here. Then I'm going to start in on your daughter. She's very pretty, isn't she? Be a shame to see her face all sliced to ribbons like raw meat."

Sky believed him. There was a cold, impenetrable hardness in his tone that demanded belief. He would do exactly what he said without a flicker of remorse. This afternoon, the police had wondered if a professional killer had been hired. The answer was yes. Too bad she'd never be able to tell them so.

"I—I p-put it in the bank."

He squeezed her again, hard. "I told you not to lie."

"I'm not lying!"

He shoved her face into the comforter. Once again, she couldn't breathe. She struggled frantically for air until he let her turn her head.

"Keep your voice down," he whispered harshly. "If you bring them in here, I'll kill them. I mean it."

"I believe you. But I'm telling you the truth," she panted breathlessly. Her brain churned, stumbling for a lie he would believe. If he had believed the truth, she would already be dead.

"When I saw all that money inside...I knew someone would come looking for it. I checked out of the hotel immediately after I jammed up the toilet. I tried to go to the bank, but it was already closed. I found another hotel to stay in and waited until the bank opened in the morning. I rented a safety deposit box and put the money inside. I even kept your weird modeling clay, but I threw away the computer case."

She could feel his breath against the back of her neck while he considered her whispered words. Her body trembled uncontrollably, going from cold to hot and back again. Her shoulder throbbed. Absently she wondered if he'd torn open the stitches.

"If you're lying to me—"

"I'm not. I swear I'm not!"

"Be quiet! Stay right where you are. Don't move until I tell you."

His weight was suddenly gone. She drew in a long, shuddery breath and tried to stop shaking. She heard him move to the window, then to the door. He was listening, trying to determine where everyone was, she decided. But how had he gotten inside? Noah had checked the house.

What did it matter? He was here and he was going to kill her. She couldn't stop him, but she could lead him away from here. Away from Noah and Lauren.

"All right. You're going to get off the bed. We're going for a little walk. At the first sign of trouble, you're going to die."

She nodded. When she scrambled off the bed, she got her first real look at him. He was covered in black from head to toe. A black ski mask, black jacket, black pants, black boots. Only the knife gleamed, wickedly silver with a smear of red blood.

"Walk in front of me. Do exactly what I say. Open the bedroom door and step out into the hall."

Sky did as he told her. The other two bedrooms gaped emptily. She walked down the hall until they came abreast of the kitchen.

"Hold it!"

He stepped into the kitchen and grabbed something off the end of the table.

"Whose keys?"

"I don't…" She saw the dog and cat charm on the end of the key chain. "Lauren's, I think."

"All right. Walk to the front door. Move!"

She came to a jerky halt just short of the door. He sidled along the nearest window and peered outside.

"They're inside the barn. The dogs, too. So here's what we're going to do. You're going to run to the girl's car. You're going to start the engine and wait for me to get inside. You can take off," he said, his dark eyes glittering beneath the eyeholes, "but if you do, I will see that your daughter and her father both die a very painful death. If not today, another day. They will never know when or where, but I promise you they will die and they will know you are the reason."

"I...believe you." She couldn't swallow. There was no saliva left to swallow with.

"Good, because I mean every word." He pressed Lauren's keys into her hand. For a second, she thought about trying to use them and go for his eyes, but something in the way he watched her told her exactly what would happen. "Smart. Go. Now!"

Sky opened the door and ran.

## CHAPTER FOURTEEN

THE DOGS WHIMPERED in sympathy, clustering around Lauren and whining in agitated commiseration. Noah was botching this discussion with his daughter and he knew it. Lauren had shut down right before his eyes. Her expression was as lost and hopeless as it had been the night he had tried to explain that Beth wouldn't be coming back to them ever again.

Lauren wrapped her arms tightly around her chest, a gesture so like Sky's he couldn't believe he had let himself be blinded to their similarities.

"But why? Why'd she have to come here? Why now?"

"I don't know, honey."

"She didn't want me. She never wanted me. She just gave me away."

Helplessly, he stared at his daughter's anguished features, so very like her mother's. "And I'm so glad she did," Noah told her. "Beth and I weren't your biological parents, but our lives would have been so empty without you. In fact, I can't imagine my life without you as my little girl."

Even as he said the words, Noah knew it was the truth. How could he hate Sky for giving away her child? "Sky did us an enormous favor when she agreed to let you be adopted. We couldn't have children together, but Beth had so much love to share, she wanted you desperately. I was gone a lot doing undercover work."

"I know. I remember. But—"

"Do you remember what you said to me that day after you finally understood Beth wasn't ever coming back?"

The silvery thread of tears glistened on her cheeks as she stared up at him. Mutely, she nodded.

Noah swallowed past the lump in his throat. "I was sitting in your mother's favorite chair just staring at the wall. I didn't know I was crying. You reached for my hand and said, 'Don't cry, Daddy. I won't go away and die. I'll stay with you forever.'" His voice broke as he envisioned the soft child's hand reaching for his all those years ago.

"Oh, Daddy!"

Noah folded Lauren into his arms, rubbing her back as she sobbed while his eyes burned with the effort to hold back his own tears. Listening to Sky recite that letter to his daughter had broken his anger. He'd realized then that it didn't matter why Sky had felt it necessary to give away her baby. There were so many reasons why a young girl would find that the right choice. And it *had* been the right choice. For all of them.

Sky had given him the gift of his daughter. Her presence wasn't a threat except in his mind. She could do nothing to change the bond that existed between him and his child.

Lauren brushed at her tears, but he saw that her hurt was still an open wound. She stared at him just as she'd done when she was five, looking for answers he didn't have.

"I don't want another mother."

Noah pulled her against his chest and closed his eyes as he stroked her hair the way he had done countless times when she was younger and in pain. Like then, he wished he knew what to say or do now to make things easier for her.

"We need to talk to Sky."

Lauren stiffened. "I don't want to talk to her."

"I know. But I've always taught you to face a problem head-on, haven't I?"

Her head bobbed slowly in silent agreement, her hair shadowing her features.

"Then let's go back to the house. We'll face her together and find out what she wants from us. You and I are family, Lauren. Neither Skylar Diamond nor anyone else can take that from us."

Lauren gave him a hard squeeze. "I love you, Daddy."

"I love you, too."

Abruptly, Limpet, who had been pushing against his leg impatiently, stiffened. The dog's posture became tense and alert. Noah released Lauren. A horse whickered inquiringly as the other two dogs followed Limpet out into the yard.

"Daddy?"

Limpet let out a sound that was half growl, half bark. Warning given, he streaked back toward the house, the other two animals in pursuit.

"Stay here!" Noah ordered Lauren. He'd never seen the animals act this way. He didn't need to be told something was wrong. He was reaching for his weapon even before he got outside the open barn door.

In the driveway, Lauren's car jumped to life. Dust flew as it sped toward the road. Sky's blond hair was clearly visible behind the wheel. She was running from them!

Then he spotted the dark shape sitting beside her. She wasn't alone.

*But she should have been.*

Noah swore bitterly and sprinted for his truck. His heart pounded in bitter recrimination. Someone had gotten to Sky.

He didn't get half a yard before the back of his truck exploded in a fireball. The three dogs scattered in different directions at the deafening sound. The living room window shattered.

"Daddy!"

Lauren ran toward him. He waved her back. "I'm okay! Get back!" He reached for the radio on his shoulder. "Marissa, I need the fire department at my place right now. Put out an all points bulletin on Lauren's car!"

Changing direction as he gave her the necessary information, Noah ran toward the back of the house, thanking the fates that he had parked his squad car there before he went chasing after Skylar the other night.

Sliding behind the wheel, he started the sports utility. Then he realized he couldn't leave Lauren here alone. He drove across the lawn to where she stood clutching Puddles and Leo with Limpet at her side. None of the animals appeared injured.

"Get in!"

"But the dogs—"

"Leave them!"

Lauren obeyed, her face paper-white with shock. He realized he'd never spoken to her so harshly before. He would apologize later. "Are the dogs okay?" he asked more gently.

Lauren nodded, her bottom lip quivering. "What's happening, Dad?"

"I'd guess another pipe bomb. Fasten your seat belt."

"Skylar blew up your truck?"

"No. The man with her blew up the truck. Marissa," he radioed his dispatcher, "see if we can get a helicopter up."

A second later she came back. "The helicopter is covering a bank robbery."

"Okay, patch me through to Terry."

"Tach eight."

"Terry, what's your location?"

"East on Swallow Lane, passing Jackson Bagley's place."

"We have to stop Lauren's car before they can reach a highway."

"There's only one route he can take from your place unless he knows the area well."

"Not likely."

"That's what I figured."

"What about the road near Cricket Creek where it narrows?'' Terry asked. ''We've got banks on each side. I can try to block it with my squad car. I'll be coming up on that spot in a minute.''

Noah pictured the area in his head. ''I don't think he'll stop for a single squad car. He'll probably make her ram it. I've got a safer idea. Marissa told me Jackson moved his herd to the pasture that runs along there.''

''Yeah. I see them.''

''Use the cows to block the road where it narrows.''

''The cows?''

''There's a steep path down the side of the hill there. If you can get them started moving in the right direction, they'll cross the road, heading for the creek.''

''Yeah. I see where you're going with this. I'll give it a try.''

''And, Terry, keep your distance. The person inside the car with Skylar may be a professional hit man.''

Lauren gasped.

''How is he armed?''

''I don't know. He just blew up my truck so possibly more pipe bombs, maybe a gun. We know he carries a knife.''

Terry began huffing slightly into the radio. Noah realized he must be out of the car, running up the hill. ''I put...the car sideways,'' he puffed. ''I'm getting the...gate.''

''Try to get them out of that car, Terry. If she's seen his face, he's going to kill her.'' Noah tried to keep his tone impersonal. He didn't succeed. Terry might not have noticed, but he knew Lauren did.

Noah was sick at the thought of Sky trapped by a killer. He didn't know how it had happened unless the man had been watching the house, waiting for him to leave. It didn't matter. What mattered was getting to Sky before it was too late.

''Stupid cows won't move,'' Terry muttered in frustration.

"Okay. It was a long shot. I'll hem him in from behind. Stay on the ridge and don't take any chances."

He spared a glance at his daughter. Lauren stared at him, wide-eyed and silent, her fear tangible as they raced along the narrow lane toward Cricket Creek.

THE MAN sometimes known as Norman Smith smiled in satisfaction as they sped down the driveway. The back end of the pickup truck exploded with a satisfying bang. Too bad he hadn't made up more of the pipe bombs. Tossing that one in the truck's bed had been a spur-of-the-moment decision. He only wished he could have left behind a few more surprises for the sheriff.

He didn't like thinking this fancy woman was sleeping with the lawman when she'd so coldly rejected him. He stroked the knife handle absently with his thumb as he studied her. Despite the blotchy evidence of recent tears, she really was quite attractive in a cool, ice princess sort of way. Too bad he had to kill her, but those were the breaks. He was a professional. He couldn't leave any witnesses behind. Besides, there were lots more, younger women who were every bit as beautiful and eager to share what he had to offer. He would have no trouble finding someone more amenable once he got to Hawaii.

"Why did you blow up his truck?" she asked nervously. Her hands gripped the steering wheel so tightly he was surprised she wasn't leaving dents in the hard plastic.

"To buy us some time. Or did you want me to wait until he got inside and kill him?"

She shivered, biting at her bottom lip. He suspected the lack of menace in his tone made the impact of his words all the more frightening to her.

"H-how did you get inside the house?"

"I'm good with locks," he said, pleased.

"But Noah checked everything."

It was hard not to gloat. Even harder not to brag just a

little. After all, she wouldn't be telling anyone what she knew.

"No one ever thinks to look up," he told her in amusement. "Your sheriff looked under the beds and inside the closets, but he never thought to check his attic crawl space. There was even a convenient opening right there in the closet where your suitcases were stored."

"You killed that man at the hotel the other day, didn't you?"

His eyes narrowed. The ski mask was hot and itchy, but he found himself reluctant to remove it. Wearing the mask gave him a psychological edge over the woman. He could feel her fear. That made her easier to control.

"His death was your fault. If you'd left the computer bag alone, we wouldn't be having this discussion."

"Because I'd be dead," she said softly.

"True. A case of being in the wrong place at the wrong time. Just like the maintenance man."

"You made the switch at the airport, didn't you? Not the hotel."

Alarm shot through him. "How did you know that?"

She flinched. "I saw airport security chasing you."

"Very observant."

"Too bad he didn't catch you," she added boldly.

Sudden suspicion made him glance at the speedometer. She was distracting him, gradually decreasing her speed.

"If you don't want me to slice a strip down your cheek, shut up and hit the accelerator right now."

Fear flashed in her eyes. She did as ordered and they rocketed into a blind curve going much too fast. The roadway was a moving wall of bovine flesh in front of them.

"Ohmygod!"

He gripped the dashboard as she frantically turned the wheel. The antilock brakes kicked in, pinning her against the seat belt. He wasn't wearing one. The force threw him against the windshield. He cracked his head with stunning force. The car came to a dead stop on the wrong side of the road. At that, she nearly hit one of the massive beasts milling in the roadway.

He swore viciously and swiped at her suitcoat with the blade of the knife. "Keep going!"

"I can't drive through them! They're bigger than we are!"

Cows stood on the road as well as the grass. More poured from a gap in the fence up the embankment on their right. Others were making their way down a narrow path that led toward the creek on their left. But what chilled him was the sight of a sheriff's car squatting sideways across the road just beyond the cows.

"Go around him!" he ordered, fighting a surge of panic.

"How?"

Her eyes rounded in fear. The car was surrounded by massive bovines.

He reached a black gloved hand across her and laid on the horn. A startled cow mooed, bumping the car, jarring them. He couldn't see the officer, but he knew the guy was nearby. He'd known there was a risk the sheriff would radio ahead.

Memories of his last botched job haunted him. He'd come close to getting caught then, too. Furious, he stared around, looking for a way out.

"Back it up!" he yelled, fury escalating toward outright panic.

"There's a cow behind us!"

"I said go!"

He yanked at the gear shift. His head pounded in pain. He swallowed against a momentary dizziness and put his foot over hers, pressing down. The car rocked, rolled a few inches and stopped.

"It's in neutral," she quaked.

He tried to slam the lever back up. His foot was still over hers. The sedan surged forward and bumped the cow standing in front of them. The airbags deployed with a loud, explosive sound. He was thrust back between the two seats as the car came to a shuddery halt once more.

A fine white powder drifted everywhere. Before the bags had even deflated, he reached for his door handle. Several cows pressed up against the car. He couldn't see around them. While most ambled contentedly away toward the path that led down to the stream, they weren't in any particular hurry.

"Get out!" he screamed at her. "Now! Move!"

His head throbbed. He'd twisted something when the airbag threw him backward. His back hurt. This was her fault! He pushed at her furiously.

She struggled to open the door on her side. The cow nearest her door danced forward several mincing steps and stopped. He added his weight to hers.

Half falling, she stumbled from the car and was instantly surrounded by the massive beasts. She gave an involuntary yelp of fear when a cow bumped against her shoulder.

"Move!"

"We'll be trampled!" She cringed against the side of the car.

He cursed wildly as he climbed over her seat and burst from the car. The animals were huge, heavy and they smelled. Did they also bite?

The sedan rocked as several cows bumped against it. He lunged for the woman. The cop had to be nearby. He needed the woman for a shield. He was not about to be caught because of some stupid cows.

Pressing the tip of the knife against the side of her throat, he gestured for her to start walking. She stood there shaking, eyes wide with fear.

"Move!"

A bovine head swung in his direction. The beast opened its mouth and mooed mournfully. He jumped back, startled.

The animal didn't move. Embarrassed at his show of weakness, he prodded the woman with the knife.

"I said move!"

"Being stabbed is better than being trampled!"

Damn her! She was more afraid of the cows than of him. He released her, shoving at the nearest animal. Instead of moving away, it lumbered several steps closer to him, nudging the hand that held the knife. Swearing, he stabbed at the huge animal, thinking it was trying to bite.

The cow bellowed in outrage. It bolted away, bumping into another animal. The cows that had been milling around the car began to panic.

A different, deeper snort of rage came from above and to the side of him. He didn't bother to look, having concluded the animals were too stupid to be anything but harmless. Desperately, he began shoving at them, trying to forge a path through the herd.

The cow he'd stabbed continued to make a racket.

And the woman screamed.

He turned toward her, but she was clambering back inside the car. And then he saw the bull. Horror held him riveted in place as the enormous beast charged down the embankment straight at them. Cows scattered out of its path.

Like the rodeo bulls on television, the beast's head was lowered. But unlike any rodeo bull he'd ever seen, this one was enormous. It probably weighed as much as the car. And it had the largest rack of curved horns on its head that he had ever seen. The deadly horns easily spanned five feet. And the bull was enraged.

The man sometimes known as Norman Smith turned to run.

NOAH BROUGHT the SUV to a halt. The road was blocked by scattering animals in full panic.

"Stay here and stay down!" he ordered his daughter.

He started running, carefully dodging cows. The scene

was utter chaos. Lauren's car was a spot of colored metal surrounded by bovines intent on flight.

"Noah, look out!"

He spotted Terry racing down the embankment behind an enraged Franklin. Noah had seen the huge bull upset any number of times, but he'd never seen the beast like this. Surly and annoyed, yes, but never in full charge. Panicked cows scattered madly as Henry's bull charged straight toward the car sitting on the wrong side of the road, dangerously close to the edge.

Sky let out a terrified scream.

Panic clutched him. Noah knew he'd never reach her in time. His heart all but stopped when he spotted the black hooded figure beside the car, holding something shiny in his hand.

Knife? Or another pipe bomb?

Sky was inside Lauren's car now and the figure turned to run.

Franklin hit the vehicle like a demented freight train.

The car must have been in drive, because it moved effortlessly several feet, twisting sideways from the impact on the narrow road. The fleeing figure fell, struck by a fender he couldn't avoid. The bull charged the car a second time and the vehicle slid along the embankment.

The figure scrambled awkwardly to his feet. He staggered, then ran, limping badly, toward a pair of nearby cows. Franklin lowered his head and veered to intercept.

Noah didn't remember aiming his gun. It was useless against an animal the size of Franklin, particularly at this distance, but he fired several rounds, trying to deflect the bull. If any of them hit, they made no impact. Franklin never broke stride.

The bull reached the fleeing figure before the man could dodge between the two cows hurrying to get out of the way. Using his powerful horns, Franklin tossed the man into the air. The body landed at odd angles.

Noah yelled for an ambulance and backup as he rushed forward while the bull gored the broken figure in a horrifying display of animal rage.

Terry was running forward as well, his weapon also drawn. Sensing new prey, Franklin raised his massive head.

"Terry, freeze!" Noah took his own advice and stood completely still, totally exposed. He willed Terry to do the same, while fear demanded he turn and run.

The bull snorted. He pawed the ground and eyed the two humans balefully. They wouldn't have a chance if Franklin charged them, too.

Franklin shook his massive head defiantly. His nose tested the air. Noah was too close. Close enough to hear the harsh sound of the animal's breathing. Franklin snorted. He butted the still figure on the ground once more but the man didn't move.

A cow mooed plaintively. Noah would have sworn the huge bull was debating whether it was worth the effort to chase them down, or if he'd made enough of an impact on the foolish humans. With an angry swish of his tail, Franklin turned and trotted after the herd.

Only then did Noah remember to exhale. He waited long enough to be sure the bull wasn't going to change his mind, then rushed forward, reaching the fallen man only seconds ahead of Terry. The man had clutched a knife, not a pipe bomb, and he wouldn't be moving again anytime soon—if ever.

"Oh, man. What a mess," Terry muttered.

"He's got a pulse." Noah stood and depressed the mike. "Marissa, we need a medevac unit right now or this guy isn't going to make it."

"I'll get the first-aid kit," Terry called out.

"Noah!"

He looked up at the sound of Sky's terrified voice and fresh fear washed over him.

"Dad, the car!"

Noah was startled to see his daughter running up behind him. In her hands was his shotgun. She must have taken it from the lockbox in the back of his patrol unit when Franklin began his charge. Noah didn't know whether to hug her for her bravery or yell at her for taking such a dangerous risk. She didn't give him a chance to do either as she handed him the weapon and pointed.

Her car teetered precariously, perched on the edge of the embankment where it had come to rest. The wheel on the driver's side hung over empty air.

Noah raced toward it, his heart literally in his throat. The car could go down the side any moment. While it wasn't a horribly steep drop, there were large rocks. If the car rolled... He choked off that image.

Sky was twisted behind the wheel. Her face was pasty white and her eyes were enormous.

"Don't move!" he ordered.

"The thought never entered my head," she managed to reply weakly through the shattered window on the passenger side. The door had been bashed in by the bull's initial charge. Noah wouldn't be getting her out that way.

He saw her shaking, yet there was fierce determination on her face. She tried for a smile that failed miserably. He could all but taste her fear.

"Sit still. I'm going to reach in the passenger window and try to pull you out—"

"No!"

The car wobbled ominously.

More softly she said, "Any movement will send it over, Noah."

She was right. The slightest shift in her weight would be enough to tip the balance. The only thing holding the lightweight sedan in place was sheer luck.

"Terry! We've got to get a line on the back of this car."

Terry nodded and turned back to his cruiser at a dead run. Noah gritted his teeth in frustration. They needed something a lot bigger than the cruiser to keep Lauren's car from sliding over. "Never mind! I hear the fire truck coming. Sky, sit tight, help's on the way."

"Sure," she said shrilly. "I've got nowhere I have to be." Her teeth chattered in reaction. "Besides, I haven't run out of prayers quite yet."

The weak attempt at humor tore at his heart. He had to get her out. His SUV had a winch and cable. But did he have enough time to run and get it?

He discovered his daughter was already sprinting back to the SUV. He looked around for Franklin, but the bull was nowhere to be seen. Taking a chance, he set the shotgun down.

"Sky, I've got a winch on the front of my unit. I'm going to put a line on your car and haul it away from the edge."

"Sounds terrific. Do you think you could hurry?"

"I'm working on it."

The sirens were closer now. Noah was afraid to wait for the better-equipped rescue team. He could hear dirt shifting, beginning to roll down the incline. The weight of the car could cause that entire section to crumble away any moment.

The SUV roared over to where he stood. Lauren stopped when he indicated she should come no closer. The sedan was definitely slipping. He had to act fast. Tying the winch to a bumper would only pull the bumper off. There was no help for it. He took up the line, got on his back and squirmed under his daughter's still-running car.

"Daddy, no!"

He heard Terry curse. It almost sounded like a prayer. Noah hoped his guardian angel was paying attention. If the car went over now, he wasn't going to walk away. He worked fast, bringing the line over the axle, securing it as quickly as he could. The ground was unmistakably crumbling. The car was going to go.

He started scooting back out. He was pretty sure he wasn't going to make it.

# CHAPTER FIFTEEN

SKY FELT the car going. Noah had disappeared from view. Her heart lodged in her throat. His deputy had abandoned the man in the grass and was racing toward them. She clutched at the dangling seat belt, so frightened it was hard to think.

Sirens screamed to a stop nearby. Lauren was yelling at someone to hurry. Sky felt, rather than saw, people running toward the back end of the car. Did they think they were going to pull it back from the brink by hand?

"Pull him out!" Lauren screamed. "It's going to go over!"

Noah? Where was he? Dear God, surely he hadn't done something stupid.

"Look out!"

And the ground gave way.

Sky screamed. The car dropped, coming to a jolting stop as it slammed against something hard. Like a pebble in a can, Sky was flung about inside the car. Suspended almost vertically, the vehicle came to a stop.

"Tire's jammed against a rock," someone yelled.

Bless all rocks.

Dirt shifted around her, pinging off the metal of the car. The water and several boulder-sized rocks were only a few dizzying feet away. Sky inched her way toward the driver's door. Every movement threatened the car's attempt to defy gravity. Her throat was parched with fear.

"Hold still!" someone shouted at her.

A large chunk of dirt and stone rushed down the hill, splattering against the back of the sedan. Holding still wasn't an option. She had to get out. Any minute now the tire would slip off the rock, or whatever had brought it to a halt. If the car flipped over she would be crushed.

"Skylar!"

Noah's imperious tone knifed through her terror.

"What?" The word was a croak of sound.

"We'll have you out in a minute," he yelled to her.

"How…nice."

Panic threaded her voice. She could hear it. Taste it.

"Sheriff, back up," someone said. "More of this hill's going to collapse."

"I'm going down there."

"It isn't safe. This whole edge could go at any minute," someone else said. "Lon, get another line. Let's—"

The voices trailed off, or maybe she simply tuned them out. Sky shivered so hard her teeth clacked together. She reached the door handle and pushed. For a moment, nothing happened. Then the door swung open. The car rocked crazily.

"Sky! Wait! Get that line on me now!"

More dirt shifted. If she waited, she would die. Her arms ached with the strain of holding the seat belt.

"Try not to move," came another voice. "We're coming to get you."

Sky hesitated. "Please hurry!"

Time inched forward uncaringly. Grimly, she hung there. Suddenly, dirt began falling rapidly. She couldn't wait any longer. She would have to jump. It wasn't far. She could do this. She braced a foot against the car door.

"Sky. Don't move!"

"Noah?"

She dared a look. Dirt was falling because he was climbing down beside the car.

"Noah, get away! The car's going to fall!"

"It's not going to fall. We've got a line on it. Just hold still. I'll get you."

"You can't!"

Panic filled her. They would both be killed.

"Listen to me! Skylar, listen!"

The firm demand in his voice got through her panic.

"Grab this. Do it. Now!"

He swung a line toward her. There was no choice but to grab it as it landed against the deflated air bag. A harness of some sort.

"What do I—" Her knee bumped the steering wheel under the deflated airbag. The car shuddered. It shifted and began to move to the side. She grabbed the harness in both hands and threw herself out the door. Hands reached for her, grabbing her and holding tightly. The car rolled free of the rock and fell another foot, dangling and swaying only feet from the ground below.

Voices shouted meaningless words. Noah gripped her tight enough to hurt and yelled back. Without warning, they began to drop. She clutched him in terror, unable to hear through her panic.

Abruptly, her feet touched something solid. The ground was there. She was standing, but she couldn't make her fingers release the harness.

His fingers pried hers and the rope fell away. Noah supported her with one hand, releasing his own harness with the other.

"Come on."

He led her stumbling toward the herd of cows milling along the bank of the stream.

"That was close, sheriff. Are you two okay?"

Sky stared without seeing the man. Her lips formed meaningless words. "I've been better."

"I can imagine." A grin came and went. "Sit her down over here."

Sky froze in rigid terror. Looking straight at her was the

giant bull. His expression was not friendly. When he snorted, she found her voice.

"Run!"

Noah swore. A cow standing beside the bull butted the huge animal demandingly. Sky told her legs to run, but they wouldn't cooperate. Noah spoke sharply. He sounded distorted and far away. The world was suddenly becoming entirely too fuzzy.

She tried to tell him to run, but her mouth wasn't working. In fact, her entire body had stopped taking orders anymore. Sky felt her knees start to buckle. Then she didn't feel anything at all.

SKY PUSHED ASIDE her uneaten breakfast and closed her eyes in despair. She opened them wearily when someone pulled back the curtain again. She wasn't prepared to see Lauren hovering there uncertainly, her expression angry, hurt and defiant all at once. Gazing at her daughter, Sky wished she could change so many things—starting with the way Lauren had learned the truth.

Not knowing where to begin, Sky tried for humor. "If you were planning to check into this place," she said, relieved that her voice came out sounding halfway normal, "I'd strongly recommend better accommodations. They tend to come by at all hours and wake you up."

Lauren didn't crack a smile. She proffered a paper sack. "I brought you some clothes. May I come in?"

"Of course. Hospital white is definitely not my color."

"How are you feeling?"

Lauren's tone was distant and formal. Still, she'd come— even if Noah hadn't. Sky buried that thought. She would not think of Noah and what might have been. Lauren was here and that was what was important. She had even brought flowers. That had to mean something, didn't it?

Sky tried to squelch a rising hope.

"I didn't know it was possible to ache in places I didn't

even know I had. Still, I'm not complaining." Her voice thickened with emotion that seemed to hover right beneath the surface today. "Thanks to you and your dad, I'm alive."

"He thinks it's his fault you were nearly killed."

Sky tried not to gape. "What are you talking about?"

"He got sidetracked with me when he was supposed to be watching out for you." With deliberate care, Lauren set the vase of yellow roses beside the tray of untouched food without meeting her eyes. "Aren't you hungry?"

Sky shook her head and immediately wished she hadn't. While it didn't hurt unless she touched it, the lump on the back of her head made her feel dizzy if she moved too fast.

"Are you okay?" Lauren asked quickly, concern flashing in her eyes.

Lauren might not want to care, but she did.

"I'm just a little dizzy. There are people who will tell you I've always been that way."

Lauren looked away again without returning her half-hearted smile.

"The doctor says you have a concussion," she said emotionlessly.

"That was their excuse for keeping me here last night." And she'd stayed, hoping Noah and Lauren would come to the clinic to get her. But the hours had ticked past and they hadn't come.

"Concussions are tricky." Lauren stated.

"Spoken like someone who's been there."

"Not me, but Dad's had a couple," she admitted. "The worst was when he fell off a barn roof during a storm trying to rescue Fluffball."

Sky could easily picture Noah muttering curses as he climbed onto a barn roof after a cat.

"He said you were asleep when he got here last night," Lauren continued.

Sky forgot to breathe. "He came?"

"Sure, but it was really late after he got through with everything."

Noah had come. Sky exhaled quickly. "Did your house catch fire?"

"No. But his truck was totally destroyed."

"I'm sorry."

"You didn't throw the bomb in it."

But there was a hint of accusation in her tone that made Sky flinch inside. "No. I didn't."

"At least we don't have to worry about him anymore. He didn't make it through surgery. They said he had too many internal injuries."

Sky had barely given the kidnapper a thought since she'd awakened in the ambulance. Maybe it was wrong, but she couldn't work up any sympathy for him. He'd intended to kill her.

"Do they know who he was?" Sky asked.

"Dad said he called himself Norman Smith, but they don't think that was his real name. I heard Terry tell someone he was probably a hired hit man."

Sky nearly nodded agreement until she remembered how dizzy it would make her. She didn't want Lauren to leave and get a doctor. There were so many things she needed to say to her daughter, but she didn't know how to say them. Maybe they weren't saying anything important right now, but at least Lauren was talking to her.

"What happened to the bull?" she asked. "Did anyone else get hurt?"

"No."

"Thank God. They didn't…have to shoot him, did they?"

Lauren shook her head. Abruptly, she crossed the room to sit in the only chair beside the window.

"They didn't shoot him, but not because Dad wasn't tempted." For a moment, the trace of a smile hovered at the corner of her mouth. "Dad was pretty disgusted. Especially when Henry and Jackson showed up and led Franklin away like a docile lamb. He only wanted to be with his favorite cow," she added earnestly. "As long as they had a lead on her, Franklin was willing to go wherever she went. That creep stabbed the wrong animal."

"I didn't know he stabbed one of the cows."

At least on the subject of defenseless animals, they had a common bond.

"Henry says that's why the bull charged the car. He was trying to protect his cow."

"Is the cow okay?"

"Uh-huh. We had to put a couple of stitches in her, but she'll be fine. Jackson agreed to sell her to Henry to keep Franklin happy."

"A happy ending, then," Sky said tentatively.

Pain skittered across Lauren's face. "I guess."

Taking her courage in her hand, Sky started to bring up the subject they were both avoiding, when a woman bustled in to collect the tray, tsking over the untouched meal. Inwardly, Sky sighed over the lost opportunity. Lauren sat back, her face once more remote.

"So what did you bring me to wear?"

Lauren's momentary hesitation was all the warning she got. The girl reached inside the bag beside the chair. Instead of clothing, she withdrew a familiar file. Her hand trembled and her eyes filled with emotion.

"Dad found this and your opal jewelry in the car that man left down the road from our house. We thought you might want this back."

Sky didn't move to take the folder. Inside were the pictures the adoption agency had sent her every Christmas for the first five years of Lauren's life. Obviously, Lauren had seen the contents. She held her daughter's gaze. "Thank you. That folder means everything to me."

"Why?" Lauren demanded.

"Because it's all I ever had of you."

Lauren's bottom lip trembled, joining her hands. Her eyes became twin gray pools of hurt. "So why did you give me away?"

The question seemed to suck all the air from the room. Sky searched for the right words, but Lauren didn't give her time to find them.

"When my *mother* died," Lauren went on quickly, placing deliberate emphasis on the word *mother,* "I couldn't understand why she left us. I was only five, but I knew it had to be my fault. Dad was so upset. I thought my mother must not want me anymore, either."

Flailed by the hidden blades of those words, Sky swallowed hard against the pain. "I'm sorry, Lauren."

"Yeah, well, eventually I got big enough to understand about cancer and dying."

"No one ever understands about cancer and dying. My mother and I were close, too. She died not long after your mother did. I was old enough to understand. I even knew it was coming, but it hurt just the same. I felt abandoned, too."

"What about your father?"

"I never knew my father. Mom said that was just as well. He'd been a mistake."

"Was I a mistake?"

The anguish hidden beneath the question threatened to rip Sky apart. Instinctively, she knew everything in their relationship hinged on her answer. Lauren was hurt and angry, and perhaps without realizing it, she was seeking a target for those emotions. It would be so easy to accept that position and ask for forgiveness. Too easy. Sky couldn't undo the past.

She drew on every bit of the New York veneer she'd endeavored to acquire, keeping her face and voice as neutral as possible. "Do you think your father believes you were a mistake? Do you think your mother did?"

Surprised, Lauren rose to her feet, trembling all over.

"We aren't talking about my parents. We're talking about what you thought. You gave me away."

"Yes. I did." Oh, God, this was going to kill her. "And I've spent every day wondering if I did the right thing."

"Your mother didn't have money or a husband, but she didn't give you away," Lauren accused.

"No, she didn't. She worked herself into an early grave to provide for me, giving up everything to give me a chance at the life she always wanted."

"And you didn't want to struggle like that."

Sky fisted her fingers in the sheets, then forced them to relax. "Anger, like guilt, is a destructive prison, Lauren. But it's one you don't have to live in. I've spent most of my life wondering if I made a mistake. Wondering if maybe eventually I could have met someone like your dad who would have wanted both of us." She gave a small shrug. "I'll never know. I was younger than you are right now, pregnant and scared. The boy who fathered you wanted nothing to do with me or a baby. He denied he was the father and I never saw him again. The design institute was dangling my mother's most cherished dream right in front of me. I saw my mom growing weaker every day. I had to make a choice. Give up my baby sight unseen to a couple who would love it as their own, or give up our dream of a future and the chance to repay my mother for all she'd given up for me. What would you have done?"

Tears glistened in her eyes. "I would *never* give up my own child."

"Really? Not even to save your dad?"

"What?"

"If giving up a baby you had never seen or held meant your father might live a little longer, what choice would you make?"

"I—"

"Don't answer that right away. Think about it. I had almost seven months." Sky sank back down against the pillow and closed her eyes. After a moment, she heard Lauren leave on a sob.

Well, she'd screwed up her life. Why not this conversation? She'd never been a parent and it was probably much too late to try to be one now. Lauren obviously would never understand or forgive.

"You were pretty rough on her, weren't you?"

Sky opened moist eyes. Noah stood there in full uniform, a brooding expression on his handsome features. She blinked back the tears, even as hope withered and died inside her. She only had to get through the next few minutes. Then she could go back to New York and try to find a purpose to her life. Sky set her jaw. "It's a tough world, Sheriff."

"Why did you come here?"

She flinched, despite his gentle tone. "To see what had become of my daughter."

"In other words, now that she isn't a needy child anymore, you suddenly decided you wanted to be her mother."

"No," she said calmly, refusing to be provoked by his quiet words. "I came to see if I made the right decision all those years ago."

He rocked back on his heels, his chocolate eyes peering into her soul. "And what did you decide?"

Sky took a deep breath. "I did what I had to do."

It was true. For the first time in her life she accepted that fact. If she had to do it all over again, she still would have made the same choice.

The lines around his eyes softened first. The smile grew slowly, deliberately. "Yes. You did. Don't you think it's time to stop punishing yourself?"

His presence filled the room, obliterating everything else. "I'm not."

"Really? Inside, where the world can't watch, haven't you been castigating yourself for the choice you made?"

The smell of the roses seemed to fill her head. They suddenly reminded her of funerals.

"Why didn't you tell me the truth?" he continued. "Why the lie about wanting her to model for you?"

Sky wondered if a person's soul could bleed. She didn't understand what he was getting at. Did he want his pound of flesh as well?

"I was attracted to you," she said flatly. "I didn't want to be, but I was. I planned to go back to New York without telling either of you the truth. After meeting you both I realized I had no right to interfere in your lives."

He didn't look angry. If anything, he looked sad. Her stomach felt queasy and she wished she could toss the flowers out the window. Their scent was making her ill.

"I see. I thought maybe you were having a midlife crisis after breaking up with your lover. I thought maybe you'd decided you'd missed out on motherhood, so you came looking for the family you never had."

She would not cry. She would bite off her tongue before she shed a single tear. Her eyes burned, but she couldn't refute his words.

"Lauren is your daughter, Noah," she managed to say calmly. "Not mine." She couldn't meet his eyes so she stared at his tie clip without seeing it. "I did want to know what I'd missed out on. It hurt when those letters and pictures stopped coming. I didn't know what had happened to my daughter and the agency wouldn't tell me anything."

"You didn't come looking for her then."

"Because my mother was ill."

"And then she died."

"Yes. I was starting to have some career success so I threw myself into my work, trying to make her dream for me come true."

Noah surprised her by walking over to the chair and sitting down. "One of the hardest things about being a parent is that we're expected to have all the answers. Show me a parent who thinks he does and I'll show you an ignorant fool.''

"Don't be cryptic, Noah. My body hurts starting at my toes and working up to the ends of each strand of hair. What are you trying to say?''

He stood and moved to the side of the bed, towering over her. Masculine, decisive, in charge.

"You aren't a horrible person for giving up your baby, Skylar. But you aren't some noble martyr, either.''

Sky sucked in a breath.

"You were a young girl with a difficult decision to make. I realized in the barn yesterday what a precious gift you gave me. My life would have been empty without Lauren. A lot like yours has been, I suspect.''

Sky couldn't think. "Lauren is—''

"Trying to come to terms with her own insecurities. She and Beth were very close. I wasn't home a lot in those days so they pretty much only had each other. She took her mother's death pretty hard. Until today, I never realized she blamed herself. I guess I should have. It was just one of the many mistakes I made over the years.''

"You did a terrific job raising her," Sky defended.

"Thank you. I think so, too. She's a bright woman. Right now she's a little emotional, but when she calms down and starts thinking again, she's going to realize you did the right thing. I think you're the one I have to convince.''

Sky tried to steady the wild thumping of her heart. "Maybe yesterday that might have been true, but a few minutes ago I realized the truth. I came here looking for answers and I found them. I can get on with my life now.''

"Good.''

"But I hate leaving here knowing Lauren is upset and confused.''

"As I said, give her some time. Doug was waiting for her outside. He has a steadying effect on her. I know she's young to be getting married, but she really does have a level

head on her shoulders most of the time. The doctor is going
to release you. What are you going to do?''

''Go back to New York.''

''Would you stay for a while if I asked you to stay?''

Sky couldn't breathe. ''Why? Because of Lauren?''

''No. Because I'd like to get to know you better.''

For a moment she thought she was hearing things.

''Since Beth died...there's never been anyone else that
made me feel the way you do. Part of me feels guilty, almost
disloyal for being attracted to you. The other part knows
that's a crazy reaction. I'm not sure what's happening between us, but if you run back to New York—''

''I wear heels. I seldom run,'' she managed to say, trying
to stem the swell of hope filling her chest. ''I'll have to go
back at some point.''

''Because your career is there,'' he said without inflection.

''Yes.''

''Mine's here.''

''I know.''

His jaw tensed. She could see the vein in his neck throbbing. ''Stay for a while.''

''All right. For a while.''

# *CHAPTER SIXTEEN*

NOAH STEPPED from the cab. He ignored the drizzling rain and the noise of the busy street. New York was Skylar's town, a place of frenetic energy, noise, dark streets, large crowds and overpowering buildings. He fingered his duffel bag and wondered if he'd made a mistake coming here unannounced.

In the past three and a half months, it was Sky who had come to him, spending long weekends when she could, talking on the telephone when they couldn't be together. They were picking their way through the land mines of their relationship while he taught her to ride and to shoot, opening his world and his heart to her.

"Noah?"

He turned at the sound of his name. Skylar stood on the sidewalk, a wide red umbrella nearly obliterating her features, a familiar briefcase clutched in her arm. He watched her lips part in amazement as she realized it really was him, and then she ran to him, almost taking off his Stetson with her umbrella as she flung herself into his arms. Her expression of delight erased his uncertainty.

"I'm so glad to see you! What are you doing here?"

"I figured if you could learn to ride, I could learn to hail a taxi. Do you think we could go inside?"

"Yes! Oh, yes. I'm so glad you're here, but I can't believe it. My apartment's a mess. I don't think I even made my bed this morning."

"Good." His body hardened in anticipation. "We'd just mess it up again anyhow."

Her face glowed. "Good point."

It had been so long since they'd found a time and place for intimacy. He saw nothing of her apartment. Skylar shut the door and came into his arms so eagerly they barely made it to her bedroom before stripping away the barriers of clothing. Warm satisfaction moved through him as he drew her against his aroused body, reveling in the taste and scent and feel of her. He couldn't get enough of her.

A long while later, Sky stirred languidly beside him. He laid his hand across her bare stomach, feeling her muscles contract at his touch. "Ticklish?"

"Don't you dare!"

"Hmm."

"Noah, I'm warning you."

And the telephone rang. "Who on earth?"

He watched her sit up, her nipples still puckered and pink from his mouth. He loved watching her. He decided he could get used to watching her on a permanent basis. The thought made him pause. He studied the intriguing slope of her back as she reached for the telephone.

"Hello? Who? Oh, no! No. I mean yes. Send her up," she said, obviously flustered. "Send them both up."

She hung up, gazing at him frantically. "We have to get dressed!"

"Why?"

"Your daughter and Doug are on their way up right this minute." She was already searching the bed for her bra.

"What? What the devil are they doing here? They're supposed to be in Dallas this weekend."

"Don't tell me, tell them." She paused in the act of stepping into her panties. A fresh surge of desire sparked a reaction he would have sworn was impossible.

"The apartment is a mess. I haven't even vacuumed."

"I didn't notice." He pulled on his shorts and reached for his shirt.

"You didn't notice anything."

"I noticed you."

Her frantic look melted momentarily. "We don't have time for that right now. They'll be here any second."

He tipped his head as he was about to fasten his jeans. "Are you ashamed of being here with me?"

"Of course not! But I'm not about to flaunt our affair in front of your daughter and her fiancé."

She was so careful to call Lauren *his* daughter. It annoyed him almost as much as her word choice. "Affair? Is that what you call what we just did?"

She closed her eyes and quickly opened them. "Don't do this. Not now. They'll be here any second."

There was a knock on the door.

"Oh, no. Quick! Finish getting dressed. I'll stall them. You can pretend you were in the bathroom."

Noah watched her tuck in her blouse and run a brush through her hair before rushing down the hall to answer the summons. He debated pointing out that her blouse was buttoned wrong, and she'd forgotten her shoes. He decided he didn't like her reaction. Not a bit.

An affair sounded cheap and tawdry. The feelings inside him were anything but. His daughter was an adult. It was time she accepted that her parents were adults, as well. He finger-combed his hair and strode down the hall, fastening his shirt.

"Lauren! Doug! What are you doing here?" Sky said brightly.

"Uh, are we catching you at a bad time?"

"Actually," Noah drawled, "it could have been worse."

Sky's face flamed as she turned and found him in the hall leading to the bedroom.

"Daddy!"

Lauren gaped. Doug looked amused and slightly embarrassed. He tipped his head with a rueful smile. "We could come back."

"Doug!" Lauren gasped.

"Noah!" Sky admonished at the same time.

The men shared a small smile. "Sky, I think you should invite them in unless you're waiting to invite your neighbors in, as well."

"Oh, God." Quickly, she ushered them inside, the state of her apartment completely forgotten. "This isn't what it looks like."

"It isn't?" Noah asked.

"Noah!"

"Hey, we're the ones who came calling without calling," Doug said.

"We noticed," Noah told him.

Sky sent him a red-faced glare. He walked over and slid his arm around her. "Lauren and Doug aren't children and neither are we."

"I give up. You're determined to make this as awkward as possible. Can I get you two something to drink?"

"Actually, we were going to invite you out to dinner," Doug said.

"Sounds like a good idea," Noah agreed. "I'm starving. Just let us finish getting dressed."

"Don't bother," Sky said through clenched teeth. "Dead men don't need shoes."

He chuckled. "Maybe not, but I think you'll be more comfortable if you button your shirt the right way."

Amazing. He hadn't thought her face could get any redder. She closed her eyes and shook her head. "Excuse me while I go to the bedroom and plan your father's demise."

"I don't blame you," Lauren said. "He's behaving outrageously, even for him."

"We'll be right back," Noah promised.

"How could you do that?" Sky demanded as soon as the bedroom door closed. "Why did you do that?"

"Because I don't like the idea that we're sneaking around. I'm sure Lauren and Doug know we're sleeping together."

"Knowing is one thing. Thrusting our affair under their noses is something else."

She walked in the bathroom and slammed the door. Broodingly, he tried to decide what it was about the word that set his teeth so on edge. He finished dressing and went out to join the kids. Sky followed on his heels, once more looking smoothly elegant except for the flush of red on the side of her neck. The memory of how it got there made him smile. Making love with Sky was heady stuff.

"Please, sit down," she said graciously. "Make yourselves at home. I apologize for the condition of the apartment, but I've been a little busy lately."

For the first time, Noah gazed around with real interest. The blue-green-and-white decor was soothing, unlike the stark image he'd been imagining. Then he remembered she'd had to completely redecorate, and he frowned.

"We're the ones who should apologize, Sky," Lauren was saying. "Doug wanted to call ahead, but I wanted to surprise you."

"And it's a very nice surprise," she said warmly, without looking at Noah.

"Hey, I'm surprised," Noah said. "Now, what are you doing here?"

"Noah!"

Lauren fished inside a large handbag and pulled out a manila envelope. Noah recognized it immediately. One of the wedding invitations she'd been addressing all week.

"I wanted to deliver this in person," Lauren said nervously.

He should have known. Maybe he had expected this. Wasn't the fact that the invitations had gone out part of the reason he'd chosen to come to New York this weekend? Lauren glanced toward him anxiously. He winked at her in support and watched as Doug slid a comforting arm around her shoulders.

Noah focused on Sky's expression as she opened the envelope. "Oh, how lovely. Your wedding invitation."

He knew the moment she read the line.

*Skylar Diamond and Noah Beaufort invite you to attend the wedding of their daughter, Lauren Marie Beaufort...*

Sky's lips parted in shock. Her gaze flew from Lauren to him in consternation.

"I asked Daddy if it was okay and he said yes," Lauren told her quickly. "I know I should have checked with you first, but I wanted to surprise you. I hope it's okay."

"It had better be. We mailed the other invitations out yesterday," Doug told her.

Noah had never been more proud of his daughter than he was at that moment. Sky's eyes filled with tears. "Oh, Lauren!"

She drew her daughter into her embrace. Noah wasn't surprised to see a shimmering trickle on Lauren's cheek, as well. His own throat felt scratchy with emotion and he noticed Doug clearing his throat.

Sky wiped at her eyes with the back of her hand. "Thank you." She turned to him with her heart in her eyes. "Thank you."

"Hey, it was Lauren's idea."

"Come with me," she said to her daughter. "I have something to show you."

Noah and Doug trailed the women down the hall to the second bedroom. A glance inside revealed her office turned workroom. Lauren gasped. The white dress sitting on the dressmaker's dummy glittered beneath the bright light of a halogen bulb.

"Wow," Doug said. "It looks like you sewed diamonds right into the gown."

"They're Austrian crystals," Sky corrected. "But I can take them off, if you think it's too gaudy."

Lauren hugged her, laughing and crying at the same time. "No! I love it! Really! Can I try it on?"

Noah nudged his soon-to-be son-in-law. "I think we'd better go see if Sky has a list of nearby carryout places posted in her kitchen. I don't think we're going to get dinner otherwise."

"There are places down the street," she said distractedly. "Pick something."

Noah grinned. They left mother and daughter discussing hair styles and veil choices. Lauren refused to let the men see her in the dress, but she fairly burbled over the Chinese takeout Noah had delivered.

"Wait until you see. I look like a fairy-tale princess in it. It fits me perfectly!"

"Except for the hem," Sky corrected, setting down her glass of water.

Noah had never seen either woman look more lovely or more happy. Sitting here in Sky's cozy apartment like this felt right. Being together as a family felt right. This was the way things were meant to be.

"I want you to try on the dress with the shoes you plan to wear before I set the hem."

"It's so incredibly beautiful. How can I thank you?"

"You already did." There were tears in Sky's eyes again. "I never married, so I don't have a wedding gown to pass down to you."

There was a moment of silence, then Lauren smiled. "Why don't we start our own tradition? As your daughter, I'll pass my dress to you. You can wear it when you and Dad get married."

The room went utterly still.

"Uh, Lauren—" Sky began nervously.

"I like that idea, Lauren," Noah interrupted. "Although I'm not sure we'd really want that to become a family tradition."

She laughed. "Maybe not."

Sky rounded on him. "What are you saying?" she demanded. "We aren't getting married."

"We are if you say yes."

Her lips opened and closed. Lauren squeezed Doug's arm and beamed. "All right!"

"Hey, you two could get married with us," Doug suggested. "We could have a double wedding. The minister will be there, most of your friends are already invited—"

Noah shook his head. "No. That day belongs to the two of you. If Sky says yes, we'll have our own day."

"What do you mean *if?*" Lauren asked. "Of course she's going to say yes. You are, aren't you?"

Sky didn't respond. Noah gazed at her uncertainly, the pit of his stomach growing cold with sudden fear. "As a cop, I'm sure I can get a job here in New York," he offered.

Sky shook her head. "I don't think the city of New York is ready for a Texas lawman like you."

Desperation clawed at his insides. She was going to say no.

"But I can design clothing anywhere."

His heart began pounding much too fast. "Is that a yes?"

"I haven't heard the question yet," she said softly.

"Will you marry me?"

"Yes."

Noah released his pent-up breath. He discovered a heart really could swell as he pulled her into his arms right there on the couch, smiling in satisfaction.

"All right!" Lauren crowed.

Doug stood, pulling Lauren to her feet. "I think we need to go now."

Sky looked up. "You haven't finished eating. You don't have to go. You can both stay here tonight."

"No, they can't," Noah said.

"Uh, thanks anyhow, but we, uh, have a hotel room—

rooms," Doug corrected quickly, red crawling up his neck. "That is, we're already booked at the Hilton."

An immediate objection rose in Noah's throat. He barely managed to contain it when he saw the laughter reflected in Sky's eyes.

"Rooms, huh?" He touched her face lightly. "The sooner we get the two of them married off, the better." He pinned the kids with a hard stare. "Just remember, we don't want to be grandparents for a couple of years yet."

"Daddy!"

Doug's head bobbed, his face now a deep red. "Yes, sir. Come on, Lauren. Hey, maybe Henry will give them Franklin as a wedding present." He closed the door on her laughter.

"We'll serve him to the guests," Noah threatened.

But Sky wasn't smiling. "Noah, just because the kids know about our—"

"If you dare use that word *affair* again, I will turn you over my knee and paddle you."

"What?"

"I don't want an affair, Sky. I want a wife. I want to wake up to you every morning and go to bed with you every night. I want to laugh and cry with you, even argue with you, because we'll have so much fun making up."

"What about Beth?"

"Beth died over fifteen years ago. She won't haunt our marriage. In fact, I think she'd be very pleased for all of us. What about you?"

"Darn these tears. I never cry. But then, I've never loved anyone the way I love you—irritating habits and all."

He cupped her face, fusing their lips in a kiss that was both tender and deep. Her arms wound about his neck, seeking to draw closer. She was his.

"What irritating habits?" he whispered against her hair, delighting in her soft chuckle.

MOTHER AND DAUGHTER stood in the chapel and gazed at one another. Sky hugged Lauren, careful not to crush her dress. "I love you, Lauren."

Noah stilled.

"I love you, too."

"Oh, hell, you made her cry again," Noah said.

"It's a wedding. The mother of the bride is supposed to cry," Lauren told him, dabbing at the corner of her own eyes.

"Go take your seat," he told Sky as she brushed at her tears before they could streak her makeup. "We're ready to start."

She left with a poignant smile and Noah turned to his daughter. "Have I ever told you how proud I am of you?"

"I love you too, Daddy."

"Stop crying or you'll smear your makeup. You do look like a fairy princess," he told her.

"I feel like one. Thank you, Daddy, for loving me. I'm so glad you're my father."

He settled the veil over her face, feeling a well-being of peace settling over his heart. Her groom was waiting and so was his bride-to-be.

The music began. Her bridesmaids started up the aisle.

"All set?" he asked.

"Uh-huh."

"Be happy, Lauren."

"You too, Daddy."

He took her arm and proudly walked his daughter down the aisle.

"Who gives this woman?" the minister asked.

"Her mother and I do," Noah replied. He hugged his daughter, shook hands with Doug, and then went to join his lady—the mother of the bride.

**TRUEBLOOD TEXAS** *continues*
*next month with*
*SURPRISE PACKAGE*
*by Joanna Wayne*

*Kyle Blackstone had been lusting after Ashley Garrett for months. Who would have figured that getting a baby dumped at his door was going to be Ashley's ticket to his bedroom? Of course, there were a few obstacles in the way of romance...like needing to find the baby's mother, providing round-the-clock baby-sitting and disposing of a secret admirer of Ashley's who seemed to be turning pretty sinister....*

*Here's a preview!*

# CHAPTER ONE

HE LEANED AGAINST the door frame, half in the shadows, half in the glow from the lamp in the living room. The teasing smile he usually wore so well had been replaced by a facial expression that made him seem older, deeper, more complex. She sensed a seriousness about him that hadn't surfaced before.

He turned to face her and took her hands in his. "I couldn't have taken care of Casey the last two days without your help, Ashley."

"I'm sure you would have managed."

"No. Finding out that I might be a father has been an incredible experience. It's not easy to explain, but I feel drawn in two opposite directions. I feel a bond with Casey that can only be explained by our being blood kin. Yet part of me refuses to accept the fact that she could be my child. At times I feel that the life I knew doesn't exist any longer and that no matter how this turns out, I can't go back to being the man I was."

This was a different Kyle than the one she was used to. Less cocky. Far more honest. The feeling that swept through her now was different, as well. Almost like an ache, a longing that she had no idea how to fill. And even though the baby was definitely not her child, she had the same bizarre feeling that her life would be different from this point on. Perhaps that was the main reason she was afraid to get involved with Kyle. She liked her life the way it was.

"I guess I'm just overwhelmed," he said. "Casey is totally dependent, and I'm not used to looking out for anyone except myself.''

''I'm not sure I could have handled it as well as you have.''

''I guess none of us are sure what we'll do until we're put to the test.''

**SILHOUETTE** *Romance*

Escape to a place where a kiss is still a kiss...
Feel the breathless connection...
Fall in love as though it were
the very first time...
Experience the power of love!

Come to where favorite authors——such as
**Diana Palmer, Stella Bagwell,
Marie Ferrarella** and many more——
deliver heart-warming romance and genuine
emotion, time after time after time....

Silhouette Romance——
stories straight from the heart!

Silhouette®
*Where love comes alive*™

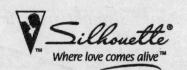

*Silhouette*®

*Where love comes alive*™

SILHOUETTE *Romance*™

From first love to forever, these love stories are
for today's woman with traditional values.

*Silhouette*® *Desire*®

A highly passionate, emotionally powerful
and always provocative read.

 *Silhouette*®

# SPECIAL EDITION™

Emotional, compelling stories that capture the
intensity of living, loving and creating a family in
today's world.

 *Silhouette*®

# INTIMATE MOMENTS™

A roller-coaster read that delivers romantic thrills
in a world of suspense, adventure and more.